The Mystery at Love's Manor

by

D. W. Thompson

An Emma Love Mystery

The Mystery at Love's Manor

COPYRIGHT © 2024 by David W. Thompson

Cover Art by *Lea Schizas*

The Wild Rose Press, Inc.
PO Box 708
Adams Basin, NY 14410-0708
Visit us at www.thewildrosepress.com

Publishing History
First Edition, 2024
Trade Paperback ISBN 978-1-5092-5898-7
Digital ISBN 978-1-5092-5899-4

An Emma Love Mystery
Published in the United States of America

Dedication

To my ever-understanding wife, Ter; my literary father, Leonard; my confidence-building mother, Mamie; my best fans- Andy, Terri, and Christy; and of course, my editor, Dianne Rich. Posthumously to Edgar Allan Poe and Agatha Christie. And always to you, my dear readers.

Acknowledgements

I'd like to express my thanks to Jason Babcock of the St. Mary's County Sheriff's Department (aka The First Sheriff). He was quick to answer my questions regarding rank structure and medical examiner processes in a rural area. Any errors of omission or inaccuracies are the product of my imagination alone, not that of the finest sheriff's department in the country.

Chapter One

A feeling of dread squeezed my soul in its dark grip. I bolted upright in bed and searched the darkness for the source of my discomfort. Was it a sound, real or imagined? A consequence of my first week's stay in a new home? I was chilled to the bone, and goose bumps rose on my flesh. Too many of my premonitions proved well founded to ignore…something was wrong. My thoughts went to my estranged family. Nana, in the sunset of life, was in a battle with the demon possessing her—Dementia. Her curse weighed heavily on my brother, Daniel, and his wife, as well as their relationship. If something was as wrong as my churning gut indicated, was it Nana?

No, if it was Nana, Gwen would have called to let me know. Wiping the crud from the corners of my eyes, I crawled out of bed. Last night's mystery novel fell from its hiding place between my flannel sheets. The day's traumas and the two-hour drive to gather the last of my possessions from my old digs had overwhelmed my curiosity about the fictional "who-done-it." My brother used to mock my choice of literature. I considered it professional reading.

I glanced out of my bedroom window. Raindrops slithered down the glass, and the filtered dawn cast its shadowed light. I wished the window faced east for the sunrise, like my childhood bedroom in the old house.

Nana is staying there now. It was the closest one to Daniel and Gwen's bedroom. I hoped Nana would find more peace there than I had.

Sliding my feet into cheap imitation fur-lined slippers, I set the book on my nightstand and made my way to the kitchen, and the coffee pot. The old-fashioned percolator began its flirtatious dance, and the scent of the fresh ground coffee teased my nostrils. I glanced around the room, noticing all the work needing to be done. The condition of the place made it affordable for me. The paint was chipping from the walls, and the kitchen cabinets were stained with decades of accumulated grease. The sink's constant drip kept time with the ticking of the kitchen clock, a throwback black cat with rolling eyes and a swishing tail. But it was home, and it was mine. Well, mine and Old Joseph's—the name I gave to the source of falling objects and bumps in the night. What I only somewhat jokingly referred to as my resident ghost. I wasn't sure I believed in ghosts, but I was a firm believer in my vivid imagination.

As I poured my first cup of the day, the phone rang, and my teeth clenched. I hated the sound, the nerve-rattling jangle, and the irrational call to immediate action it demanded. I wished the telemarketers would at least allow me to enjoy my morning coffee. Who else would call so early?

At the second ring, I felt an ice-cold trickle creep up my spine, like the time Sammy Mattingley threw ice cubes down the back of my blouse. My hand trembled, hesitating to answer when I recognized the number. It was my brother, Daniel.

At the third ring, I wished he hadn't discovered I

was home. Last month, Gwen spotted me leaving the crappy hotel I used as my temporary local residence while I house-shopped. This phone call meant the cat was out of the bag. I felt disloyal anyway, not letting Gwen in on my secret return, but Daniel? My ten years away hadn't healed all the old wounds. Creating a new life and forging my independence provided a much-needed salve to my soul. Still, I wished he didn't know.

By the fourth ring, I'd convinced myself his call was to bitch at me—feigning hurt for not telling him I was back. My finger brushed against the phone's "ignore" button…but what if it was about Nana? And he was my brother…the DNA test said so.

I answered before the fifth jingle when the voicemail would kick in. Might as well get it over with—in case it was about Nana…

"Hello?"

"Emma, I need you at the house as soon as you can get here."

"Daniel? How about 'Good morning, Emma. Did you pass the test and get your license, Emma? I'm so glad you're home safe and—' "

"Not now, Sis. Please get here as soon as you can. It's important. I need you."

"Is something wrong with Nana? Is she—" But the line was already dead. Typical of my brother. His needs came before anyone else's.

Pouring coffee in a go-cup, I threw on a pair of well-broken-in jeans and a sweatshirt, hopping toward the door as I pulled on my soft rubber clogs—as fancy as I get to go to the family farm. They needed me, and from Daniel's perspective at least, they needed me now. He must figure even the black sheep of the family is handy in bad times. I brushed my hair with one hand and backed my old soft-top Bronco down the driveway with the other.

My recently purchased cottage on the outskirts of Newtowne was seven miles from the farm. The home place was a sprawling acreage with a creek bed running along one border and a pond at the bottom of the hill from the main house—what some called Love's Manor. Many of those same folks claimed the place was haunted. At times when I lived there, hearing the scratching in the walls and the bumps in the night, I almost believed the stories to be true. Locals claimed the hauntings were from the deaths occurring in the house over the past century—not least of which were my parents, my older sister, Maya, and her best friend, Jessie. Others widened its haunted origins to include the entire town. These candidates included Benjamin Hance, the young black man who was lynched on June 17, 1887, for allegedly attempting to assault a white woman. An even older tragedy was that of the legendary witch, Moll Dyer, whose cabin was set ablaze on the coldest night of the winter of 1697 by village vigilantes. Moll froze to death. It is rumored she still roams the area and wishes to reclaim the lands she once walked. I put little stock in such things. It wasn't the supernatural that had pushed me away from my ancestral home, nor was it the reason for my return.

The half-mile driveway followed the contour of old tobacco fields—now covered with stubble from this year's crop of soybeans. Not much appeared to have changed in the years I was away. Driving past the pond, I smelled the honeysuckle vines, and an unexpected tear slid down my cheek.

"Miss you always, Maya," I said to the ghost of my sister claimed at Love's Manor.

Flashing red and blue lights flickered through the trees as the Bronco sputtered up the hill toward the house. Cops were everywhere. Three squad cars and a lone ambulance were parked in front of the house.

The car groaned as I slapped it into Park and raced to the house to beat the rain. Daniel met me, holding the front door open.

"What the hell's going on?" I asked.

"Emma, it's Gwen. I don't know what's happened. The house was broken into, and she's nowhere to be found."

"What's Sheriff Wathen saying?"

"Just what I told you. The glass in the side door was broken, and that's how they got in. There's no note from Gwen saying she was going anywhere, and if she was taken against her will, there's nothing from the kidnappers."

"The sheriff thinks she was kidnapped?"

"I don't know what he thinks, but he suspects me of something, the way he's putting me through the third degree. That's why I called you. You're a private investigator now, right? You passed your test?"

"Where were you and Maria when the house was broken into? You didn't hear anything?"

"No, but we weren't in the house, Emma. Maria can vouch for that. She heard me driving the tractor to check on the cover crop in the backfield. I offered take her along as Gwen suggested. She said a break from Nana might be good for her, but Maria wanted to weed Nana's flower bed. She said she'd promised her."

"When was this?"

"Last evening. I got back around dusk and parked the tractor in the barn. Maria was still in the backyard in the flower beds. We came in together through the back and went up to check on Nana. She was agitated about something, but I couldn't make much sense of it and didn't pay her much mind. You know how she gets. After I calmed her down, I went to bed. Gwen wasn't there, but she often stays up late. She curls up by the fireplace with a glass of wine and a book. I tried to wait up for her, but I must've passed out as soon as my head hit the pillow. I woke up this morning, and she wasn't in bed. I went through the house calling for her. That's when I saw the broken glass."

"So, after you came home, you never saw her before you went to bed?"

"No, I told you—"

"Have they found anything yet?"

"They found blood on a broken necklace outside in the grass, Emma. The clasp snapped like it was ripped from her neck. It was the one I gave Gwen on her birthday last year." Daniel's face was pale, bloodless, and his eyes swollen.

"Deep breaths, brother," I said.

"Right. So, did you pass your test? Did you get everything unpacked in the new place?"

"I did, and I have. Thanks."

"What do you think happened to her, Emma?"

"I don't know, but here comes the sheriff. Maybe he found something new."

"He's been grilling Maria for the last hour as if she would know anything…"

Sheriff Wathen stepped toward us. His footfalls were as silent as our father taught us to be when stalking game, like a true predator. John Wathen was Daniel's age, but young to be sheriff—even in a community as small as ours. It helped that he ran unopposed in the last election and that his family went back as far as ours. His ancestors were also passengers on the Ark at Maryland's beginning. They'd lost some local standing in recent times over a scandal involving his younger brother Robert and drugs. The family's wealth and social standing meant Robert got off with less than a slap on the wrist, but it did rub some muck on the family's name. I heard Robert was running for County Commissioner next year. He'd probably win too.

"Emma," the sheriff said. His hand gripped my shoulder, and I felt his nails dig in through my sweatshirt. He twisted me around to face him.

"How have you been, girl? I've heard good things."

"I'm doing well, Sheriff." I grabbed his hand, lifted it off my shoulder, and dropped it as if it were repulsive, rotted flesh. I wiped my hands on my jeans.

"Same old Emma, I see."

The sheriff smiled as if it hurt his face, and his jowls shook at the effort. He was a bull-in-a-china-shop sort of man and kept his dark receding locks slicked back like he owned stock in several hair products. His girth had grown proportionate to his arrogance since I'd last seen him.

"Congratulations on winning the election, Sheriff. Do you have any clues about what happened to my sister-in-law? This isn't like her at all."

"I'm hoping your brother can help me with that. What do you say, Mr. Love? Would like to chat here or back at the Newtowne station?"

****

I knew better than to ask the sheriff's permission to sit in on the "chat," AKA interrogation. There was bad blood between our families as far back as anyone could remember. My school years with the younger Wathen brother, Robert, did nothing to dissuade me from my family's low opinion of the clan.

Deputy Sam Mattingley (yes, that same Sammy Mattingley—he of ice cube notoriety) was a different story altogether. Sam was a tall lanky man with a face full of freckles and an aww-shucks way about him. Despite our childhood pranks on each other, we became good friends over time. It only took a wink and a smile, and Sam had a chair set up for me just outside of the door. I could hear every word…

The sheriff started slow, and I'll give him the credit due—he knew how to get an interviewee to open up.

"Can you give me a description of your wife, Mr. Love? Or a picture for our case file? I knew her, of course, but a detailed description with any unusual identifying features, that sort of thing, would be helpful."

"Okay. Gwen is five foot, five inches tall, and weighs about a hundred thirty pounds. I know because she was just saying the other night that she'd gained a few pounds and needed to go on another one of her crazy fad diets. She has shoulder-length wavy black hair. Two weeks ago, she had two pink streaks put in the front of her hair at Brandy's beauty parlor out on Route 235. She said it framed and accentuated her face or something. I thought it was a little strange at first, but it looks good on her. She has a small mole at the base of her neck that she wants Doc Johnson to look at on her next appointment. The only other thing is a birthmark. Where I won't say…"

"It could be important, Mr. Love, if we need to identify…Never mind. We'll let that go for now. Mr. Love, what do you think happened to your wife?"

"I wish I knew, Sheriff. I'm afraid for her. There's the blood on the necklace, and her purse is still here. I think she's been taken."

"We shouldn't jump to conclusions, Mr. Love. Ordinarily, we wait twenty-four hours to follow up on a missing person's case when it's an adult, but for now, at least, her disappearance appears to be involuntary. I understand your pain, Mr. Love, and we'll do everything in our power to find her. I'd like to monitor your phones in case any ransom demands are made. Is there anything else the sheriff's office can do for you during this horrible time? I know, I know—catch the perp—but would you like a police presence at night, for instance? You know, to keep an eye on the place? I can spare a deputy…"

"Thank you, Sheriff. I don't think that's necessary."

"That'll be fine then. Mr. Love, besides the broken door glass, did you notice anything else different in the house this morning?"

"No, except my wife wasn't anywhere to be found. Otherwise…wait, there was a half-empty glass of milk on the kitchen counter. That wasn't unusual for her though. Do you think she got up in the middle of the night and that's when they nabbed her?"

"It is certainly possible. How long have you known Miss Maria Clements?"

"A year or so, maybe. She was recommended by a family friend. Honestly, we couldn't ask for a better live-in companion for Nana. Maria's been a godsend. She sees to all of Nana's needs…and our grandmother can be a handful in her condition. Why do you ask?"

"Did she get along well with your wife? Any tension between the two of them? You know what they say about two women not being able to live peacefully in the same house. Was there anything like that?"

"No. They got along well."

"I'm surprised. Miss Clements is quite a looker. I'm sure you've noticed, and you know how women can be. Young Deputy Abell got all tongue-tied when she opened the door this morning. Young and shapely, yes sir…not that your wife wasn't a lovely woman herself. But no jealousy there at all?"

"No, Sheriff, and I don't see what this has to do with—"

"So, she's just an employee of your family? Nothing more? Ever tempted to stray a bit, Mr. Love? Nobody could hardly blame you."

I heard my brother's sharp intake of breath and a soft growling sound. The sound he learned to make to control his ill temper. "No, I have not. What are you implying, John?"

"Well. It's just that the both of you live here but were conveniently absent when the break-in occurred and you're each the other's alibi."

"My wife is missing, Sheriff. There's nothing convenient about this situation. Is that all or is there another bee in your bonnet?"

"I reckon that's about it for now. You know what they say in the movies, Mr. Love—'don't leave town.' "

I heard the sheriff's chair scrape against the floor. I gestured to Sam to grab mine before the sheriff cleared the door.

"Oh, one more thing, Mr. Love," the sheriff said. "Did you know Miss Clements has a police record? Seems she was picked up over in Chapman County for prostitution ten years ago."

Chapter Two

I hurried back to the kitchen before the sheriff discovered my eavesdropping. Maria was there flipping pancakes for Nana's late breakfast. Maria was a stunning woman even without trying, but she made the extra effort. I looked at her mass of wavy blonde curls and wondered how long it took staring into a mirror to achieve the look. *Geez, Emma—envious much?* Still, I'd trade those waves of gold for my straight auburn tresses in a heartbeat. When Maria entered a room, all heads turned, male and female, for different reasons.

"How's Daniel doing in there with the Gestapo?" she asked.

"I think the Third Reich is done with Daniel for now. I wouldn't be surprised if he was up in Nana's room questioning her."

"He won't get much out of the old gal, I'm afraid."

"Can I be upfront with you, Maria?'

"Of course, you can, Emma. We've known each other for a long time since you used to babysit me."

"Okay, then…the sheriff seemed very interested in your relationship with my brother. Is that something we need to be concerned about?"

Her face flushed red, and the pancake she was adding to Nana's plate slipped from the spatula, hit the edge of the stove, and dropped to the floor.

"I think I got my answer. Not judging, but it may

have ramifications with this case. I thought…I mean I think a lot of Gwen. I hope you haven't…No, never mind."

"Emma, you don't understand. It wasn't like that…"

"We're all selfish in our desires sometimes, Maria. We forget or ignore the people our choices hurt."

Her eyes welled up, and her lips quivered as she searched for a response.

At the sound of footsteps in the hall, I held a finger to my lips to hush her. The door flew open, slamming into one of the cabinets, and the rogue bull—Sheriff Wathen—stuck his head in the door.

"What are you two hens in here cackling about?"

"Our total lack of confidence in our elected officials," I replied.

"Yup, same old smart-mouthed Emma Love. One of these days that mouth's gonna get you in trouble. Well, ladies"—he raised one eyebrow, and stared at Maria—"we're starting a search party. Got some men from town and my deputies are ready to go, so if you'd like to join the search? We can use the extra sets of eyes."

"I'm in," I said.

"We're meeting out front. Everyone is already gathering."

"Will Nana be okay if I come along too?" Maria asked.

"Gwen said there's a monitor in her room and you can access the feed from your phone?"

Maria nodded.

"Let's go then."

Snatching rain parkas from the hall closet, Maria

and I hurried to catch up. The yard was full of volunteers from many walks of life: bankers, farmers, and lawyers. I smiled to see the town drunk there, swaying in his tracks, yet eager to help. A horse and buggy pulled up, and three of our Mennonite neighbors stepped out and joined the milling crowd.

The sheriff clapped his hands, and all conversations stopped. "Okay, everyone. First, thank you for coming out on this nasty day to help us look for Gwen Love, a friend and neighbor to us all. I don't know what we'll find, but any sign out of the ordinary: cloth, footprints, or heaven help us—blood, yell out to me or one of the deputies. I'd like everyone to join up with a partner as we move through the field toward the tree line over there by the county road." The sheriff pointed toward the far property line. "Try and keep about five yards or so between yourselves and the next pair of searchers. Any questions? No? Okay, let's move out."

"Emma?"

I turned toward Sam's voice. "I'd like to join up with you to search if that's all right?" He glanced at Maria. "But if you two are going together, that's okay too."

I slipped my hand into the crook of Sam's elbow. "We'll just go as a trio, then. The sheriff won't mind…much. I'm not sure he can count to three anyway, and he did tell us the more eyes the better."

"I wouldn't sell him too short, Emma. John Wathen is smarter than he acts, but he does have a hidden dark side. He's an angry man."

"I don't think his dark side is so artfully hidden, Sam. Oh, do you know Maria?"

Maria held out her hand and smiled her dazzling smile, reminding me of a toothpaste commercial. Flirting came naturally to her.

"I'm so pleased to meet you, Sam. Is that short for Samuel? Weren't you at the oyster festival? I read in the county paper that you are the Assistant Sheriff now. Congratulations. You're so tall and handsome in your uniform too."

Sam's face turned the shade of red that our sunsets are renowned for. "Yes, ma'am, thank you."

I stopped and stared at the two of them. "Seriously? Can we please remember why we're here?" I barked. They both dropped their eyes to the ground and Sam turned an even deeper shade of scarlet. Seeing their lips pout and noting the awkward silence, I regretted my outburst, but for the love of God, Gwen was missing! This wasn't some love connection. Maybe, just maybe, I was a bit jealous too. Nah, there was no room in my life for a boyfriend.

We traversed half the field before another word was spoken.

Sam stopped in his tracks and held out his arms, so we'd do the same.

"Got tracks over here, Sheriff."

The sheriff was fifty yards or so behind us and I marveled at how a man his size could cover so much ground so fast. He glanced at the tracks.

"Looks like the ones we found closer to the house. Same deal though. Rain washed out any tread marks from the shoes. Can't even tell if it's a man's or a woman's shoes; they're too distorted."

"It looks like they're headed to that patch of woods where the creek runs through. Not a good sign. The county road is just on the other side," Sam said.

The search continued, and Sam's concern proved to be true. The footprints entered the creek bed, and although we searched the opposite side, we could not find where they came out of the thicket.

The three of us followed the creek for hours as the search party's numbers dwindled.

Ahead of us, I spotted the Dawsons' house and suggested we stop there and see if the family had noticed anything odd.

Abigail, the family matriarch, answered the door after the first knock. Dressed in a flower print dress that barely contained her, she swooped me up in her arms.

"Emma, child, you haven't changed a bit. You're still cute as a button. I see big city life didn't change you any, or not that I can tell. They didn't corrupt you up there, did they? Turn you away from the ways of our Lord?"

"Thank you, Mrs. Dawson, and no, at least I don't think so."

"I'm still Abby, child, same as always. Why did you leave here so quickly? I've missed your visits, especially since Jessie…"

"There wasn't much for me to do…" I began.

"And is that you, Sammy Mattingley? Why, aren't you a sight for sore eyes? I always thought the two of you might end up together."

I glanced at Sam. He was staring back at me.

Abbie looked past me, and her eyebrows shot up when she spotted Maria. Her lips contracted into a hard thin line, and her voice became raspy.

"Why don't you young people come in for a cup of coffee? Or would you prefer tea or a soda? I'm afraid we don't have much else to offer. No alcohol in this house, I promise you that. My husband would have a fit."

"No, ma'am, I think we're fine," Sam said, but I'd known Abigail Dawson for a long time and knew she'd never be satisfied if she couldn't offer her unexpected and uninvited guests something. She was the closest thing I had to a mother after my parents died…her and Nana.

"I think we could all use a cool glass of that fresh well water you have, Abby."

"Now there's my girl. Nothing like a cool drink of Earth juice, is there? Just the way the good Lord intended."

"We can't stay long, Abby. I'm not sure you heard, but Gwen is missing. The house was broken into, and we're searching for any sign of her or what happened. Have you noticed anything strange lately?"

"Oh my, no. I hadn't heard anything about that, the poor child. Mr. Dawson will be devastated to hear this. You know my husband Michael, don't you, Sam? He thought a lot of Gwen, often meeting up with her for coffee and chatting. He taught her way back in elementary school, you know?"

"Yes, ma'am. So, you haven't noticed anything odd lately, Abby?" I asked.

"Well, now, as a matter of fact I did, now that you mention it. I woke up in the wee hours last night. I thought maybe there was a fox after the chickens and that was what woke me up. The moon was full, and I could see clearly as day before the rain started. There was a man at the edge of your field walking away from the trees, a big man. Looked like he was searching up and down for something. You know me. I was too nosy to leave that window, but I finally went back to wake my husband. The big man was long gone by the time Michael dragged himself out. I swear my husband moves slower than molasses in January when he first gets up. He told me I was imagining things, and we went back to sleep. It was still dark when Michael left the house this morning. I guess I'll be a bachelorette for a few nights."

"Where did Mister Dawson get off to?" Sam asked.

"He's off to the same place as every other year about this time. He and a couple of his old teacher buddies get together and go trout fishing up north, somewhere in Allegany County, I believe. He never brings home any fish to speak of. I think it's an excuse to get with the boys and do manly things. I don't worry too much. My Michael's not a drinker, but I don't know about the rest of them."

"I don't think you have to worry about Mr. Dawson, Abby. I do hope he has some luck fishing this year," I said.

Abby snorted and rolled her eyes at the ceiling.

"Do you have any thoughts on what the man might have been doing last night?" I asked.

"I had Jack walk out there when he finally got up. You know teenagers—they like to sleep in. I told him to see if he could find anything that man might've been up to…"

She walked over to a basket sitting by her stairs and reached inside.

"Jack found something. I don't know if it means anything to you or not. It might have washed down from the county road. People are always tossing their trash out of their car windows. Trashy people do trashy things, I guess."

She held up a single shoe. One of the pair of pink fur-lined clogs I'd sent to Gwen for her birthday.

****

We said our goodbyes at the door and thanked Abby for her hospitality.

"You're welcome here any time, my young friends. It's so good to see you both." She glared at Maria. I knew the "both" wasn't said by accident and wasn't intended to include her.

"Young people forget about us old folks sometimes. I hope Gwen turns up soon."

Sam and Maria went out the door first, and Abby pulled me back inside behind the door where they couldn't see.

"Wait, Emma. I have some fresh-baked cookies for you. Chocolate chip is your favorite, I believe?"

"That took a while," Sam said when I rejoined them several minutes later. "What was going on besides cookies?"

"Nothing. Just girl talk. Abby hasn't seen me in a while."

Sam raised one eyebrow and pursed his lips but said no more about it. We walked back to the house, entertained by our thoughts. Again, Sam stopped and held out his arms, then pointed into the brushy hedgerow at the field's edge. A man stood there watching us. He was small in stature, but easy to see despite his attempt at concealment. His lime green hoodie drew the eye and the pine sapling he stood behind couldn't hide even his thin frame.

"That's Jack, Abby's son," Maria said. "Should we

go talk to him?"

I was already walking his way.

"Hold up, Emma," Sam said, falling in step beside me. The young man never moved from his position, reminding me of a rabbit in its form. *Can't see me. I'm invisible.*

"Hello, Jack. Could we talk with you for a minute?" He looked as if he might run away now that he accepted the inadequacies of his hiding spot.

He stepped out from behind the pine and took a few steps across the field to where we stood. He nodded at Sam and me but saved a special gaze for Maria.

"How have you been, Maria? I'd hoped we could have lunch together again."

"Hi, Jack," Sam said. "Your mom showed us this shoe you found this morning." He held up the shoe in its evidence bag. "Can you tell us where you found it?"

"At the edge of the creek," he answered. His eyes never left Maria. "Ma said she'd seen some dude out here last night, but her eyes ain't all that great anymore, but I looked just the same."

"Well, this may be an important clue you found. Did you see anything last night or discover anything else this morning?" I asked.

Jack swiveled his eyes to look at me. I don't think he'd noticed me until that moment.

"Who are you?" he asked.

"Emma Love. I'm Daniel's sister, Jack."

"Uh huh, Gwen's sister-in-law then?"

"That's right."

The teenager pulled a comb from his pocket and ran it through his slicked-back blond hair.

"She's quite a looker. I'd like to enjoy a few

lunches with her if you know what I mean, but I think Pops had the hots for her, so you know—can't keep everything in the family. It's a shame really…"

"You knew Gwen was missing then?" I asked.

"Missing, umm, no. What do you mean?"

"You said, 'it's a shame?' What is? And then you said your dad 'had the hots for her,'…past tense?"

"Like I'm some English major or something? But Dad, yeah, maybe he had one of those crisis of conscience things that Ma and the Rev are always preaching about. Yeah, that's it. Look, I gotta go now. I heard Ma calling me in for lunch. Real nice seeing you, Maria." He winked at her and ran across the field toward his house. We stood staring after him.

"Maria, what the hell? He's what, all of sixteen years old?" I asked.

"No, no, no. A thousand times—No. Nothing like that happened, Emma. I'm not that…I'd never…well, you know."

"Why don't you tell us then, Maria."

"We did have lunch, I guess, but that's all it was. I was out walking on the edge of the field one afternoon. I often do. Daniel will tell you. I have a little spot where I take a bag lunch and have a little private picnic, except it wasn't private that day. Jack showed up, and we shared my sandwiches. He must have misread the situation and put the moves on me. I was as gentle with him as I could be while making sure he knew—there was no way! He apologized, and that was that. I feel sorry for him."

"Sorry? You were lucky. It could have gotten ugly fast."

"She's right," Sam agreed. "Why didn't you report

it?"

"Report what exactly, Deputy? Nothing happened. I told you. I explained some things to him, and he was embarrassed. He didn't act like this then either. I think he's on something, high or drunk maybe?"

"Explained what things?" I asked.

"I just told him he was young, and he was like a little brother."

We fell silent again as we approached the house, keeping our counsel as Nana used to say, or downloading the events of the day. I thought about what Abby had whispered to me as we were leaving.

"I don't like to speak ill of anyone, Emma," she'd said, "but I warned Mister Love about that wife of his. He was always good to us. With God as my witness, I told him to keep an eye out. I always thought it was men who couldn't be trusted, but the women in that house…the shenanigans. It wasn't natural, and I told him so." She wiped her palms on her apron. "I know I keep a watchful eye on my man and my little wannabe man. Mister Love thanked me. Said he had his suspicions and would take care of it soon. I'm a God-fearing woman and I'll not be the first to cast any stones. I'll not be mentioning any of this to the sheriff or around your deputy friend, mind you. They might get the wrong idea."

****

The house was quiet after the excitement of the morning. No police car bubblegum lights flickered in the yard. It was an odd feeling as if the house was waiting for something or someone. But I get these feelings sometimes.

"This is the house I always think of when people

talk about places absorbing strong emotions and events over the years. The walls seep with memories, don't they? I can't imagine growing up here," Sam said. I guess he felt it too.

"Looks like the sheriff decided you didn't need your cruiser. I can give you a ride back to the station after I visit Nana for a few minutes. If you don't mind being seen in my dilapidated old Bronco, that is?"

"That old yellow Bronco is a classic, Emma, just like you. I'd be honored, thanks."

I looked at him and bit back a smile—pretty sure he considered calling me a classic to be a compliment.

"I'm going to make a fresh pot of coffee," Maria said. "I need it after being out in the dampness so long. Anyone else up for some?"

"I'd love some," Sam said. I flashed Maria a thumbs-up as I climbed the stairs to Nana's room.

I knocked at her door, but knowing she didn't hear well, I opened it and went in. Despite the vase full of garden flowers on the nightstand, the room smelled of old people and moth balls. Nana was sitting at her usual spot, her easy chair by the window.

"Nana? How are you feeling today?"

"Sarah, is that you? Where have you been?"

"No, Nana, it's Emma, Sarah's daughter."

"Of course you are. Come closer, sweet girl. Let me look at you."

I rolled the desk chair over to sit by her side.

"You look just the same, Sarah. Why haven't you visited me? Is that husband of yours keeping you too busy on the farm? You tell my son Dan that I said you need a break now and then to come to see me."

"Nana, Mom and Dad are both…" I started but

thought better of it. I moved the chair closer, hoping she'd recognize me. Her eyes were clouded with cataracts, but I still saw the love reflected there. "It's me, Emma. I'm sorry I haven't been here lately."

"Emma?"

"Yes, Nana, it's me."

"You're such a lovely girl. Daniel Junior drove you off, poor child." Her eyes misted over.

"It's okay, Nana," I said and took her hand in mine. "I'm here now."

"Your son can be a prick sometimes, Sarah."

A giggle threatened to burst forth, and I bit my lip to maintain composure. Nana never used expletives.

"Poor boy got that from his father. All self-righteous, prim, proper, and tight-assed."

"Nana!" I said, shocked.

"I'm sorry. It's Emma, isn't it? I shouldn't use such language around a young girl like you."

"It's okay, Nana. Tell me what you've been up to. Have you read any good books lately?"

"Land o'Goshen, child. I wish I had the time to read. Agatha Christie has a new mystery out, you know? I do love Miss Marple."

"What's been keeping you so busy?"

"Keeping up the house, of course. Today your father and I dug up the potatoes from the garden. After they cure some, we'll load them up in the root cellar. Lordy, I hope there's room. So much has been put in there already."

"What have you harvested?"

"We've stored the usual things: carrots and turnips, and some winter squash. Your father even planted some parsnips this year, though Lord knows why. Nobody in this house eats those nasty things. Probably Gwen's idea, some new fad diet of hers. Everybody's putting their favorites in there, I guess."

"Well, you can't be too prepared with winter coming."

"That's right. Will you take me home now, Sarah? I'm tired and want to get to my bed."

"Nana, you are home. This is your room. See? There's the window you love looking out of."

"I do love my window, and they don't like me seeing everything that I see, but it's still not my room. It just looks like my room. Somebody's trying to trick me, Sarah. There are all these people outside day and night. This isn't my home."

"We did have a lot of company today, Nana."

"At least I don't hear all the voices at night like I used to. Maybe the ghosts are too old to be wandering about."

"I didn't know you believed in ghosts, Nana."

"Well, I talk to my husband Frank all the time, don't I? And there's an old woman too, old as me. Sometimes I hear Maya scrambling around. Do you remember her, Sarah?"

"I sure do. I talk to her sometimes in my dreams."

Nana turned in her chair and clutched my arm until it hurt. She stared at me with a disturbing intensity. "You saw something, didn't you…that day?"

"When Nana?"

"When what? Did I tell you about the potatoes? We had a good crop this year. We won't go hungry this winter."

Maria came in with coffee for Nana then, and I said my goodbyes. I met Sam in the kitchen and filled my go-cup with the fresh-brewed coffee.

"Ready to head back?" I asked.

"Yes, ma'am. How did it go with your grandmother? Good visit?"

"It was good to see her, but she's gone down so much since I saw her last, poor thing."

The corners of Sam's mouth curled down. "I'm sorry to hear that, Emma. I always liked your grandmother. She was always a lot of fun."

"She was that."

"By the way, Daniel came in and said he wanted to see if you'd stay the night. Something about presenting a unified front. I guess he's feeling picked on by the sheriff's office."

"I'll grab an overnight bag at the house and head back here. If nothing else, I have my carry permit. The only gun in this house hasn't left its spot over the mantel for twenty years. It might hurt the shooter more than the target."

"Your P.I. training might come in handy too, especially if the kidnapper calls with ransom demands. The sheriff has the phone bugged—just so you know."

The ride back to town went fine until Sam ruined it. After a long period of silence, he opened with, "Whatever happened to you, Emma? We had a good thing, or I thought we did. My folks threw that party for me when I graduated from the Southern Maryland Criminal Justice Academy. After that, you were gone without saying a word."

"Let's not do this, Sam."

"Please let me finish, Emma. I think you owe me that much at least. There wasn't even a goodbye from you. When I asked, even your brother acted like he didn't know anything. After several days of worrying about you, Robert Wathen, of all people, told me you'd left town for good. Surprising after the events of that night. I admit, I was hurt. Was it something I did?"

"Look, I'm sorry if you were hurt, Sam. I never wanted that. It wasn't my intent, but there were things you don't know…"

"So, tell me now. What things?"

"I can't."

"You don't trust me enough?"

"Don't feel bad, Sam. I don't trust anyone enough, but you're the only one I trusted to tell that I've been back in town for these past six months. Not even my family knew."

"Who or what were you running from, Emma?" he asked.

I shook my head.

The silence stretched out, and with a sense of relief, I pulled into a parking space in front of the sheriff's office. Sam grabbed the door handle but seemed in no hurry to get out.

"Emma, I just want—" he started.

"Sam, what did you mean by 'the events of the night?' Did something happen with Robert Wathen that I don't know about?"

"You don't know? Well, I'm not sure I can trust you enough to tell you."

My lips pouted and I gave him what I hoped was a soulful look.

"All right already. You can quit with the hurt face. He was saying stuff…crap about you."

"What did he say."

"Stuff that I won't repeat."

"So, nasties then."

"It doesn't matter. He didn't say them long. I told him to shut up. When he didn't, I broke his nose. He deserved it, but it almost kept me out of the Field Training Program."

"Sam, I'm so sorry, but you shouldn't have." I reached out and held his hand. "My hero, defending my honor." The look in his eyes changed…softened, and he leaned over and pursed his lips. I wasn't sure where he planned to plant that kiss, and I turned my head to accept it on the cheek.

"You're the best friend I have here, Sam. Let's not ruin it."

Sam nodded and got out of the Bronco without another word. The rain started falling in earnest.

Chapter Three

In less than an hour, I was back at the house, the so-called Love's Manor, that is. I'd packed enough clothes for two nights, just in case. My Ruger 9-millimeter was tucked away inside my waistband, also just in case. I'd never had cause to use it—other than showing some good old boys that girls can shoot. This particular girl could shoot better than they could, in fact. My Private Eye training emphasized that it was better to have and not need than need and not have. The same with most things in life, I guess.

Again, this evening, Daniel met me at the door.

"I'm glad you could come, Emma. Thanks for that and welcome home."

I think he missed the irony in his statement, considering how and why I'd left home to begin with. My brother's memories of past failures were as accurate as Nana's memories about everything.

"Why don't you get yourself settled in. The downstairs bedroom is yours. I asked Maria to put on fresh sheets, then maybe we could talk a bit?"

"Sure. I'll meet you in the great room."

I knew the bedroom well. It was the master suite, Mom and Dad's old room, and stepping in brought back a flood of memories. Mom's hairbrush rested on her bureau, as it had for years. How many times had she brushed my hair while I sat on her bed? I picked it up and saw her hair and mine entwined in the bristles. I went into the bathroom to store my toiletry bag. For a moment, I imagined the scent of my dad's Old Spice cologne filling my nostrils.

My parents were never the same after Maya died. For a few years there, it was Nana who raised me. My parents became more and more distant, spending more time with the bottle than they did with Daniel and me. He was older and didn't seem to mind much, only showing up for dinner anyway. Their blood alcohol level was never mentioned in the papers after the crash. Having clout in the community pays off. Their car left the road and struck a huge oak head-on. They said our folks died instantly and thankfully, no one else was hurt. I was eleven when Maya had her accident. I lost my parents at thirteen. Before I left to talk with my brother, I allowed myself a few minutes to grieve yet again. I sat on their bed and cried.

I found Daniel in the great room. A small fire flickered in the river-rock fireplace. He sat in an overstuffed chair with his elbows on his knees and his head in his hands. Despite our past, I felt sorry for him. I walked over, placed my hand on this shoulder, and squeezed it.

"What are you thinking about, Daniel?"

"About Gwen, of course. I know that every hour that passes after an abduction, the odds of finding them alive diminishes."

"Are you sure that's what's happened here, Daniel? The tracks in the field don't mean a lot. They could've been anyone's from any time. Maybe they're Maria's footprints. She says she walks that way often, and they're soggy and distorted from the rain. Plus, there's no ransom note. Why would anyone kidnap Gwen if not for ransom?"

"I don't know, Emma, but what else could it be?"

"Did anyone have a grudge against her?"

"No. You knew Gwen, Emma. Do you think she was the type of woman someone could hate that much?"

"Were you and Gwen getting along okay? Did you fight? It will come out you know. Any ill word you've said against her, even in jest, will be brought to the sheriff's attention, and he will be asking."

"No, nothing like that. We had our ups and downs. Of course, we did; everyone does. We weren't puppy love teenagers anymore, but we were in it for the long haul, Emma."

"The sheriff may act oblivious, but he doesn't miss much. I'm sure he noticed the door glass was broken out from the inside also. You know what that means?"

"Wait, what? No, that can't be right. It would mean…"

"That whatever happened to Gwen started with someone inside this house."

"I can't believe that. Who would've—"

"How did you get that cut on your finger, Daniel?"

"I was sharpening the kitchen knives and—"

"Were you having an affair, Daniel? Was she?"

Daniel's eyes moved around the room but would not meet mine. He was hiding something.

"Of course not. Only you would think like that."

I felt the blood rise to my face. My nostrils flared. *Keep your cool, Emma*. I jumped up from my chair and stared at him, my teeth grinding together.

"I think we'll leave it at that for tonight, brother.

You may want to think long and hard about those questions because I'm sure the sheriff will be asking them repeatedly until Gwen is found."

"Wait, Emma. I'm sorry," Daniel whined as the door closed behind me.

I slipped into my bedroom and closed the door without a sound, mindful that Nana's room was right above mine. This long day was behind me, but I knew more were waiting over the coming days. I slipped under the Egyptian cotton sheets, pulled Nana's homemade patchwork quilt up to my chin, and was asleep as soon as my head hit the pillow.

****

I woke in a cold sweat and sat up listening for whatever woke me from my troubled sleep. Sleep marred by dreams about Maya, as usual, and the last moments I saw her alive.

There was a scratching sound behind the headboard that I knew must be a mouse. There were too many gaps in the old house's foundation to keep them all out, or the heat in, for that matter. A few of the nasty rodents crept in every year when the air began having a bite. I slapped the wall to silence the mouse and heard a thump and scraping from below me in the basement. *Lord, I hope there aren't rats too*. I'd ask Maria for traps in the morning.

I slipped from the bed, rubbed my arms over my chill-induced goosebumps, and glanced out of the window. It held the same view as Nana's window but from a much lower perspective. I could only see as far as the edge of the fields, but enough to see sheets of rain falling. There was nothing amiss outside, or nothing that I could see anyway. My mouth was dry, and I decided to slip down the hall to the kitchen for a glass of water.

I don't remember much after that. As I walked past the basement door, I heard a creaking sound. As I turned, I caught a glimpse of a dark figure swinging something at me. I raised my arm to fend it off, but I was too late. My head exploded with pain, and you indeed see stars…for a moment, then you don't see anything.

The next thing I recall was hearing Sam's voice and feeling an icy chill on the back of my head.

"Emma, are you okay? Can you hear me?"

I nodded, but even that small movement caused fresh throbbing pain. I tried to open my eyes, and blackness skirted the edges of my vision, and the room swirled.

"Can you open your eyes for me?"

"I don't want to…hurts."

"Okay. The EMTs are on their way."

The next several hours remain a blur. An ambulance transported me to St. Merriam's Hospital. The doctor there said I had a mild concussion and would admit me for overnight observation. I remember the nurses coming in and out of my room. They were very kind each time they led me back to bed after I tried to get dressed and leave. I had to know what was going on and what had happened to me—beyond the gash and thick knot on my head. Finally, I accepted my fate and their expertise and fell asleep.

I'm not sure what time it was when I woke again to a scratching sound. I opened my eyes to see Sam at my bedside, his fingernails clawing at something on his uniform.

"Hey there," I said.

"Emma, thank God. How are you feeling?"

"I'm a little worse for wear, but I'll make it. I'm ready to get out of here though. Are you here to take me home?"

"The doctor said sometime tomorrow morning. I guess he wants to make sure you didn't shake any more screws loose in that hard head of yours."

"Ha-ha. Oh, ouch. Geez, Sam, don't make me laugh, not even a pretend laugh. That hurts."

"Sorry, Emma. Bad habit. I joke at times like this. You do remember me, right? The class clown? But you could've been killed, Emma." He cleared his throat. I glanced at him and saw a tear slipping down his cheek!

"I'm all right, Sam. Thank you for worrying about me, but really, I'm fine."

He took my hand in his and patted it a couple of times. I had to smile, though even that small amusement caused pain. He excused himself and slipped into the bathroom. I heard the spinning of the toilet paper dispenser and then the great honking nose-blowing that Sam was known for at school. He was two years ahead of me, but "the honk" was famous. I'd always believed the blaring goose call was something he did for comical effect, but apparently, it was standard nose-blowing procedure for him.

"So, catch me up," I said when he returned to his chair.

"From what your nurse said, I shouldn't do that. She said no physical or mental strain for a minimum of forty-eight hours, and I don't think I want to be on that lady's bad side."

"Nurse Coombs? She's a sweetheart, Sam. But

forty-eight hours? Seriously? Being out of the loop for that long will cause serious mental anguish."

"Well, there's a lot to tell."

"Apparently, but I have no place to go."

"Well, where do you want me to start? There's the matter of your attacker, the bloodhounds the sheriff brought in, and the ransom note…"

"Wait. There was a ransom note?"

"I guess you would call it that. It was left on the foyer table. We assume it was from the guy who attacked you, but it didn't shed much light. It said, and I quote, 'We have Gwen. She's safe. Stop searching. Demands will follow.' "

"That's not at all cryptic. So, what was the deal with the bloodhounds?"

"We brought in John Russell's bloodhounds to see if they could pick up anything from yesterday's trail. We didn't expect much, and that's exactly what we got. I did hope they'd do better with following your attacker with the trail being hot, but Mr. Russell said the rain washed away the scent. The dogs didn't pick up a thing."

"I think I'm in over my head here, Sam. I'm scared for Gwen. Can I ask you something in confidence?"

"Always."

"Do you think Daniel could do something to her? I've been away for so long. You probably know the current version of my brother better than I do."

Sam shook his head. "I wish I could say, Emma. The man is a bit standoffish on his best day and a self-righteous snob on his worst…no offense."

"None taken."

"Still, I have a hard time seeing the man get

emotional enough to do anything like this, but you just never know with people. There is a lot of evidence pointing at him or Maria. Take your pick."

"I'm trying to keep my focus off Daniel, he is my brother, but it's getting harder. I'm willing to let bygones be bygones, or so I keep telling myself, but I fear that our past conflict might be why my suspicions keep pointing back at him."

"It's your training. I knew you'd make a great P.I., and there's a lot of evidence supporting an inside job. I don't know what happened in the past between the two of you, but I know you."

"An inside job? So, you noticed that the glass was broken out from the inside?"

"Yes, and to be honest, Daniel's refusing a deputy's presence at the house last night struck us as suspicious too. His house was just broken into (or out of) for goodness' sake. I talked to the sheriff, and we set up posts at both ends of your road and one on the county road behind your farm. The only vehicle that came in or out was your Bronco. I was first to the scene after the 911 call about you because I was only two hundred yards away. All the doors were locked then. I verified that after checking on you. This is of course in confidence."

"So, Deputy Mattingley, are we sharing secrets now?"

He winked, and we said our good nights, Sam promising to be back for me in the morning. I tossed about on the hard mattress for some time, hearing the crackling of the plastic mattress cover with every movement. *Should I tell him what Abigail Dawson said? Did it matter? There were so many other things I could never tell him.*

****

Nurse Coombs made one visit to my room to check my vitals and left me alone for the rest of the night. I enjoyed a rare night of dreamless sleep and woke when the rising sun burned through my eyelids. The day nurse wanted to be sure I got plenty of vitamin D and threw open the curtains.

"Good morning, Miss Love. Can I call you Emma? Okay, Emma, and what is your pain level this morning?" She pointed at a chart. One end had a clownish smiley face and the other looked like someone after weeks of hell's most inspired torture.

"Somewhere in the middle there between Mr. Rogers and Dante's Inferno."

"Would you like some meds? You're due some if you want. No? Can I get you anything? Well, I hear you're going to be released today, and it's going to be a gorgeous day. The rain has finally stopped."

After Nurse Bubbly left, I switched on the television—soap operas and cartoons. I opted for cartoons. Breakfast was served, and I changed the channel to a different cartoon. Vital signs checked…watched more cartoons. Got up to use the bathroom and suffered a moment of vertigo on the way back to bed, then watched more cartoons. I wished I'd asked Sam to bring my mystery novel to read.

Then the doctor made her rounds.

"Mrs. Love…"

"It's Miss."

"Oh, sorry. Miss Love then. You have a substantial concussion. I'm not aware of the cause of your injury. Weren't you asked at check-in? It's not on your chart.

A car accident?"

"I was hit with something. I think maybe it was an anvil. Was Wile E. Coyote at my house last night?"

The doctor gave me a strange look. *No more cartoons, Emma*, I thought.

"I see. What do you do for a living, Miss Love?"

"I'm a private investigator. Freshly ordained."

"You might want to consider another line of work."

"Thanks, I needed that affirmation."

"I'm sorry. That's none of my business. I'm not a fan of violent professions. Given my profession, I hope you understand."

I nodded. I did understand, and it was none of her business.

"I will be releasing you today, but I don't want you to think that means you're fully recovered. Your brain had a serious injury. You must take it easy for a day or so and stop any activity that makes you feel unsteady or uncomfortable. No driving or operating heavy equipment until this time tomorrow minimum. Follow up with your regular doctor in a week. They should be able to remove the stitches then too. Any questions for me? No, then have a great day."

Despite my warning to myself, I watched more cartoons until Sam showed up. I was so happy to see him, I could have kissed him. Might have too, but luckily Nurse Bubbly walked in with my release paperwork.

"Are you ready to get out of here, Emma?"

"With a police escort? Sure. Can I play with the lights and siren?"

"Sorry, but no. I took the day off, so I could keep an eye on you. No cruiser, so you'll have to settle for the Mustang. You can play with the radio though if you'd like."

Chapter Four

Sam opened the door for me and stood by the car door, poised to catch me if I fell flat on my face.

"I can manage, Sam. It is just a little bump on my head."

"Yeah, right. Where to, lady?"

"Home. Before I do anything else, I want to get the dried blood out of my hair. It's driving me nuts."

"Okay, home it is then, and I'll help."

"You'll help with what? Washing my hair? Seriously?"

"I told you; you're stuck with me all day."

"Something tells me you are going to be a royal pain where the sun doesn't shine."

He smiled. "I'll check in with the sheriff's office later today to see if there are any new developments. Otherwise, I don't want you to even think about this case."

"Yes, sir, Doctor Mattingley."

Sam was great though. As gentle as any professional hair stylist, he massaged the shampoo through my hair and dried it with tender hands that were used to rougher jobs. I'm not sure why he stuck by me over the years. It's not like I deserved his loyalty after the way I treated him…and the way he treated me.

"What would you like to do today?"

"Hmm, I don't know. Reexamine my life choices

maybe? That's the doctor's recommendation."

"Any particular one?"

"I'm not sure I'm cracked up to be a private investigator, Sam. I mean I work better alone. Five different teachers wrote on my report cards, 'She doesn't work well with others.' So, it seemed like a good fit for me at the time, but I'm not so sure now. I've botched everything. If I'd been on my toes last night, the kidnapper would be in a holding cell and Gwen would probably be safe and sound at home. I hoped to set things right; and help people…My first unofficial case, and I just wanted to get Gwen back safe and my brother in the clear. Knowing Daniel, a tainted reputation is as much of a concern as Gwen is. All I've done is further incriminate him, and Gwen is farther from home than ever. She may die because of my amateurish blundering…"

I don't know where it came from, but my heart dropped, and my chest constricted. Tears streamed from my eyes from nowhere. I hadn't had a serious cry since I watched *Old Yeller* as a child, but I blubbered like an infant who'd dropped her pacifier in the dirt.

Sam scooted closer to me on the couch and put his arm around me. He didn't say a word. He was just there. After a moment, he put a hand against my face and pulled it into his shoulder, and so we sat until my trembling subsided.

"Emma, it's okay. Everything will be all right."

I brushed at the tears soaking Sam's shirt. "I'm sorry, Sam. I don't know what came over me."

"You've had a lot on you, lady, and nobody can be a rock twenty-four seven, not even you…certainly not me. I doubt the concussion helped much either."

I smiled my thanks for helping me save face, but I still felt weak wiping the wetness from my cheeks.

"As for your life choices, there are some I might question, but not that one. If you'd asked me last night when I saw you on that hospital bed with dried blood clotted in your hair, I might've said something different. I was worried about you, especially knowing you were never afraid of anything. You'll be the best private investigator this state has ever seen. The main job of an investigator is getting to the truth, and you're like a bulldog on a bone—you don't let up, ever. I cannot think of a better quality to have."

"Only the best in the state, Sam?"

"Let's start with that. Is there something you'd like to do today, remembering there are limitations on your activities?"

"How much will you let me get away with?"

"Every bit as much as Nurse Ratchet recommended last night."

"Figures. A nap might be in order then. Hospital beds are not conducive to a good night's sleep. I might finish reading the last two chapters of my mystery novel. If you have anything you need to do…"

"Not a thing. Maybe I'll slip out and pick us up some steaks. I noticed your grill on the deck. If you want to turn in, I'll be back in twenty-five minutes, and I promise I'll be as quiet as a mouse."

"Not as quiet as the mice at Daniel's, I hope."

Sam waited for me to climb into bed before he left. When I heard his Mustang start up (not hard to do with his exhaust system), I jumped up, grabbed my laptop from the living room, and pulled up my emails. Halfway down the unopened ones, mostly spam, I saw the one I was looking for from "Cocky@somd.net," the address Robert Wathen used for himself.

My original email to him read:

Robert, I don't know if you remember me, but I readily recall you and your threats against Sam Mattingley and me. I wanted you to know I'm back in town and have been for over a month. I've been busy during that time, as the attached photos will attest. I don't know your wife, Amanda, very well, but well enough to know it's not her in them with you. I especially liked the picture of you modeling your lady friend's undergarments. That was a turn-on and so politically correct too—diversity and all that. For now, I'll be discreet in my handling of them as well as the evidence of misallocated funds from your non-profit drug abuse referral program. I believe its creation helped you after your recent transgressions. What a noble gesture. Please reply with confirmation that you've received this advisement. Otherwise, I wish you a good life as I know you'll have a "warm reception" waiting for you at the end of it. Your friend for-never, Emma Love.

Hours after I'd hit send, I received back:

Dear Emma, I appreciate your candor as the pictures would indeed ruin many lives. I'm confused as to the threats you refer to; however, I beg your continued discretion. I'll check into any malfeasance at the non-profit, but rest assured, neither of you has anything to fear from me. Welcome back to Newtowne! Your old classmate, Robert Wathen.

I shut down my email account, opened the NeighborsSnoop.com site, and logged in. The access there was more limited and costly than what the sheriff's office could discover for free, but I had a lot of questions, and nobody was safe from my prying keyboard. I had surprises in store. You think you know people…but Michael Dawson?

When I heard the Mustang pulling back in the driveway, I shut my laptop, scurried off to bed, and slipped under the sheets.

Sam peeked in at me moments later, and I feigned sleep. I wanted some time to collect my thoughts without distractions, and as much as I hated to admit it, Sam was becoming a distraction. I wondered when he'd filled out, no longer the skinny scarecrow teen he once was…and why I hadn't noticed before today.

While I planned out my next moves, I tried to read the last of my novel, but I was unable to concentrate or keep the words in focus. I read one paragraph five times before I slipped off to sleep.

I woke to the sound of a knock at my bedroom door and the scent of freshly grilled beef massaging my nostrils.

"You awake, Emma? Hungry?"

"I am now."

"Awake? Sorry."

"No, hungry."

Sam's grill skills did justice to the T-bones. Grill marks on the outside with a hint of crispness to the thin margins of fat and a perfect bright pink in the center…a steak lover's dream. I did my best to show my appreciation by devouring every morsel. I was tempted to lick the plate—it was that good, or I was that hungry.

"It's awesome to see someone love my cooking so much, but how can you put away a twelve-ounce steak, a baked potato, and green beans and still have the same shape you did when you were seventeen?"

"I don't always eat quite as well as this, but for the sake of argument, let's just say it's good genes."

"Maybe you need someone to cook for you more often?"

"Maybe…did you reach out to see if there are any new developments in the case?"

"I did while you were napping. There's not much more to go on. No further communication from the kidnappers. The sheriff assigned two deputies to canvass the rest of the neighbors up and down your road to see if any of the folks farther out saw or heard anything. They reported nothing of note, just a few old men and women sharing gossip."

"Anything juicy?"

"They spoke with Mrs. McGee and Mrs. Dawson again. I assume it was the two of them anyway. The deputy said she questioned the lady in the flowered dress and the cat lady, whose house smelled of cat urine. Those two women are convinced there's some hanky-panky, as they put it, going on in the house. They both affirmed that they're devout Christians and won't speak ill of their neighbors. They then invited the deputy in for milk and cookies."

"That sounds like the two of them." I laughed. "I'd like to have another chat with Abigail. I'll think of some excuse to visit."

"Something you'd like to share?"

"Not yet, just a gnawing feeling I have. Anything else?"

"That's about it. Seth Hill didn't have much to say. Talked about how safe the neighborhood used to be and that the country was going to hell in a handbasket. The rest of them said they didn't know anything. One couple wasn't sure who your family was until the deputy mentioned the manor on the hill. They haven't lived here long, and Daniel must keep to himself. Oh, one fellow did say he'd been treated poorly when he did some work for Daniel but wouldn't give any details. That one might warrant looking into, a Mister Brian Hodges. That's the end of my report, Detective."

Sam stood up from the table and began collecting the plates.

"Don't tell me you even do dishes?"

"Ah, the trials and tribulations of bachelorhood. Indeed, I do. What's the plan when I finish cleaning up?"

"We could watch a movie before you go home."

"I'd like that. It sounds like a solid plan, but I meant later. There are two options. If you stay here tonight, I am too. I've scoped out the couch, and it seems comfortable, though a tad short. Or I'll take you home to Daniel's. The point is you shouldn't be alone tonight."

"In my delicate condition?"

"Exactly."

"I won't have you crunched all up on that lumpy old couch. If the depleted stuffing didn't keep you awake all night, that awful stained lavender fabric would. No, I'll head back to Daniel's if you insist. You've already gone well beyond the call of duty, Deputy. The couch came with the house, in case you were wondering."

Sam made a show of wiping sweat from his forehead. "Oh, what a relief."

We looked through the movie selection on my

streaming service. Sam gravitated toward horrors. I was a mystery girl. We settled on a thriller, and *Silence of the Lambs* flickered to life on the wide screen. I'd seen it before, but a few moments still caused me to catch my breath. The first time it happened, Sam reached out, held my hand, and smiled. I wondered which it was he enjoyed—my momentary vulnerability or his role as some sort of media guardian. Neither seemed very positive to me, but it was nice having him there. Clarice Starling might not approve.

****

Sam dropped me off at Daniel's house and walked me to the door. He said it was late, and he didn't want to disturb anyone. We said our goodnights, and he gave me an awkward kiss on the cheek.

"Thank you for everything today, Sam. See you tomorrow?"

"Sadly, yes, as it will be in a professional capacity. Remember you shouldn't do anything strenuous. I have spies, and I'll know if you do."

"Goodnight, Sam." I closed the door and stood there for a moment.

"Guess you and Sam picked back up right up where you left off," Daniel said from behind me. "Remember, right now, he's the enemy. They're trying to railroad me, Emma. That's bad enough, but it's taking time away from searching for whoever has Gwen. I don't think you should spend any more time with him."

"Thanks for your unsolicited advice, brother. I'll keep it in mind."

"Don't go off half-cocked, Emma. I do appreciate all you're doing. Guess I'm a bit overwhelmed. How's your head? Are all your marbles intact?"

I nodded.

"I would've gladly picked you up this morning, you know. Sam insisted on doing it. I agreed because I'm already on the sheriff's department's crap list and I don't want to get in any deeper."

"Don't worry about it. Sam took great care of me."

"I'll just bet he did," he said under his breath.

"What was that, Daniel? Speak up if you have something to say."

"I apologize. I have no moral high ground in relationships. Seems everyone is out to get me, and I'm lashing out at the only person supporting me."

"Apology accepted, but the world isn't against you, and Maria's been—"

"Maria is pissed at me too. I think we're both worn thin and starting to suspect each other."

"Where is she? I'll talk to her."

"We got in an argument, and she went to her room early."

"You need to curb that temper of yours, brother. What were you fighting about?"

"Something from a while back. Not worth mentioning. Silly really."

"Go on…"

"It's a personal matter and unrelated to any of this. That's all I care to say."

"Very well. I'll see what Maria has to say."

I made a fresh pot of coffee, decaf as it was almost bedtime. The high-test stuff won't let my brain shut down at night. I fixed Maria a cup too—cream with no sugar, though she didn't need to worry about her weight. Maybe that's why she didn't.

I climbed the worn carpeted stairs, past Daniel's room, then past Nana's, stepping with care to avoid the loose floorboard on the center-left. I learned about it the hard way as a teenager when I tried sneaking in after my curfew. Nana only caught me that first time, or if she did again, she never let on. She was my guardian after my folks died, and she didn't miss much. After all these years, the floorboard still squeaked like a demon's claws on a blackboard.

I tapped at Maria's door, softly in case she was asleep.

"Yes?"

"It's Emma. Can I come in?"

I heard footfalls on the chestnut wood floors, and the door swung open. "Hey, Emma, come on in. How are you feeling?"

"I'm coming along, unabated pounding headache and all. The doctor said to expect it for a few days though."

"I wanted to come see how you were, but Mrs. Love has been in a bad way lately. I couldn't sneak out for more than five minutes before she yelled at me. First, strangers were coming again tonight to take Daniel. She says she always hears them talking when they come. Then she asked me to please take her back to her house. At least she didn't say I'd hidden or stolen her jewelry this time. Dementia is awful, the poor dear. She's such a sweetheart too. Nobody deserves that hell."

I nodded and handed her a cup.

"Oh, you brought us coffee…"

"I thought we could both use some after a long couple of days. It's decaf."

She took her cup and set it on her nightstand and invited me to sit on the bed beside her. There was a mystery novel by one of my favorite authors there. I commented that I'd read it and enjoyed the author's work too. We talked for a while, a pleasant friendly conversation. I lost track of time until I heard the anniversary clock chiming the eleventh hour downstairs. I needed to cut to the chase.

"Do you like it here, Maria?"

"Wow, Emma. That came out of nowhere."

"Sorry, I think my thoughts are a bit scrambled from my concussion. Plus, Daniel said you'd fought."

"He told you about that?"

"Yes, but—"

"It's all just so horrible, Emma. I didn't mean for it to happen. It just did." Her body shivered, and she took my hand and shook it. "That's why I got so upset when you asked me if Daniel and I had an affair."

"So, you were?"

"What? Daniel and me? No, we weren't…it was Gwen and me. I thought he told you. We were falling in love. Daniel walked in on us. Nothing had happened yet, but he knew…"

I was at a loss for words and stumbled over the few I had available.

"Oh…Okay, well hmm. I…I didn't see that coming…"

"We didn't either. It just happened. Gwen is so beautiful and not the skin-deep beauty either. You know she was the "Queen of Tolerance" at the county fair a few years ago. She is a kind and loving woman. Daniel never saw that."

"But you did?" There was an unintentional edge in

my voice.

Maria sobbed. "I thought you would understand if anyone did, Emma. You were his victim too."

"Hey, I'm a 'glass house, no stones' kind of girl. Daniel is my brother, but Gwen is my friend too. She supported me at a bad time in my life. I will get to the truth of what happened here though. How did Daniel react to seeing you together?"

"It was bad. Daniel slapped Gwen and told me to pack as I'd be leaving in the morning. Gwen ran out crying, and the two of them yelled and cursed at each other for hours. The next morning, Gwen told me I wasn't going to go anywhere. She told Daniel to plan on a bitter divorce and that she'd get her share. She said Daniel begged her to reconsider. Everyone avoided everyone else the rest of the day. Neither of them spoke to me after that, but there wasn't any more yelling either. Even Nana knew something was wrong and didn't speak a word, just stared out of her window. The next morning, Gwen was missing."

Chapter Five

Sleep came in fits and starts that night. My mind wouldn't shut down, and it wasn't from caffeine. My brother could be a jerk and was most of the time. He was not an even-tempered man, but did I believe he was capable of kidnapping or worse? If it was Daniel who'd dragged Gwen off somewhere, was she alive and suffering—or worse? Jealousy was a powerful motive, and there was the specter of an ugly and expensive divorce looming ahead of him.

All the evidence pointed squarely at him, or Maria. If they'd fabricated the Maria-Gwen love story, I had to consider the possibility that Daniel and Maria were both involved in doing away with Gwen. I didn't know Maria that well, but what I did know didn't add up to a conniving murderous villainess. She was kind and gentle with Nana, and I believed the story she told me, but was she so afraid of what I might find out that she attacked me? Or had Daniel swung the bat?

I fell asleep to the weirdest dream with my case notes in my lap.

****

I was a child again, at the pond below the house, snooping on my older sister, Maya. She hadn't wanted to play games with me today. She said she had things to do, and I wanted to know what was more important than playing. Hiding behind a patch of multiflora rose,

I spied on her as she sat at the pond's edge.

Mom said I needed to give Maya some space now because she wasn't a little girl anymore. She was a young woman. I said I was a young woman too, but Mom said that was different. I think it was because I didn't have the bosoms yet.

Maya spread a blanket out on the grass and wildflowers and slipped off her shirt. She was wearing a yellow bathing suit underneath. Mom appliqued tiny bumblebees across its top. I thought Maya was going for a swim. I started to get up to ask if I could swim too, but I was afraid of the snapping turtles Daddy said lived there. I sat back down behind the wild roses. Maya didn't swim though. She stretched out on the blanket like she was taking a nap. Every few minutes, she'd sit up and look around like she was looking for someone. I hoped she didn't know I'd snuck up on her. She'd tell Mom, and I'd be in so much trouble for spying.

The next time Maya sat up to look around, I saw a figure walking toward her from the shallow end of the pond. It was a girl, and she seemed familiar. As she got closer, I recognized her. It was Jessie Dawson, our nearest neighbor. Maya stood up, waved, and Jessie ran toward her. Maya gave her a hug and Jessie pulled off her top to reveal her bathing suit. Hers was white, and it was decorated with bumblebees too. The two of them sprawled out on the blanket staring at the sky. They were talking about something. I couldn't hear what they were saying, but they sounded excited about it. I'll bet it was about a boy at school or some silly movie star.

They were like that for a long time, just being lazy

and doing nothing.

'Let's go play Space Invaders*, Emma,' I thought.*

I watched for a while longer, but it was pretty dull. So much so that I nodded off for a second. I slipped forward into the roses and a hooked thorn scratched across my cheek. I made a noise, then remembered where I was and looked toward the pond. Both girls sat up. Did they hear me? Oh no, I'll be in trouble. Then they did the oddest thing.

Maya said something to Jessie, and Jessie put her hand behind Maya's head and pulled their faces together…their lips touching. They were kissing like in the movies, the kind of movies we stole peeks at from behind the doorway when our parents thought we were asleep.

I stood up with a big grin, planning to tease Maya about what I saw, but everything got fuzzy. The flowers around the girls swelled up and grew huge before my eyes. The flowers swarmed around them, as fast as a snake's strike on a mouse. It was the reverse of nature—a huge ball of flowers devouring the little bumblebees. Then the flowery ball with its captive bees rolled into the pond with a splash…and sank.

Maya!

I heard the last note of the clock chiming in the great room and bolted up in bed.

"Maya? Where are you?"

I took a deep breath. From the corner of my eye, a shadow flitted across the room and disappeared into my closet. "*Easy, Emma. It's just that dream again,*" I assured myself.

A whisper in my ear. W*hat else did you see that day, Emma? Remember…*

"Maya?"

Of course, there was no response. I shook my head to clear out the cobwebs. The concussion must be worse than I realized.

The nightmare was so real I could smell the sweet scent of honeysuckle in the air, Maya's favorite. It was the same haunting dream that disturbed my slumbers since I was a child. Some people claim that dreams hold meaning or forgotten memories, but this one made no sense to me. I didn't remember any of it in my waking life.

I do recall sobbing at the dining room table the day after Maya's funeral—also the day after I first experienced the nightmare. Mom said I kept repeating in my sleep, "I should have saved her. I should have saved Maya."

"Emma, we were shopping in town for your new shoes that day. Remember? There was nothing we could have done," she'd reminded me.

So, it wasn't a deep dark secret I'd unconsciously squirreled away in a hidden recess of my mind. I did love playing *Space Invaders* as a child, and I remember Mom sitting on the couch sewing the bumblebees on Maya's swimsuit, but they were the only parts of the dream that rang true to me. My big-city shrink said it was due to so-called survivor's guilt. Maya died, and I was still here. God, I missed her.

I wiped the wet from my eyes and walked over to look out my window. The full moon hung low in the night sky. It looked swollen, mysterious, and somehow ominous. Would today be the day we solved the puzzle and brought Gwen home? Every day brought more clues, but we were no closer to the truth, no closer to saving my sister-in-law and friend. Something fuzzy and green flashed by the edge of my vision nearest the house. Was it my imagination—again? I stared outside for several minutes, but there was nothing to see. As I turned away, my vision swirled. I steadied myself with my hands along the wall to make my way back to bed. I fell into the mattress and held my hands against my temples, waiting for the spell to subside.

Scratch. Scratch. Thump. The sounds seemed to come from the basement, or was it the sound of my head pounding? I tried sitting up, but the swirling got worse. Blackness edged into my peripheral vision, and I dropped my head back to the pillow gently.

Clouds drifted over the moon and the room fell into total darkness. I concentrated on hearing any whisper of sound. My eyes were getting heavy when I was rewarded for my efforts—footfalls ascending the stairs from the basement. I wanted to go investigate and catch them in the act, whatever that act might be. I thought it might be another arrow in my proverbial quiver if they didn't know I knew. I listened to hear when the late-night prowler crept back upstairs to see which bedroom door they opened. Was it Daniel? Maria? Who would be rummaging around in the basement in the wee hours of the morning…and why?

I stood at my bedroom door with my ear against the wood. After a while, when my equilibrium was tested, I kneeled and listened—still no movement was heard. I began to think I'd missed an opportunity. My procedural instructor would've called it a rookie mistake, and that's what it felt like.

Whoever it was must have been aware of the loose floorboard above my head. It was still too early to get up and wake the household, so I pulled out my laptop and logged into my NeighborsSnoop.com account. So many of Daniel's neighbors had secrets to hide. I wanted to know them all.

I fell asleep never having heard the night prowler climb the stairs to the bedrooms.

****

I woke to the sound of the rooster crowing, slipped on my robe, and went to the kitchen to make a big pot of coffee. I suspected I'd need more than one cup today. Maria was there ahead of me, and the scent of fresh brew tickled my nostrils as soon as I opened my bedroom door.

"Perfect," I said. "I need some of that."

"Almost done. I'm rather in need myself."

"Long night?"

"I didn't sleep at all well. I tossed and turned all night. You?"

"Crazy dreams and all the banging around in the basement." I watched for her reaction. The raised eyebrows and slight downward turn of her lips looked more like puzzlement than guilt.

"Who knows what that was? We get mice in there all the time. Once, Gwen discovered a baby raccoon down there. It was crying for its mama, I guess. I'll find those traps you were asking about."

"Let me know if you find them. I'd like to look around down there to see if there are any old family pictures or mementos."

"Sure, whatever you want."

"Are you okay, Maria?" Her eyes were so puffy, her eyes were little more than slits.

She shrugged her shoulders, and I saw tears

forming. I'd leave her to her grief.

"I'm going up to check on Nana."

Maria nodded and took her coffee into the great room where she stared out the windows in silence. I climbed the stairs and was pleased to find Nana in a cheerful mood. The house's gloom and doom weighed heavily on my soul. She was sitting at her usual spot by the window.

"Morning, Nana."

"Good morning, child. Did you come home for a visit?"

"I did. I needed to check up on you and see if you were behaving yourself. How have you been?"

"Well, the old bones are creaky, my muscles are weak, and my mind is slipping. Stay young as long as you can, Emma."

"You recognize me?"

"Of course, I do, silly girl, and don't you worry about Daniel. He'll probably sleep all day. He was up all night storing veggies in the root cellar."

"I didn't even know we had a root cellar. Where is it?"

"Why in the basement of course. Where is your sister, Maya? Is she coming to visit with me too?"

"Not today, Nana. I think she's off visiting the neighbors."

"Last evening she promised to come see me again, but she only comes at night you know. She's probably over at the Dawson's house unless I miss my guess. She's too close with that Jessie girl. Jezebel is more like it if you ask me. The whole pack of 'em. That family doesn't come from good stock, Emma."

I bit my lip to subdue the smile threatening to

bloom on my face. Nana was never one to hold back or to forget past slights.

"They're friends, Nana, and Jessie has always been nice to me, a sweet girl."

"Your grandfather helped them out, and they treated him like dirt in return."

"What happened, Nana?" Nana's face went slack, expressionless, and distant.

"Where's your mother, Maya? I worry about you. Did you ask Emma about that day?"

"I'm Emma, Nana. Remember?"

"Of course, I remember Emma. Daniel ran her off. I was her guardian, but her parents left the house to Daniel, and I couldn't do a thing about it." Tears ran unabated down her face following the lines of well-earned wrinkles. I reached over and took her in my arms.

"It's all right, Nana. I'm home and doing fine. I'll never forget how hard you fought for me." My tears threatened to fall, and I shuddered.

Nana patted my back. "There, there, child."

After we collected ourselves, I stood up to leave.

"I'm going to check with Maria on your breakfast, Nana. You ring your bell if you need anything."

I found Maria in the great room where I'd left her. Other than the spot at Nana's window, it was my favorite part of the house. The big, overstuffed furniture just begged to be sat in while your troubles floated away.

Maria had lit the river-rock fireplace. A bearskin rug stretched out in front. The bear was one my Papa killed in West Virginia. Nana said it was digging through a trash can at their West Virginia cabin one fall and growled and snapped its teeth at her when she came upon it unawares. Papa heard Nana scream and shot the bear with his old 30/30 lever action. Most of the hairs were worn off the bear's ears, and there was a patch of fur missing from its back, but it evoked a cherished memory, and Nana wouldn't allow it to be disposed of. The fireplace held gas logs now. Daniel installed them after I left, and it lessened the ambiance somehow.

The cathedral ceiling was covered with fine planks of red cedar and stretched out, reaching for the sky. Most of the house was dark and gloomy, not unlike many houses of the era, but not this room. The floor-to-ceiling windows brightened it up on the cloudiest of days. They faced the main road going past the property and allowed a view almost as sweet as Nana's.

Maria turned toward me when I entered the room.

"How's your grandmother, Emma?"

"Nana is doing good this morning. She's in a great mood."

"I should see about getting her some breakfast. I'm being neglectful to her, the poor lady. I'm sorry. I have been so out of sorts of late, and it's hard staying here without Gwen and with Daniel hostile toward me."

"It's been a lot on you, I'm sure. I appreciate all you do too."

"Thanks. What are you planning to do today? Does the sheriff have any new leads?"

"Not to speak of. I do want to check out the basement. Does Daniel still have that scanner-printer combo in his office? I want to print out a stack of missing flyers for Gwen and put them up in town. You never know—someone might have seen her or seen something. I thought I'd add that picture of her from the foyer."

"That's one of my favorite pictures of her."

I thought, *Sure it's your favorite*. It was the only picture in the house without Daniel in it with her, but I kept my thoughts to myself.

I met Daniel in his office and asked if I could use his machine for making the posters.

"Of course, that's a wonderful idea. I'm not sure if the sheriff thought to do so or not. I doubt a small-town sheriff has a lot of experience with kidnappers. I don't recall one in all my years here."

"Were you by any chance rummaging around in the basement last night?" I asked.

"At night? No. I can't say that I slept very well, but I doubt crawling around in the dust and spiderwebs would've helped me sleep. I haven't been in the basement in years. Why?"

"I thought I heard something down there last night."

"Probably a mouse or something. Gwen heard a raccoon one night six or seven years ago, a baby one. She had a fit over it. Wanted me to catch it. I threw an old coat over it and tried to carry it up the stairs. It slipped its head out and bit my thumb. I dropped it then, of course. and it bared its teeth and growled. That was enough for me. Those things can get rabies you know. I finally caught it in a live trap using sardines as bait. No, I won't be going down there at night."

"It was probably hungry. Maybe it was after the vegetables in the root cellar?"

"What root cellar?" Daniel looked puzzled at the question.

"I don't know. I thought all the older houses

around here had them."

"I wouldn't know. I'm not a fan of dark, dank, and musty places."

Daniel left me to my own devices while he made a phone call to the county agricultural agent. The posters were printed out in short order, and I was off in the Bronco.

Most of the stores allowed me to put a poster in their window or on their bulletin board if they had one. Newtowne is a small country town, and most folks knew each other. Normally this is a fine thing, but not today. Everywhere I went, people wanted to chat, reminisce, or just plain gossip. I thought I'd never finish before dark until Abigail Dawson came to my rescue.

She stepped out of Baker's Five and Dime and I'm ashamed to say—I tried to avoid eye contact. She was hard to miss in her yellow top adorned with daisies, and hard not to hear, yelling her thanks to Mr. Baker at the top of her lungs. I didn't have time for her idle chatter.

"Emma? Emma, is that you? Over here."

For a woman of her size and age, she moved fast— like a cat pouncing on its prey. She showed me the curtain material she'd bought for her kitchen windows and described, in horrific detail, the tribulations of her gastronomic distress.

"Oh, did I tell you about the handsome young pastor at Mercy Church? He's a bachelor, you know. Should I pick you up for church on Sunday?"

I explained the hurry I was in and held out the missing person posters, and she reached out and grabbed the remaining stack.

"Now, don't you worry about a thing, Emma.

Boys, come here," she yelled at three pre-teens on the other side of the street. They looked at each other and back in the direction they'd come from. It seemed they decided flight wasn't in their best interest, and they crossed the street toward us.

"Yes, ma'am, Mrs. Dawson."

"I want you young men to do me a favor." She handed each boy a third of the pamphlets. "Take these and tack them to every phone pole from here to the end of the street. Stop and ask at the last few stores too. See if they can put one up in their windows."

"Yes, ma'am," they said and were off in a flash.

"Thank you, Abby. That was so kind of you."

"Just a neighbor helping another neighbor. No need for thanks. I'm sure your family would do the same for me."

"You mean like my grandfather?" I asked.

Abby's eyebrows shot up, and her lips were drawn in a tight line.

"Don't believe everything you're told, sweetheart. I meant your mother. She and I were a great comfort to one another when our girls passed on to be with our Savior. I don't know how I would've gotten through it without her."

"I didn't know."

"Well, you weren't much more than a sprout then, were you?"

"No, ma'am."

"How's everyone doing up at the big house, Emma?"

"As well as you'd expect, I guess. Did Mr. Dawson get home all right? How was his fishing trip?"

"Lord, Emma, that man. He isn't home yet. He

called last night while they were out gathering supplies in Flintstone. They're staying up there another week."

"Are they filling their coolers with trout then?"

"You know, I didn't even ask. I know the Good Lord fed all those people with the loaves and fishes, but I'm afraid if I'd been there, I would've had to go hungry. Forgive me, Lord, but I can't eat fish. Makes me downright gag."

"That's a shame. It's good for you."

"Don't I know it, but there are things we should do but don't, and a lot of things we do that we shouldn't. Wouldn't you say?"

"Yes, ma'am. Well, I better get along. Thank you so much for your help." I turned and started walking away. I thought I was in the clear when her voice called me back.

"Emma, wait."

I turned back and it felt like my shoes were full of lead walking back.

"I forgot to mention it, but you might want to pass along to Sam something else that Michael said. He saw a strange car, an older dark-colored Buick four-door, maybe late '60s, parked on the back road behind our property that morning when he left to go fishing. It was dark so he didn't recognize the gentleman or the car. The man was shutting his trunk when Michael drove by."

I had to catch my breath—a strange vehicle parked so close to our house on the night Gwen was abducted. Finally, a lead. "Thank you again, Abby," I said. "That's something I'm sure the sheriff's office will want to know."

****

I was excited when I got back to the house. I didn't take off my coat or hang up my keys before I had Sam on the phone.

"Sam, I got a lead. Maybe the first one that doesn't point at Daniel or Maria." I described Abby's revelation.

"That's good to know. I wonder if he noticed anything else?"

"Abby said she'd ask Michael for any more information about the car. He might have the color or know what state it was tagged in."

"That's a good idea. I can't recall a Buick of that vintage around town. Older cars stand out. If it's an out-of-state vehicle, the FBI might get involved. The sheriff is reluctant to pull in outside resources, but each day that passes, Gwen's prospects are bleaker."

We talked for a good half-hour and not entirely about the case. We hung up intending to meet the next day and put our heads together. I had one item left on my agenda for the day. The basement beckoned.

At the bottom of the stairs, I flicked on the light switch. The weak yellow bulb did not reach far into the darkness. It reminded me of a Neanderthal cave dwelling. Primitive animal art on the walls wouldn't have been at all out of place. I decided to do a cursory inspection and try again in the morning. Cobwebs covered all the corners of the walls. In front of the wall closest to me, a stack of boxes waited. Beside them were several suitcases. A bright yellow one at the top of the pile caught my eye. Attached to it was a name tag—Maria's name tag.

At the edge of my vision was a huge trunk. I think the style is called a sea trunk. From what I could see, it was very old and would warrant checking out…tomorrow with better light. I opened the nearest box and saw hundreds of old pictures, a cornucopia of family remembrances. I sifted through a few but stopped again, anxious to see what other treasures awaited me.

The next box contained old documents. It was apparent from the damage to the pages that silverfish and book lice discovered them before me. I slapped my hands together to shake off the dust and noticed something black and shiny between the boxes. I reached for it and the black snake uncoiled and did a mock strike at my hand! In hindsight, I knew the snake was bluffing. It had me dead to rights if biting was its intent. But its intentions mattered little to me. That was enough for tonight…

Chapter Six

I was exhausted and hit the sack early. As usual, my dreams took me to places I didn't want to go. There was the old familiar one at Sam's graduation party. Sam was there, of course, and "dream" Sam ignored me just as he did that night years ago. What had I done to receive such a cold reception? I'd thought he loved me, although he hadn't said the words yet.

When I got to the part of the story where Robert Wathen entered it, I punched my headboard and jerked myself awake. Some memories are too dark even for the subconscious mind to dwell upon. I sat up in bed and looked around my room, for a moment believing the dream was real. It was real, all too real, just not in my present. I shook off the tendrils of sleep and the haunting nightmare. I listened for any sounds of movement in the house or below. There wasn't a sound from man or beast or slithering reptiles. I looked out of my window. Nothing stirred there either. I curled up in bed and pulled up an extra blanket. The meteorologist predicted a cold wave coming for us, and I missed my flannel sheets.

I slept the sleep of the dead (as Nana described it in my teenage years). Not until Rachel the rooster crowed his approval at the rising sun did my head leave the pillow, and yes, Gwen named her rooster Rachel. The Mennonite farmer sexed the chicks when she bought them, and apparently, he got one wrong. Our neighboring poultry expert and conspiracy buff, Mr. Hill, said the government put testosterone in the feed and the bird swapped genders between hatching out and full-fledging. Rachel didn't care one way or the other.

When I heard sounds of movement from the kitchen, I slipped on my robe to join Maria for a cup of coffee.

"Morning, Maria," I said as I stepped into the kitchen, but it wasn't her standing by the stove.

"It's just me, sorry to disappoint you," Daniel said. "I haven't seen anything of Maria. Unusual. She's usually an early riser."

"I'll take her up a cup when it's done and check on her."

"If you must. I'd just as soon not to see her."

"You have a snake in the basement."

"What's that you say?"

"I said there is a snake in the basement. It's only a black snake from the looks of it. I know they can't hurt you unless they give you a heart attack when they surprise you."

"I should say so. When you go upstairs, ask Maria for a box of mothballs. I mean, if you're still determined to investigate the depths of the basement."

"I'll do that."

With two cups of coffee in my hands, I went upstairs and tapped Maria's door with my knee.

"Maria? I have two cups of go-juice, liquid caffeine—breakfast of champions. Are you awake?"

I waited until the heat from the cups became uncomfortable. Placing the cups on the floor, I knocked again, harder this time. Still no answer.

"Maria, are you decent? I'm coming in." I knocked one more time and tried the doorknob…locked. I jiggled the knob and tried again with no luck.

"Daniel, do you have a key?" I yelled, but there was no reply from Daniel either.

I started back down the stairs and heard tires on the gravel driveway. I ran down the hall to look through the replacement glass that Daniel had installed. Sheriff Wathen and Sam were climbing out of their cruisers. I pulled open the door without a thought of my fancy attire—pajamas and an old robe.

"Has something broken on the case? Have you found Gwen?"

The look on Sam's face did not fit with the bearer of good news.

"What is it? What have you found?"

"Miss Love, please go back inside. For the moment, we just have some additional questions for your brother, and I think we'll do that downtown. Major Mattingley will take any additional statement you may have until the other deputies arrive."

"Other deputies?"

"Yes, ma'am." He reached into his uniform jacket, pulled out a folded piece of paper, and handed it to me. It was a search warrant and allowed a search of Daniel's bedroom and common areas in the house. Any items believed to be associated with Gwen Love's departure may be seized with particularity any items with potential DNA evidence. It was signed by Judge Thomas Allen.

"This is rather open-ended, isn't it? Is that normal?" I asked.

"It is unusual, but this is an unusual situation.

Kidnappings don't happen around here," Sam said.

"You don't have anything to hide, do you, young lady?" the sheriff asked.

"No, but my rights are something I hold dearly."

"Where can I find your brother?"

"I'm here," Daniel said and stepped into the foyer. "What's all the commotion about?"

"We are going downtown to have a chat, Mr. Love."

"I'd rather not. I have a lot going on today."

"You must have misunderstood me, Mr. Love. That was not a request," the sheriff said. He pulled out a pair of handcuffs and shook them at Daniel. "With or without. Your choice this time."

"I didn't do anything to Gwen, Emma. Believe me," he said, as he was pulled through the door. "Call my lawyer, Henry Stone."

I watched in silence as the sheriff and Daniel pulled away in the squad car and turned to Sam.

"What is going on? Is there some new development you haven't told me about?"

"I think it's a matter of desperation at this point because there isn't anything new. I know you don't care for his family, but the sheriff isn't a bad guy and he's good at his job. Finding Gwen is his priority. He'll probably be back to take Maria in for the third degree when he's done with your brother."

"Oh my God, I forgot about Maria."

"What about…?"

I ran to the kitchen and found one of the tiny keys for interior doors hanging on the hooks by the back door.

"What are you doing?"

"Come on," I answered.

Up the stairs to Maria's room. I knocked hard, and hearing no answer, unlocked the door.

The room was empty. Her bed didn't look slept in, but the bedspread was rumpled as if she'd spent time tossing and turning on it before…whatever happened. Sam held out his hand to stop me from entering.

"I know you know what you're doing, but I better do this by procedure. I wouldn't want it said that the evidence was compromised."

Sam pulled out an evidence bag. He picked up the hairbrush on Maria's nightstand.

"I know the warrant didn't mention Maria's room, but do you mind?"

I shook my head. "Not if it will help."

He searched the room for any indication of foul play or hopefully, a note saying where she'd gone, but came up empty. He looked for scratch marks around the door, as there was no forced entry, but perhaps forced removal?

"Sam, look in her bathroom. Her purse is missing. She keeps it right there on that stand." When it went undiscovered, I breathed a sigh of relief. Maria would be back with us soon.

Sam put on gloves before he picked up her phone and dialed the *69 sequence to see who she last called, then put the call through. He placed the phone on "speaker," and I could hear the phone on the other end ringing. A high-pitched young voice picked up. "Brandy's Beauty Parlor. Lilian speaking. How can I help you?"

"Yes, ma'am, this is Deputy Mattingley with the Sheriff's Office. Can you tell me if Maria Clements has been in today or if she has an appointment later…?"

"Well, hello, Deputy. We haven't seen you in a while. How have you been? I'd love to do your hair. It's free for law enforcement you know, but in your case, it wouldn't matter if you weren't—"

"Hi, Lilian…about Miss Clements."

"Oh, sure. Are you two dating now? She is a pretty one. Quite the reputation you know, but if you're okay with that…"

"Lilian, this is an official inquiry. Please answer my questions."

"Official, hey? I'll just bet it is too, but wait just a minute. Don't get your shorts in a knot. Let's see…Clements…Clements…There she is. She has an appointment in one hour, Deputy. If there's anything else I can do for you, don't hesitate to call."

"Thank you, Lilian." He hung up the phone and turned back toward me.

"What's so funny?"

"Nothing, Deputy, but if there's anything I can do for you, please let me know."

"Ha-ha."

Two more sheriff's vehicles pulled into the driveway, and Sam left to greet them. He sent one of them back to town to see if Maria made her appointment.

I called Daniel's lawyer, and he said he'd get to the sheriff's office before lunch. He was representing some kid who was caught vandalizing street signs and would be out of court by then.

The phone rang as I replaced the receiver.

"Hello, Miss Love. This is the sheriff. Put one of my deputies on, please."

Sam was standing nearby and took the call. He nodded a few times, hung up, and pulled out his cell phone to dial. I could tell he was speaking with one of the deputies, but he ducked his head and took several steps away where I couldn't hear the conversation.

"What was that all about?"

"The sheriff said the blood analysis results from the necklace are back from upstate."

"And? Was it Gwen's blood on the necklace? Daniel's?"

"That's another conundrum. The DNA from the blood sample identified it as from a male, but there's no match for it in the system."

"And the call you made?"

"The sheriff asked Daniel for a blood sample. Daniel refused, and that looked a little suspicious. With the way the sheriff has grilled him though, I don't think the man knows which end is up. He did say he might submit one to his doctor after he consulted with his lawyer. The sheriff asked about other possible males in the area, and he mentioned Mr. Hill, your other neighbor up the road a piece. I understand Hill does some handyman work for your family. I asked Deputy Douglas to stop and ask Mr. Hill after checking on Maria at the beauty parlor."

"That's barking up the wrong tree. Mr. Hill wouldn't hurt a fly."

Sam put crime tape across Maria's doorway, then we walked down the hall to Daniel and Gwen's room. The other deputy was already there dusting for fingerprints.

"When you're done here, Deputy, dust the room down the hall too. Make sure you get the doorknob on both sides. Emma, we'll need to take your prints also to eliminate yours from the equation. I think Maria will be showing up for her appointment. I expect a call from Deputy Douglas at any moment to verify, but just in case, as we're already here."

I didn't want to see what private items they might pull from Daniel and Gwen's room, but I knew I could trust Sam to be discreet. I went downstairs and warmed up a cup of coffee. The auto shut-off had activated, and I didn't like the cold brews. I sat in the great room and gazed out of the windows to the road. I thought how lucky we were that Nana didn't know what was going on.

My last sip of coffee required chewing, and I spat the grounds into my hand. Daniel always overfills the percolator filter cup.

I rinsed my cup and walked upstairs. I peeked in as Sam was answering his phone and Deputy Joyce (as she said to call her) was placing evidence bags in two large trash bags.

"You're about done then?"

"I think so. Just wrapping it up," she said. "Sorry about the fingerprint powder."

"No worries, Deputy Joyce. I'm going to ask Maria to clean it up when she gets home to make up for making us worry about her all day. I'll be right back." I walked down the hallway to Maria's room.

Did they miss anything? I wanted to do a quick search myself, but I knew Sam would have an absolute fit. I stood at the door staring in until something caught my eye.

"Sam, come here, please."

He came out of Daniel's room with his phone at his

ear.

I heard him say, "Not there" and "Good job" before ending the call. I stared at him, waiting.

"That was Deputy Douglas on the phone," he said. "Maria never showed up for her appointment. The owner said she never misses one."

He slipped his phone back in his pocket.

"What's up? Emma?"

I pointed to the floor beneath Maria's bed. "What's that?"

He slipped under the crime tape, reached under the bed, and pulled out a pink leather diary.

"As it appears Maria is missing now as well, I hate this, but we can't take a chance. This diary is evidence."

He brought it back to me and opened it to her last entry. The heading showed yesterday's time and date. He held it out so that we both could read.

I'm not sure what to do. I feel that when Gwen is found, she'll need me, and I know in my heart that she is still alive. I can't allow any other possibility to take root in my mind. But Daniel was so angry at her, and at me. What if he did do something to her? When Emma drove Sam back to the station the other evening, he threatened me. What if I disappear next?

Sam closed the book. "This doesn't look good, Emma. I'll have to take this in."

Chapter Seven

After Sam and Deputy Joyce left, I texted Daniel's lawyer to update him on all that happened, not calling in case he was still in court.

I was at a complete loss on what to do next. I called Sam several times, but he didn't answer, and Daniel's phone was going straight to voicemail.

I returned to the hallway outside of Maria's room. If she was abducted, as it seemed, the evidence there would be the freshest. I pulled the crime tape a bit this way, then the next, trying to see anything inside that we might've missed.

I felt like such a child and yanked down one side of the tape.

"Oops," I said as it floated to the floor. I knew Sam would kill me, but I crawled under and tiptoed inside. I'd noticed a couple of places Sam had not searched. Under the pillows and the mattress were good hiding spaces. Sam was too much of the gentleman and only did a cursory search of Maria's underwear drawer. Perhaps he would've if I wasn't standing there watching? He looked like a kid caught with his hand in the cookie jar. He'd brushed the unmentionables one way, then the next, and closed the drawer.

I reached under the mattress on both sides, then slipped my fingers under and inside the pillowcases. I felt nothing. I wasn't as shy as Sam, and I pulled out and shook out every piece of undergarment. Some I admired and wondered where Maria purchased them. There were one or two I'd describe as risqué—unless you were a lace aficionado and liked strategically placed ventilation holes. Some were like most of mine, with the elastic shot and the material thread-worn. Then my hands fell on a tiny box. Ah. Her secret treasure, I thought. I lifted the lid and my mouth dropped open. There was a thick lock of pink hair that I'd bet was cut from Gwen's new hairdo.

****

I gnawed at my lip; I was that angry with myself. Emma Love, "best private investigator in the state," Sam had joked. I felt incompetent and alone. The case was no closer to being solved. If anything, I was putting the nails in Daniel's coffin, and two women had disappeared—one right under my nose. I grabbed the phone by Maria's bed, ignoring the black fingerprint powder I'd spend hours getting off my hands and out of my hair.

"Sam, I found something in Maria's room that you need to know about."

"Emma, you shouldn't have gone in there. This is serious, Maria is missing, and you're…"

"Incapable? Is that what you were going to say?"

"No. I was going to say…"

"Inexperienced?"

"You're not a cop and you are our main suspect's sister. I have every confidence in you, Emma, but this needs to be done by the book. You know what a prosecutor would do with this piece of information?"

There was silence on the phone while I calmed myself down. It wasn't right to bark at Sam just because I felt insecure. Plus, he was right.

"Anyway, what did you find?" he asked.

"I think it's a lock of Gwen's hair."

"Okay, please don't mess with anything else in that room. I just got off duty. As soon as I change out of my uniform, I'll head your way. How about I pick us up something to eat on the way? Chinese work for you?"

"Beef and broccoli would be nice. Oh, and make mine with fried rice."

"You've got it. I will see you soon."

"Sam? Just between us, does the sheriff think Daniel is behind all of this?"

"I can't speak for him, but I don't see Daniel, a man I've known all my life, being capable of hurting anyone. Professionally? All the evidence is pointing at him."

While I waited for Sam, I remembered the basement and decided to have another go at it. I was mindful of snakes and grabbed a walking stick Daniel had bought when he and Gwen went on their honeymoon to the mountains. I doubt it had been out of the umbrella stand since they brought it home. I poked at every box before I moved them but didn't find anything of importance. There were old tax records and bill receipts. I wished things were as cheap as they were when the receipts were printed out. The most recent records were over twenty years old. Daniel didn't do basements, and he stored his records in the attic instead.

I heard a thumping at the front door followed by Sam's voice calling my name. I grabbed a stack of children's drawings and old deed work from the sea chest to look at in my leisure and closed the basement door behind me.

I greeted Sam at the door. He held out two bags of Chinese carryout and smiled, but his eyes wouldn't meet mine.

"What's wrong, Sam? What has happened?"

"Emma, on the way over here, Deputy Douglas called. He informed me the sheriff officially charged Daniel. I'm hoping the bail hearing will be set for tomorrow, but I can't say for sure."

"More bad news. I guess we should be used to it by now."

"Let's eat our food before it gets cold. It might help to take our minds off all of this for a while."

We sat at the small dinette set in the kitchen. It was easier and more comfortable to talk there without the formality of the dining room. I loved the fancy cherrywood hutch and table in there, but for me, it evoked an image of old lawyer's offices and courtrooms. I wasn't up to that.

I set the table as Sam passed out the food. He went with General Tso's chicken. It was one of my favorites too, and I must have giggled, thinking I might sneak a bite when he wasn't looking.

"What's so funny? I could use a laugh about now."

"Nothing," I lied. "Hysterical laughter maybe?"

The speed with which the food disappeared was either a testament to our hunger or to the cook's prowess or both. We washed the dishes together. Sam washed. I dried.

"Where did you find the lock of hair? I'll need it to have it sent upstate to the forensics lab for testing."

"No problem, and I found it in Maria's unmentionables drawer. I noticed you were less than thorough when handling the lady's panties."

79

"Thanks for that," he said, and his face flushed.

"Oh. Look at you all embarrassed. Don't worry. If you give me an evidence bag, I'll slip the hair in there and you can forget it ever happened. Remind me, just in case, before you leave."

"Thanks a lot," Sam said, "but I'm staying here tonight if that's okay?"

I'm sure my eyebrows squinted a bit as I tried to read his face to determine his intentions.

"You think the poor little country girl can't take care of herself, Deputy?"

"No, I just thought…"

"Hmmm, so I'm entertaining a male guest who's overnighting with me—a damsel who's obviously in distress…an uninvited male guest, I might add. What would the neighbors say? Are you trying to destroy my good name, sir?"

"You'd be doing me a huge favor, Emma. My landlord sprayed the next-door apartment for bugs today. It smells awful, plus they'll all run into my apartment now."

"I see. That's totally different. It's good to know that you only want to stay because you're being invaded by an angry horde of cockroaches."

"Emma, I admit I don't want you staying alone and that all my reasons aren't of an official or even practical nature. I think a lot of you, in case you haven't noticed. I always have. I guess the dating gurus would condemn me for saying this, but I don't like playing games. I'm just going to be honest with you. It's all I know how to do. I've dated other women, but I've never gotten over you. I dream about you way too many nights. I wake up with a handful of the pillow cover, thinking it's your hair." He looked straight into my eyes then, gauging my reaction, but words would not come.

"I…I think I've said too much. I'm sorry," he said.

I don't know what came over me at that instant. He looked like a lost and forlorn soul, like a puppy after a bigger dog stole its chew toy. His shoulders sagged, and his eyes dropped. I wanted to take him in my arms and comfort him like a child, but Sam was no child. He turned his back to me and stepped toward the front hallway. I reached out and held his shoulder. When he turned to face me, I stood on tiptoes and let my lips brush against his.

"I guess I need to stop teasing you so much, Sam Mattingley. You're so flustered and cute, and you're about to leave without Gwen's hair."

"That didn't come out so well, Emma. God, I sounded so needy. Hope I didn't offend you. My tax accountant says I'm way too honest for my good."

"We're fine, Sam. I appreciate your honesty." Under my breath (or so I thought) I said, "Wish you'd always been so honest."

"What do you mean by that?"

"I'm sorry I said that. Please forget I said it."

"I will, but just for now, Emma. Promise?"

Was it possible that he didn't know already? That I meant so little, he didn't even remember that long ago night?

"Okay, I promise," I said.

Sam walked out to his Mustang and came back with a camouflage-print sleeping bag tucked under his arm.

"You know we have plenty of bedrooms. I can make up a bed for you."

"Nope, uninvited guests sleep on the couch. Besides, I'll be right down the hall if you need me."

I nodded my head. "I do find it interesting that you had the sleeping bag in your car already. Felt pretty sure of yourself, were ya, sailor? Or is it still there from the last lady you overnighted with?"

His eyebrows went up until he saw me smile.

"Of course, you know the ladies cannot resist my charms, fair maiden. It's my curse."

****

Sam went into the living room to pick a movie to stream while I popped some popcorn. I thought about the new developments with Sam and wasn't sure how I felt about it. He seemed to be the same old Sam I'd deeply cared for so long ago. If that were true, wouldn't we end up in the same place as before?

In the past year, he'd been such a good friend and confidant. That was when I'd reached out to him on a whim. He supported me when I decided to go through Private Investigator's training and prodded me when it got tough, or I dragged my feet. I needed to know where this was going. Could I trust him again? He was the only one who knew when I came home six months ago. He helped me house hunting while I stayed in a flea-bag hotel, and he kept my arrival secret. Could he be trusted for more?

It was one tiny kiss and you initiated it, Emma. Let it go.

"Everything okay out there? Can I help?" Sam yelled.

"All done. I'm coming now."

Where the Crawdads Sing was waiting on the screen for our viewing pleasure when I rejoined him.

"Does this one look all right? I've heard it's good."

"Have you been perving around my bedroom at home, Sam Mattingley?"

"What in the world are you talking about?"

"I have the book on my nightstand to read next if I ever get home again."

"A great book can be translated into a so-so movie, so we can pick another if you want. I wouldn't want to ruin the book for you," Sam said.

"You know I used to be a terrible tomboy once upon a time. I'd spend hours playing at the creek trying to catch crawdads with the tiny net from our aquarium, so it might bring back good memories. Let's roll the dice and see."

We sat together on the couch, closer than we did before. After a while, my head rested on Sam's shoulder, and I could somehow feel him smile. He curled into me to make his shoulder into a better pillow. When the popcorn was gone and the wine in my glass was low, I hit the pause button on the remote and sat up.

"Don't you think it's odd though?"

"Yeah, but she was abandoned by her family in the swamps…"

"No, I don't mean the movie; I mean the hair. If Daniel did something to either of them, why would he put Gwen's hair in Maria's room?"

"We don't know for sure what happened to Maria, or Gwen either for that matter, but I'm sure Gwen is missing. Maria hasn't been gone for twenty-four hours yet. She might have met some guy or stayed over at a friend's house. We just don't know yet."

"I don't believe that. She wouldn't, not without

letting us know, especially with what's going on here. I could understand if she wanted out of this house for a while, but not without telling someone…telling me."

"I think you're right about that. It would be out of character for her, but what's going on here could be the reason she stayed away. As for why Daniel might have put the hair there, it would make us look closer at Maria."

"If either of them was responsible, do you think they're stupid enough to keep a memento of the crime? It was tied up in a frilly bow. It was more like a lover's remembrance than a kidnapper's trophy."

"That's not necessarily an either-or. Daniel could be both things. Maria, as well."

Chapter Eight

I told Sam good night and crawled into my bed. My head was buzzing with more questions than answers and sleep didn't come easy. I rolled over and grabbed the papers I'd retrieved from the chest in the basement and started going through them.

The number of drawings done by Daniel, Maya, and me was mind-boggling. I'd only grabbed the first three packets from one side of the trunk, yet they covered our artistic efforts from our toddler years through middle school. The rest that I'd left behind must be from our more skilled (I hoped) high school years. It seemed every drawing we'd ever made was kept and treasured by our parents. It was a happy and sad moment, and I smiled even as tears threatened to flow. The packets were categorized by the artist and age, each tied together with baling twine. I assumed that was my father's contribution. I went through a few dozen of them from each of our early years. There were plenty of representations of our family standing in front of the house. Curling tendrils of smoke rose from the chimneys and smiling suns with well-defined rays dispelled the big fluffy white clouds. Some of the clouds were smiling also. Maya drew a couple of pictures in front of the church. The building was easy to identify by the huge crosses precariously mounted on the roof and the very tall man standing behind our family wearing a Roman collar and a toothsome grin. We all three attempted depictions of what I assume to be dinosaurs and elephants around the same age. We must have shared at least one art teacher in common over the years. By the tusks and huge dangly trunks, I could identify the elephants, but the dinosaurs, not so much.

I smiled at the thought of who we were back then. I set our old artwork aside to examine the documents I'd discovered next. They were stacked neatly in folders on the opposite side of the trunk from the drawings. The folders were labeled and held together by dry-rotted rubber bands that flaked apart when I tried to remove them. These were organized by category rather than by year. I fished out old tax returns out of curiosity. I saw the one from the year before my parents died. It would be a miserable existence to try to live on their combined adjusted income now. The next bundle held insurance policies from over the years. Another stored receipts, manuals, and warranties for various items. The instructions for my mother's KitchenAid mixer were in there—right beside the one for the new-to-us tobacco planter my father bought second-hand from Mr. Charles Hayden. The last folder I'd retrieved was the thinnest of the lot. It was marked "Deeds and Contracts." This one contained the oldest documents I'd seen so far. I flipped through the papers, not expecting much from the yellowed dog-eared pages. One caught my eye, and I slipped it out for a closer look. The top of the document was marked in heavy print "Quitclaim Deed." Its stated intent was to transfer the title of twenty acres of farmland from Sebastian Dawson to my grandfather, Franklin Love. There was no monetary amount listed. I thought that odd.

I grabbed my laptop from my nightstand to find out what a "Quitclaim" deed was. The search engine results indicated it was when the title holder gave up, or quit their rights, to a property without financial remuneration. It was generally done in cases such as a gift of land to a family member. Why would Mr. Dawson give twenty acres of land to my grandfather? There had to be some form of payment made. I suspected the two men wanted to keep Uncle Sam out of their business, but it was a mystery for another day.

My eyes were heavy, but I read the final chapter of my novel to a satisfying conclusion. I fell asleep wondering what the following day would bring. I dreamt of Maya and hordes of predatory flowers.

****

The cawing of crows outside my window woke me. I rubbed my eyes and checked my cell phone. I'd overslept. Slipping on a pair of jeans and a pullover, I hurried out of my room, fearing I'd missed Sam's departure. I didn't earn any points as a hostess.

"Sam?" I yelled.

"In here, Miss Sleepyhead."

I followed his voice into the kitchen. He was standing at the sink pouring water into the percolator.

"I was hoping to have some coffee ready for you, but I'm still trying to figure out how this thing works." He held it up for me to see.

"Geez, Sam. Haven't you ever gone camping before?"

"Yeah, but I took instant."

"Yuck. Watch out and I'll make us a pot of real coffee. Nice and strong, and the last cup will even give you something to chew on."

"None for me thanks. Raincheck? I really must get going before the sheriff puts out an All-Points Bulletin on me. See you later? Lunch maybe?"

"Maybe. I need to make up some missing person posters for Maria. I haven't put anything on social media yet either, but I did see where the sheriff's department did."

"You're welcome." Sam nodded.

"I think we can call her missing now. Twenty-four hours, you said?" I asked.

"That's not an official thing, Emma, not like in the movies. We're already treating her case as a missing person. It just isn't taken as seriously in the case of an adult until then, unless there's an extenuating circumstance."

"I'd say two women disappearing from the same house is an extenuating circumstance."

"Exactly."

We said our awkward goodbyes at the door. Sam looked confused and held out his hand. I reached in for a friendly hug.

I went back to the kitchen and my percolator. I heard the Mustang roar to life and chuckled to myself. I remembered an inspection ticket Sam got upset over years ago. He'd installed noisy glass-pack mufflers on an old Chevy Chevelle. He said it made his car sound "throaty." It made my teeth clench whenever he hit the accelerator.

I sat at the table with a notebook and pencil and sipped my coffee. I tried to outline the clues in the case in the timeline they occurred rather than in the order of discovery:

Gwen and Maria were more than friends.

Daniel caught them in an embrace.

Daniel and Gwen fight.

Gwen went missing, probably against her will.

The door glass broke out from inside the house.

Blood of an unknown male on Gwen's broken necklace.

Gwen's shoe was found in the back-field well away from the house.

Vague ransom note left with no follow-up.

Maria and Daniel fight (according to the diary entry).

Maria went missing, and her purse was gone. If she was forced—yet to be determined.

It wasn't a lot to go on, and none of it boded well for my brother. I started another list of "things to do today" as I finished my second cup.

My first effort was making up Maria's posters. This didn't take long as I used the same outline I used for Gwen, only changing the picture. I called Henry Stone's office and received no answer. I guess sleeping in for me was too early for a small-town lawyer. I left a message with my cell phone number and asked him to call me back about the particulars of the bail hearing.

I found Alicia Wood's home phone number magnetically attached to the refrigerator and gave her a call. I knew she was Daniel's on-call help whenever Maria took a few days off. She was young, but mature for her age, and always eager to earn a few extra bucks. She was living at home until she finished nursing school. She answered on the second ring.

"Alicia? This is Emma Love, Daniel's sister. I was wondering if you're free for a few days. I'll be in and out a lot and I can't leave Nana alone."

"I sure am. Perfect timing. I'm between classes and at your disposal."

"How soon can you get here?"

"I can leave now if you want, or…"

"That would be wonderful, Alicia. You are a lifesaver."

"Do I need to bring anything?"

"The fridge and freezer are full. You can help yourself to anything you want. Otherwise, pack enough clothes for a couple of nights—just in case."

"Okay, I'm on my way, Emma."

Everything else I needed to do waited for me in Newtowne. With the lawyer's office closed, I could wait a few more minutes while I cleaned the kitchen. I wiped down the table and washed my coffee cup. I dumped the grounds from the day's brew into the trash can and did a double take. What was that? I pulled out a fresh white envelope, now stained with coffee grounds. I saw "MARIA" typed across the front in bold capital letters. There was no address or other markings—did someone hand deliver it?

An image flashed in my mind, and I hurried to the basement. It only took a moment to verify my suspicions…I knew something was different last night. I could not wait to tell Sam what I had discovered.

****

When Alicia arrived, I pointed out different things in the house, but I could see she knew it well. She was more familiar than I was with Nana's food and medication schedule. She knew the drug names and side effects without looking. I left soon after, giving her a thankful hug on the way out the door.

Henry Stone's office was still closed when I got to town, so I spent the time putting up Maria's missing posters. Luckily, I'd brought some extra flyers about Gwen as a few were defaced with mustaches and beards. Kids, I guess.

"I don't think I knew the other lady, but that's Miss Clements, isn't it?" a small voice asked from behind me.

I turned around, and it was one of the young boys who helped me put up Gwen's posters. He was tall and thin with blond hair and the lightest blue eyes I'd ever seen.

"Yes. It is. Do you know her?"

"Yes, ma'am. She's a real friendly lady. She doesn't talk to us like we're little kids."

"I don't suppose you've seen Miss Clements, have you? She's missing now too."

"No, ma'am. But if I do, I'll tell her you're looking for her."

"Thank you. I appreciate that."

"Who should I tell her is looking?"

"I'm Emma Love. What's your name?"

"I'm Josh Grimes, but my friends just call me Crab on account of one bit me real bad this past summer. It drew blood and everything."

He held his finger up to show me, but it was either well healed since summer or the dirt from the playground did a good job covering it up.

"I'm sorry to hear that, Josh. Did you get your revenge and eat that crab?"

"No, ma'am, it was a sponge crab. You know, the girl crabs that have the eggs? Daddy said to throw it back. Say, are you one of the Loves that live in the mansion up on the hill?"

I smiled. "Well, I am for the moment anyway, living there I mean."

"I'll be sure to give Miss Clements your message if I see her, ma'am. Do you want some help putting those up? Me and the boys will do it for you."

I told him that would be wonderful, and that I'd appreciate the help. I handed him a five-dollar bill.

"I have another five dollars for any of the other boys who want to help too. You just find me in town today and I'll pay them. I promise my credit is good."

"Yes, ma'am, Mrs. Love. It was nice meeting you." He held out his hand and we shook.

My next stop was a return to the lawyer's office. It was what one might expect the office of an old-school lawyer's office to look like. Dark cherry wainscotting highlighted the eggshell white walls. A tasteful yet elegant chandelier hung from the ceiling, and expensive carpeting protected the wood floors that I observed around its edges. The receptionist's desk had a turn-of-the-century vibe crafted from the same dark cherry. The woman was speaking on the phone and held up one finger to suggest she was almost done. Her desk held the requisite family photo: Mom (the receptionist), Dad, and two kids—a boy and a girl. She was dressed in business attire—a navy-blue pantsuit with a white button-up blouse with a wide collar. There were more buttons loosened at her top than one might expect. I had to admit, though, that she pulled it off, and the "whole face" smile she threw at me made me like her immediately.

"Yes, ma'am. Can I help you?"

"I'm Emma Love, and I'm here to see Mr. Stone."

She laughed, and for a moment I was a bit offended.

"Of course, you are, Emma." She stood from behind the desk and held out her hand and we shook.

"I almost didn't recognize you, girl," she said. "Wow, you're gorgeous. Can I have your hair? Wait until my brother gets a look at you. You were already all he talked about. Oops, don't tell him I said that."

I stood there with my mouth agape and with no idea who she was.

"Oh geez, I'll bet you don't remember me." She flashed her beauty pageant smile at me again, and I reflexively smiled back. "It's been a while, and I was a few years ahead of you both. I'm Irene Burch, well, Irene Mattingley back then. Remember me? Sammy's big sister? Well, not bigger, just older."

I looked her up and down as if she might be an imposter. She had a new hairdo, none of which had a single strand of hair out of place (Did she just come from the salon?). It was a new color too. Her makeup was flawless, in that I couldn't tell for sure if she had any on or if it was natural beauty. It was more than that though. This woman looked so mature and grounded…the proverbial All-American girl. Not at all like the girl I remembered from school.

"Irene? Seriously? Look at you. It's so good to see you again. It's been a long time."

"We will have to get together sometime, maybe have a drink together or a cup of coffee? Talk about those good old days?" The interior office door opened, and Henry Stone emerged from his inner sanctum. He was a good man, but his face would make a baby cry. It wasn't that he was an unattractive man, but his resting face looked so serious, stiff, and sour that any semblance of a smile might crack its veneer.

"Miss Love." He nodded and swung his hand toward the opened door.

"Remember, Emma," Irene said. "Let's get together soon…maybe lunch? The old tyrant does give me a couple of minutes to wolf down a cold sandwich twice a week."

Then, wonder of wonders, Henry Stone smiled.

He walked into his office behind me and stepped around an ornate mahogany desk. I wondered how many men it had taken to bring it in there or if the room was built around it. I noticed the threadbare material on his office chair. He liked the familiar and comfortable. He waved me to a seat across his desk from him.

"I'm sure you're here about your brother, Mrs. Love."

"It's Miss, but please call me Emma."

"Emma it is then. I'm afraid I have some bad news for you though. I've spent a good part of the morning trying to get in to see Judge Allen in his chambers. I'm afraid his docket is full. He has two assault-and-battery cases pending today. He said emphatically that he would not be holding your brother's bail hearing today. He has an opening early tomorrow. It will be the first case of the day due to another case being plea bargained, so be in the courtroom at say nine o'clock?"

The phone rang, and Stone glanced at the number.

"I have to take this, Emma." I nodded and gave him a thumbs-up.

"See you tomorrow?" I asked.

"One second, Emma."

He picked up the phone and answered, "Good

morning, Mr. Mayor…Yes, I know, they've been here too…Yes, I do understand…Could I put you on hold for ten seconds, Caleb? Thank you."

He pressed a button on his phone and turned his attention to me.

"Just by way of a warning, Emma, *The County Examiner* newspaper is hunting around town for a front-page headline. They've already been to the sheriff's office and visited the mayor and me. We're trying to stop this from becoming a media circus."

"Any tips?" I asked.

"Yes, even if they ask you the time of day, the answer is 'No comment.' I'll see you in the morning." Our conversation was over when he nodded and picked up the phone.

I stepped out into the receptionist's area. Irene was on a call also. It seemed to be busy times in lawyering circles. I waved as I passed her desk. She held her hand over the mouthpiece and pointed at me, then herself. "Let's get together soon," she whispered.

I walked out on the street and headed to the sheriff's office. It was lunchtime, and I thought I might catch Sam for lunch. A girl must eat. Halfway there I spotted my new buddy Crab and waved to him. I noticed the other two of my "poster boys" had joined him, and each had posters tucked under their arm. When Crab saw me, he yelled.

"Miss Love, wait up." Crab looked both ways before crossing the quiet street, and then all three of them ran toward me.

"What's up, Crab?" The other two boys laughed at my use of Josh's pseudonym.

"I think I owe you fine gentlemen some money," I

said. I reached into my purse and pulled out two more five-dollar bills.

"Thank you, Miss Love," Crab said. "These are my buddies, Eric the Red and Pete the Sneak." Crab pointed to each one in turn.

"Yes, ma'am. Thank you, Miss Love," his companions echoed.

"Pleased to make your acquaintance, Miss Love," Pete said. Eric nodded in agreement.

"There's something we wanted to tell you, Miss Love. Well, Eric did…"

I turned toward the little red-headed boy, and he smiled.

"What did you want to tell me, Eric?"

"Tell her, Eric…about Miss Clements."

Now they had my full attention.

"I think I saw the lady in the poster, ma'am. She's Miss Clements."

"That's right, Eric. When do you think you saw her."

He had a look on his face like a young math student calculating figures in his head.

"It was yesterday."

"Do you know what time it was?"

He gave me the same calculating frown. "It wasn't too late, but it was probably about when we'd eat lunch at school. 'Cept, we didn't have no school 'cause of the teachers were in the service and had a meeting there. I think that's what it was."

"He means they had an in-service meeting. We get off on those days while the teachers sit around and gab. That's what my dad says," Crab explained.

"So, around noon then. Are you sure it was Miss

Clements?"

"Almost sure. I was behind her, and she was back there"—he pointed toward the hotel—"and she had on this big old floppy hat with flowers stuck on it."

"Are you sure it was her?"

"No, ma'am. I said almost sure. It looked like her. She has that funny way of walking ladies do where they're all wiggly and back and forth." He then demonstrated a swishing backside jaunt that would make any catwalk model proud, much to the other boys' amusement (and mine to be truthful).

"My momma does that sometimes in front of the TV, and I ask her if she's all right. Then my daddy says it's time to go to bed," Crab informed us.

"Thank you, boys. You're both entertaining and illuminating, and I appreciate you more than you know."

They looked back and forth at each other. I think they were wondering if they'd been insulted until I pulled out three more five-dollar bills and handed them out.

We departed each other's company as the best of friends, and I made a beeline toward the hotel, lunch with Sam forgotten.

****

The hotel was the only one in town and was a registered state historical landmark. It was claimed to be one of many spots where George Washington once took a bath, used the toilet, or ate a slice of cherry pie before he chopped down the tree. Perhaps he bit into a pit and broke one of his wooden teeth, but I don't remember the particulars.

The brass bell over the entrance door chimed when

I entered. A matronly blue-haired lady sat behind the counter reading a book. She held it in one hand. The yellowed fingers of the other hand held a cigarette that she drew on heavily before blowing smoke rings at the ceiling. Claudia, as her name tag identified her, then turned her attention to me.

"Good afternoon, miss. Are you back again for a room?"

"No, ma'am. I'm looking for someone."

"Aren't we all, dear?"

"A particular someone. Her name is Maria Clements. Can you tell me what room she is in?"

"I can check to see if we have someone here registered under that name, but if so, I'd need her permission to provide additional details. It's a new world with all this privacy stuff. I think if people behaved themselves, it shouldn't matter to them, but what do I know."

"That would be wonderful, Claudia, thank you."

"Let me see, Maria…Maria Clements." Her yellow index finger slid down the register. "No, ma'am, I'm sorry, but there's no one here by that name."

I opened my purse and pulled out one of Maria's missing posters.

"How about this woman? Have you seen her? Maybe wearing a big hat with flowers, the kind the women wear at Preakness for the horse races?"

She held the poster at arm's length, and her eyelids opened wide in recognition.

"I'm sorry, miss. I really couldn't say."

"Can't or won't say? This is very important, Claudia. Did you read the poster? She's missing."

"She didn't act like…I'm sorry." The woman's

hands trembled when she handed back the poster. I wondered if it was Parkinson's disease or a case of nerves.

"What were you going to say? Have you seen her?"

Claudia took a deep breath, "I can't say. There's no Maria Clements registered here, miss."

I slapped my hand down on the counter, and the woman jumped. By the time the exit bells stopped chiming on my way out, I felt bad for having done so. The old woman was just following the hotel's policy…but this was more important than policies. I pulled out my phone to call Sam. I noticed young Jack Dawson exiting the bar across the street. I waved at him, but he pulled up his hoodie, ducked his head, and ignored me. I'd have to mention it to Abigail when I saw her again. Sam too, if the bar was selling to minors.

Sam answered my call on the second ring and asked if I'd blown him off about lunch. I explained what just happened at the hotel.

"Wait there," he said. "I'll be right over."

Sam pulled up in his cruiser and parked in front of the hotel. Before he got out, he switched on his cruiser's bubble gum machine lights.

"Let's go ask her again," he said.

I went through the door first, and Claudia was surprised to see me.

"Miss, I told you…" Then Sam entered behind me.

"Officer…"

"It's Deputy, Mrs. Brown. How are you this afternoon?"

She only nodded.

"I need to know anything you know about this young woman." He held out the missing poster I'd given him.

"Deputy, I can't say. My boss would fire me."

"I know your husband is your 'boss,' Mrs. Brown. What I don't know is if you want an anonymous tip sent to the Health Department about certain irregularities in this old building. I've heard reports that some rooms are regularly occupied by women of, shall we say, ill repute. I'd hate to have to open an investigation, but…"

Claudia shot a black-eyed sneer in my direction. "I suppose I could look at the picture again. We always like to cooperate with the police, and the poor girl is missing, she said."

After a quick scan of Maria's photo, she said, "Yes, I do believe I know this girl. She was supposed to check out hours ago. I went up to check, and her things were still there. She must have slipped out early this morning when I was in the back."

"We'd like to see the room."

Claudia's eyes drew down to a squint, and her lips formed a rigid line. "That you can't do without a search warrant. You can do whatever you want, Deputy."

"Thank you, Mrs. Brown. Have a lovely day."

Chapter Nine

I tried to update Sam on all I'd learned, but he said we'd catch up later. He wanted to update the deputies on the Maria situation and try to get a warrant from Judge Allen before the court day ended.

"I'll see you at the house later." He lit out in his cruiser with a squeal. I thought the county might be buying two new tires soon.

I walked to the sheriff's office to visit Daniel. I was sure he'd love some company, even mine. I hated to think about what he was going through, whether innocent or, God forbid, guilty. I checked my pistol with Deputy Joyce just inside the door, and she led me to the holding cells. Daniel sat in a tiny barred cage with an exposed toilet and sink. He sat in the corner on a lumpy cot mattress, his head cradled in his hands.

"How are you holding up, Daniel?" I asked, and he lifted his head.

"Emma? Thank God. Are you here to get me out of this place?"

"I'm sorry. Stone tried but he couldn't get bail set for you until tomorrow. You have another night in this place."

"Tomorrow? You promise?"

"I promise to do everything in my power. Stone thinks with your high standing in the community, the judge will consider you a low flight risk. Sam said the evidence is circumstantial at best, so that should help too."

"There's a bail bondsman on Maple Street, also known as Louse Alley. The bondsman is across the street from Baker's Bar."

"Yeah, I know the place."

"Maybe you could get Sam to come along? It's not in the best part of town, and the guy who runs it is a creep. Gwen told me he hit on her in a lewd way at the fireman's carnival before we were married."

"Thanks, Daniel. Don't worry, I can take care of myself."

He stared at me for a moment. "Yeah, I think you can, but be careful anyway."

"Emma, did you call in Alicia Wood for Nana?"

"All taken care of, Daniel."

Joyce, my deputy escort, stuck her head through the doorway to the cells.

"Time's up, Emma. I'm sorry, but you have to go."

We said our goodbyes with a final promise from me to see him in the morning. I retrieved my gun from the deputy and walked back toward my car. It was time to go home. With my car keys in hand and only steps away from the Bronco, I saw him, dead ahead and walking my way, Robert Wathen. This time it was me ducking my head…but it was too late.

"Hello, Emma."

"Robert."

"There's been a lot of excitement out your way, lady. I hope you're being careful…a young woman alone and all…"

"What is it you're trying to say, Robert? Is that a thinly veiled threat?"

"Oh. No, Emma. Whatever would give you that idea? Geez, I'm only concerned about your welfare."

"Like you were when I was a teenager?"

"I think we remember that night a bit differently, Emma."

"What do you want, Robert?"

"I'm not a bad guy, Emma."

"Whatever you have to tell yourself to sleep at night."

"I was at the sheriff's office earlier. I thought I could help with Maria Clements' missing person's case."

"Help how?"

"We used to date a long time ago; did you know? Maria and me? We hit it off for a while, but I guess the spark just wasn't there."

"She is a little young for you, isn't she, Robert?"

"Well, you know me…"

"Yes, sadly I do."

"Now. There's no need for that. I thought we had a truce."

I stared at him until he wiggled.

"Anyway, I was telling my brother that Maria was always talking about leaving here. She said when she had her nest egg built up, she was gonna wipe the dust of Newtowne from her shoes and head for the big city. Baltimore, I think she said. She was working at the Five and Dime then, but said when she left, she wouldn't say a word to anyone, not even her boss. She'd be here one day and gone the next."

"That's an interesting story, Robert. When did you last see her?"

"Oh, it's been a while since I've seen her…I'm a

married man, so what she told me about that was at least five years ago. I just thought it might help. Maybe she just up and left like she said she would."

"Always the conscientious citizen, huh, Robert?'

I turned my back on him and slid my key into the door.

"Be careful out there, Emma."

****

I drove back to Love's faster than I should have, blowing some carbon out of the old Bronco's engine. I was lucky none of Sam's colleagues spotted me. A rusted-out black Chevrolet Cavalier station wagon with bald tires was parked at the end of the driveway, partially blocking the entrance. Someone tried to retard the onset of rust with what appeared to be a rattle-can spray-paint job. The rear side windows were also painted out, giving the vehicle a mini-hearse look, like you might expect at a pet cemetery. A young man leaned against the driver's side door.

"Can I help you? Are you having car trouble?" I asked.

"Mrs. Love? I'm Johnny Walker." He held out his hand and I shook it.

"Johnny Walker? Your folks must have liked Scotch, huh?"

"Yes, ma'am, but they had a poor sense of humor. As you might guess, I've heard that a time or two."

"I can imagine you have. What can I do for you, Johnny Walker."

"Ma'am. I'm with the *County Examiner* newspaper, and I hoped to ask you a few questions about your brother and the rash of missing persons here."

"I'm not interested at this time, Mr. Walker."

"I promise I'll be fair. Your family and these kidnappings are big news around the county right now. It is all anyone is talking about."

"Mr. Walker, please pull your vehicle out of my driveway before I call the cops. I have nothing to say to you."

I dropped the gear shift into first gear and the Bronco's left tire flirted with the ditch, then caught traction. I accelerated up the driveway. Alicia Wood met me at the door.

"Miss Love, I'm so glad you are home," she said.

"Is everything okay with Nana, Alicia?"

"Oh, of course, she's such a dear, and she's been asking about you."

"No problems then? She can be a handful at times."

"Not at all, but the phone has been ringing non-stop. Everyone is asking about Gwen and Maria. I stopped answering it. I hope you don't mind?"

"Not at all, thank you. How did you deal with the nosy neighbors?"

"It wasn't just the neighbors. The *County Examiner* wanted an interview and someone with a '202' area code in Washington, D.C. called and wanted the same thing. Maybe call me on my cell when you need to reach me?"

"I'll do that. What did you tell the reporters?"

"I told them everything I knew…nothing. I'd just as soon to keep it that way too. Your family has been good to me, Emma."

I checked in on Nana, but she was asleep at her favorite spot, and I didn't want to disturb her. I jotted down a quick note, *Love you, Nana. See you soon*. Then I grabbed my coffee cup and night clothes and sent Sam a text that I was going home…to my home.

Johnny Walker was still at the end of the drive but had at least pulled his vehicle back to the shoulder of the road.

He tapped on my window as I stopped for traffic. "It will come out, Miss Love. I'd like to get your family's side of the story—" I missed the rest of what he said as my tires spun and threw gravel behind me. I looked in the rearview mirror; he was engulfed in a cloud of dust.

I drove back toward town and my small cottage, looking forward to a relaxing night in my bed. I took two steaks from the freezer. I thought there was time for them to thaw before Sam arrived, but I poured some cold water over them in the sink to speed up the process. I'd let Sam do the manly man and fire up the grill. What is it about men and outdoor cooking? Most of the men I knew, if you give them a smoker, a grill, or even a bonfire to incinerate some hotdogs with, and they're in hog heaven.

I glanced at my watch. It was still a couple of hours before Sam got there. I took a shower, washed my hair, and shaved my legs (why don't men have to do that?). I considered getting dressed again in a fresh blouse and pants, but, as usual, comfort beat out fashion. I slipped into long flannel pajamas. I wasn't going for sexy, and the cold front was lasting unexpectedly long.

I curled up on my bed and opened a new book. After two chapters, my eyes started growing heavy. I should've gotten up, but instead I fell fast asleep.

"It's Sam," he yelled from the front door. "The

door's unlocked. Can I come in? Are you decent?"

"I'm not so sure about that."

"What?"

"Come in. I'll be right out, Sam."

He was sitting in my small living room, his sleeping bag beside him.

"Well, don't you look…interesting."

"What do you mean? I dressed up just for you."

"I can see that." He laughed. "I was surprised to see your text about coming back here tonight."

"I wanted to sleep in my bed tonight. Besides, I ran into a reporter staking out Daniel's Love's Manor. We had a little chat, and I left. I'm not up to all that right now."

Sam nodded his head. "I guess it will get worse before it gets better. The state boys have wedged their way in now too. They've placed troopers from the local barracks on the case. I'm afraid it's going to explode soon."

"Good times," I said.

I pointed to the sleeping bag. "Why don't you go home tonight, Sam? Get some sleep on your bed. I bet you didn't get two hours of rest last night, and I'm perfectly capable of taking care of myself. I'm too old for a babysitter."

"I slept like a baby being rocked by angels last night. I know I'll sleep better here knowing you're safe, or at least, safer with another set of eyes and ears on the alert."

"Are you sure you're up to another night on a couch? Mine's not as fluffy as Daniel's, in case you haven't noticed. It has springs popping out all over the place, and they love sticking you in the butt. I need to get rid of the ratty old thing."

"I'll be fine, Emma."

"Don't say I didn't warn you when you wake up bleeding in a dozen unmentionable places."

"I don't think I have a dozen unmentionable places, Emma, but if you are just trying to get rid of me…fair warning—it won't be easy."

"Okay, hardhead. I guess you can make yourself useful then. There are two thick T-bones in the sink. As I recall, you aren't too shabby with the grill?"

"Oh, girl, are you kidding me? You're in for another treat from the master," he assured me. Yup, he was a man all right.

While Sam grilled, I microwaved two large baking potatoes and spiced up some canned green beans. After I set the table, I pulled on my heavy winter coat and stepped out on the deck to check on Sam's progress.

"Give me two more minutes on the steaks."

The beef was as good as advertised. Sam claimed it was due to his superior culinary skills. I insisted it was my keen eye for a tender cut of meat. We agreed it just wasn't steak if there was no pink in the middle. With no pink, it's a chunk of dried-out cardboard, a travesty.

During dinner, Sam told me he'd obtained the search warrant for the hotel room from the judge, but they found little inside. Prints were taken, but it might be a while before there were any matches. Plus, it was a hotel that had a hard time retaining its cleaning staff. He assigned a deputy to keep watch from the street in front of the hotel in case Maria came back.

"Besides interrogating little boys to get the hotel lead, what else did you get up to today?"

"Josh 'Crab' Grimes, and his buddies…they're

good kids. But it had to be Maria in that hotel room, Sam. As for the rest of my day, after you left, I found this." I handed him the typewritten envelope. "What do you think?"

"Strange. Maybe it's just a coincidence, but what if someone sent her a note that triggered her to leave?"

"How?"

"Could be a lot of things. Maybe someone, not mentioning any names, threatened her with what might happen if she stayed."

"Daniel wouldn't…"

"Or maybe someone suggested she wasn't safe and offered her an alternative to Love's Manor. It could have been an invitation for a date or even a job offer…That would be an odd way to make an offer, but it's too vague a clue to help us much. The prosecution would have a field day with it."

"After I found it, I was reminded of something else. When I first went into the basement, being nosy, I saw a pink suitcase with Maria's name tag on it. This morning that suitcase was missing."

"Now you're talking, Emma. That casts a whole new light on things. The kidnapper might have taken that too if it was in her closet or something, but he wouldn't know about it being down there. How could he? She must have taken it herself."

I stared at Sam. For a moment, he looked confused, and I waited. His eyes opened wide, and his jaw dropped when the full implication dawned in his eyes.

"You're right, Emma. Daniel would've known. He's the only one, besides Maria and you, who would have known it was there."

"Daniel hates basements."

We both were silent for some time after that. It seemed that every time I opened my mouth or discovered something new, I dug Daniel in deeper and deeper. Did I know what I was doing? Was I helping convict my brother? Should I drop out of the investigation and just be there for Daniel for moral support? Leave this to the professionals…to Sam? I said as much to him and as usual, he was supportive and praised my efforts.

"You've found at least as many clues, more, than an entire sheriff's department with ten times the resources you have. If anyone can get to the truth, it's you. Isn't that what a private investigator does?"

"Thanks, but it doesn't feel like that."

"I'm just praying that Robert is right and Maria just skipped town," Sam said.

"I saw him in town today. I think he threatened me." I said—to my immediate regret.

"What did Robert say to you?"

"Forget it. Just something about my being a woman staying all alone and I should be careful."

"He could have been concerned about you…well, if it was anyone else that is. Robert always has an agenda, but why would he threaten you? He hardly knows you."

"We have…history."

"You dated Robert?"

"Oh good God, no, Sam!"

"Then what?"

"It's nothing…ancient history."

"This has something to do with why you left, doesn't it? Your deep dark secret?"

"Let it go, Sam."

"You know I can't. You did promise me…"

"Are you sure you want to know, Sam?"

"After all this time, why wouldn't I?

"After all this time, why would you?"

"You know the answer to that. It's a part of you that you've kept hidden. Unless I miss my guess, it's what pulled us apart."

"It will change the way you think of me. It did my family and all my other friends."

"I'll take that chance. Will you take a chance on me?"

Chapter Ten

I wasn't ready to share the memories of that night again, but if there was any *us* in the future—Sam and I—I'd have to dredge up painful memories to put them to rest.

"The night of your party, do you remember? I got there late because I'd promised the Dawsons weeks before that I'd babysit Jack that night. Mr. Dawson had a teachers' function that involved spouses, so I knew there wasn't an option for them to change dates."

"I remember. You left a message with my folks. They told me you'd be late."

I nodded. "When I arrived, two of my friends, Janet Hill and Debbie Bailey, pulled me aside to tell me about you and a hot girl who was all over you. It wasn't long before I saw what they were talking about. She was gorgeous. I told myself if that was the kind of girl you wanted, it wasn't me. And I knew I couldn't compete with her. It wasn't just her looks. It was the way she flirted with everyone when they were dancing. She was smiling and laughing at everyone's jokes, a real social butterfly…everything I wasn't. Then I knew why you'd been too busy to return my phone calls. You should've just told me, Sam. It wouldn't have hurt so bad."

"Wait, wait, I remember. It wasn't like that…"

I rolled my eyes.

"Let me finish, Sam. I've felt guilty for so long for leaving without telling you, but you left me first. Dammit, you hurt me, and I'm so stupid to feel bad when all I did was return the favor. It's not fair."

I looked up at him and his eyes were threatening to spill over.

"Oh my God, Emma, she was my cousin from Florida, Laurie. Her dad is my mother's brother. My folks kept pestering me to take her everywhere and to show her a good time. I only saw you there for a moment that night. When I dragged Laurie through the crowd to meet you, you'd disappeared. Where did you go?

"Sam. Please, let it go…" Now my eyes were brimming with tears too.

"Please, Emma."

It was only because of my promise and the look in Sam's eyes that I continued.

"I don't remember a lot after that. Robert Wathen started hitting on me and I couldn't stand him, but I knew how much the two of you hated each other. It seems he hated you even more though. I felt the need for some childish, petty revenge. I was just a kid, Sam. Robert brought me a drink and someone, probably Robert, slipped me a Mickey. I woke up in your parents' gazebo."

Sam's face grew a darker red shade with every sentence I spoke. The look on his face was disturbing; a face I'd never seen before. His eyes were as dark as sin and reflected no light.

"What did that bastard do to you, Emma?"

"I don't think he 'did' anything, or not like I think you mean, Sam. But he said he had pictures of me making out with some guys and acting inappropriately…I don't think he showed them to anyone, but I was treated as a pariah at school the next day. I figured he'd put his spin on what happened and advertised it to anyone who'd listen, or maybe it was because I was the stupid teenage girl whose boyfriend was cheating on her. Robert threatened to show the pictures around if I said anything.

"Is that why you left?"

I bit the edge of my lip. "Yes."

"This is me, Emma. I know when you're holding back. Don't lie to me; finish it."

"Sam, I'm not sure…"

"Please."

"Ok…then no. At least not the only reason, Sam. I was pissed off more than anything. I told Robert to go to hell and do whatever he wanted. Then I'd go to the sheriff and have him charged with drugging me against my will, but it was an idle threat. I didn't have any proof. Plus, I knew it would drag my name through the mud, and he did too. His brother wasn't a sheriff way back then, of course, but his family had plenty of local connections.

"I guess my threat scared him though. He cornered me when I was walking home from school that same day. He opened his backpack. He said it was crammed full of the pictures he'd taken.

"He said, 'Any friend of Sam Mattingley is no friend of mine. I'll get even, and I'll start with you. I think I'll plaster these on every telephone pole and in every men's room stall in the county.'

"I slapped him hard, with everything I had. He fell backward and his backpack hit the concrete sidewalk.

'You wanna see how much I care about your threats, Robert?' The pictures were strewn across the sidewalk. None of them were lewd or anything…just suggestive. Guys lying beside me with their tongues hanging out. One was holding a sign saying my virtue wasn't all it should be—that sort of adolescent crap. Anyway, I grabbed one of the pictures and slapped it on a telephone pole. Someone left a handy thumbtack for me to reuse. I turned my back on him and walked away.

" 'You better watch your step,' he yelled behind me.

" 'Or what, perv?'

" 'I have the goods on yours and Sammy Boy's family too. I know things and that boy's been a thorn in my side for way too long.' "

"That's why you left, Emma? That punk was mad because I'd exposed him in a lie in front of Laurie. He had the hots for her, and he got his panties in a knot. That piece of crap had nothing on me. Why didn't you come to me?"

"Well, I didn't have a warm fuzzy about you at the time, but I didn't want to see you hurt, and he did have something on you…well, on Irene. He claimed to have pictures of your sister that were worse. I knew what those pictures would do to her and your family. He even showed me one picture of a guy covered with blood. He said Irene or one of her friends had hurt someone."

Sam laughed although his eyes were misted over.

"It's not funny, Sam."

"It is, Emma, in a sad way. I can't say for sure, but Irene was in the Drama club. You probably don't remember because she was a year ahead of me. She was a senior when you were a sophomore. In one play, her part was Charlotte in *A Murder is Announced*. You know the one? She shoots a guy who was on to her. There was fake blood everywhere. I remember it because I could never quite look at Irene the same after that. She was that good of an actor. I'd bet dollars to doughnuts that's what he had pictures of. The crew went overboard with the blood."

"Maybe," I agreed, "but there were still the other pictures."

"If he even had them. It might've been a bluff too. Irene did lose her way for a while and went through a rough patch. She had a vampire-slash-goth stage around senior year too. She and her strange friends called themselves bloodsuckers. They dressed in all black, and I mean all black. They wore black shoes and eyeliner along with black lipstick…the guys too. That could've been the blood pictures as well. I don't know, but I do know Irene never hurt a soul…even if they wanted her to, besides herself that is. It was a bad time for her and our whole family. I guess she was 'acting out,' as they say.

"It explains another old mystery from those days though. I walked in on Irene when she was on the phone one evening. She was yelling at the top of her voice at someone named Robert…I didn't know Robert 'Who' at the time. Guess I should have figured that out…some investigator I was. She said she didn't care what he did, and he could kiss her butt. 'Do your damnedest,' she said, 'and I'll pay you back in triplicate.' She turned her life around about then. Cleaned up her act; went back to school and made something of herself…just like you did."

"Thanks. I knew I liked Irene."

"So, you abandoned your life…to protect us?"

"Well, not exactly. If it was, I would've stuck around until I got to the bottom of everything. I would've made Robert pay too. I'm not above vengeance either, sad to say."

"Then something else happened?"

"Besides thinking my boyfriend of several years was running around on me?"

"Yeah."

"After school, I went home and thought about everything that happened. You know how proper Daniel was back then? Our family's reputation meant more to him than anything. Still does, I guess. I decided to tell Daniel about it, to give him a heads-up in case Robert made good on his threats. We'd had a big fight that morning over something trivial. We both blew it out of proportion, but Daniel was still angry. He was outraged when I told him and blamed everything on me. He said I was…well, let's say he used some very unsavory words to describe me. He threw in the whole 'you've always been a disgrace to the family' thing and that I'd ruin our family's name. I argued with him, trying to get him to see my side. That's when he told me to pack my bags and get out.

"I packed my things that evening and spent the night sobbing into my pillow. I heard Nana and Daniel's big screaming match that night. Nana was my guardian, but Daniel inherited the house. He was adamant I had to go. The next morning, Nana came to my bedroom and said Daniel was reconsidering. But I wasn't staying where I wasn't wanted, and I had no reason to stay. So, I went and never looked back…well, until recently."

"What changed? Not that I'm complaining, but why did you come back?"

"I had a profession that allowed me to be independent, and I had the pay-back on Robert. If he ever crossed me again, I could come home with revenge in my hip pocket. Besides, I missed the old town, the people, and the familiarity. It was time to come home."

"So, that's what all the sneaking around was about? What did you get on him?"

"Misappropriation of funds from his non-profit along with some juicy photos of him with a woman who was definitely not his wife."

"I'm sure he is busy covering his tracks now, and our hands are full with hunting a kidnapper. It's more of a state police crime though, so a well-timed tip to them might be in order. Remind me to never get on your bad side, Emma."

"Hopefully you won't need reminding, but if you do, I will."

"God, I've missed you." He had a far-away look in his eyes.

"Missed you too, dear friend."

Sam only looked at me with a blank stare.

"Hey, you. Did you have a stroke or something? Earth to Sam…you there, Sam?"

He stood and turned toward me, reaching out with both hands. When I took his hands in mine, he pulled me to my feet and wrapped his arms around me. I felt his body tremble against mine, then he held me at arm's length. His face was wet.

"I'm here, right where I want to be."

"Then don't look so sad? Smile…"

"We've wasted so much time, Emma."

He leaned his face into mine and kissed me. He wasn't my betrayer. He was the boy I remembered—turned man, my oldest friend, and my first love. That night, Sam didn't sleep alone.

My dreams that night were happy, light-hearted affairs. There were no predatory flowers or visits from familiar ghosts. It was the best sleep I'd enjoyed for as long as I could remember, until it wasn't…

****

The sound of breaking glass woke us both at the same instant. Sam was on his feet and grabbed his gun from the top of my dresser. I ran to my window in time to see a hooded figure running down my short driveway.

"There's someone out there, Sam. He's getting away."

Sam already had on his pants and ran toward my bedroom door.

"Be careful," I yelled after him.

I dressed and tucked my small pistol into my waistband in case the robber came back. I ran downstairs, considering joining in the chase, but the invader had too much of a head start for anyone to catch up with him.

Minutes later, Sam called and verified my thoughts.

"I lost him, Emma. He crossed the county road and slipped out of sight in the woods. I've called John Russell and asked him to bring his hounds. Mrs. Russell was not happy with me."

"Well, it is two o'clock in the morning." I went to the living room to see if I could see Sam's flashlight through the window.

"Sam, I found the source of the breaking glass that woke us. There's a softball-sized rock sitting on my couch that was thrown through the living room window. There's some paper attached to it."

"Don't touch—"

"Don't touch it with my hands. I know, Sam Mattingley. I'm pulling on my kitchen gloves now."

"I'll call you right back, Emma. Mr. Russell is calling me."

The paper was fastened to the rock with a heavy rubber band, like bunches of asparagus are held together with at the grocery store. I pulled the rubber band off and unfolded the paper. The note inside was made from cut-out letters from a glossy-paged magazine. It read, *Go back wear you came from or meet there fate.*

This wasn't a ransom note. It was a threat plain and simple. Why? What did it mean? Was I getting closer to an answer, and the kidnapper saw me as a risk to his plans?

The phone rang…Sam was returning my call.

"Hey, is everything okay? Sam? Mr. Russell get there yet?"

"All is good. He's on his way and should be here any minute, but I had to hear what was on the note. It was a note, wasn't it? Ransom?"

"A note yes, but if it's a ransom note, it's unlike any I've heard of, even in the movies." I described the lettering on the paper and then read it to him word for word.

"What do you make of that?" I asked.

"First, are you armed?"

"Of course, but I think you've run him off, at least for tonight, Sam."

"The spelling on the note is interesting," he said. "It reads like an elementary school dropout or someone who skipped every spelling and grammar class he ever had."

"Or someone trying to make us think that's who he is."

"Exactly," Sam agreed.

"One good thing, with Daniel in jail, it takes the spotlight off him."

"For the note, sure, but not the kidnapping. He could have an accomplice."

I heard a sound in the background and identified it after a moment. "Do I hear Mr. Russell's hounds?"

"He just pulled in. Be safe, and I'll be back as soon as I can."

****

I sat on the couch and within moments fell asleep. The sun was just breaking free of the tree line when I woke, but that wasn't what woke me. It wasn't the sound of Sam opening the front door either. That came moments after the springs I warned Sam about earlier jabbed me in the butt. I yelped, and Sam rushed into the living room.

"What is it, Emma? You okay?"

"I'm fine," I said, rubbing my backside.

"Did one of those hungry springs bite you? I guess they have good taste." Sam laughed. "I have a first-aid kit in the Mustang's trunk. I can put a bandage on it for you."

"You're just so thoughtful, but no thanks. Did you have any luck?"

"Not to speak of. The hounds went down your driveway, and through the woods on a hot trail. Howls echoed through the trees. It was loud in the silence of the night. I'm surprised you didn't hear them. I gathered plenty of the neighbors did, judging by all the porch lights flicking on. That intensity didn't last long though. The hounds lost the scent at the state road and kept circling, back-trailing. We hoped they'd pick up the scent again, but eventually we accepted the fact that the perp had a car there waiting. There's a spot there to pull off the main road that goes back in the woods a few yards. We keep an eye on it because teenagers like to go parking there. A car sitting there would go unnoticed unless a passer-by looked at just the right second."

"Someone who knows the area pretty well then," I said.

"There's a good chance of that, I'd say, and someone who has an axe to grind with you."

"That was my first thought also, and it brought a certain individual to mind. The spelling is childish but that could be to throw us off. There is another possibility. What if something I saw or did yesterday was a threat to the kidnapper?"

"Did you? Does anything stand out in your mind?"

"Only what I already told you about…not much."

"Please don't take any chances today, Emma. I know you like to rush in where angels fear to tread, but caution might be in order here. You have your handgun permit. Carry everywhere you go today, except for court. You'll have to put it in your lockbox in the Bronco then. There will be plenty of deputies, including me, in the courthouse."

I nodded. "Well, the sun is up, Sam. No sense

trying to get that extra hour of sleep now. How about a cup of coffee?"

"I'll be dragging all day today. Coffee sounds great."

Chapter Eleven

Sam left early for a shower and a fresh uniform at his place. I enjoyed the luxury of a second cup of coffee, then went out to start the Bronco to get its heater warmed up. It was another brisk morning.

I scraped the frost from my side view mirrors—the defroster never cleared those—climbed in, and turned the ignition key. The engine turned over and over…nothing. I tried again after saying a few choice words.

"C'mon, baby. You can do this. I know it's cold." But my little pep talk didn't help. The battery was running low now, and I popped open the hood to have a look.

"Sweet Jesus," I said, although I knew He wasn't involved. I slammed my hand down on the engine, and a hose clamp sliced across my knuckles. It was going to be one of those days. I pulled my phone from my best black slacks and called Sam.

"Know any good mechanics? I'm dead in the water."

"I'm just leaving my apartment. Do you need a jump start?"

"Not my battery…that sorry scumbag cut all of my spark plug wires last night."

"Oh no. Okay, I know a guy. I'll ask him to drive out with a new set. The bail hearing is in twenty minutes though, so I'll swing by, and we'll hit the courthouse first."

"You're a lifesaver."

I went back inside and rinsed the blood off my hands, then wrapped a piece of gauze around it. I called Alicia to ask about Nana, and she said everything there was fine. We chatted for a moment and said our goodbyes. By the time Sam returned, blood had soaked through the gauze.

"What did you do to yourself, Emma? Let me look at it. God, did you try to beat the Bronco to life?"

I laughed. "It seemed like a good idea at the time, but we need to get going. It's stopped bleeding now anyway."

I couldn't believe the number of cars parked around the courthouse. Sam swung his cruiser to the back of the building to the restricted court parking. He pointed across the street. I looked over to see a WMAM, channel 3 news van.

"The vultures are circling," Sam said.

"I guess we're famous in Newtowne now. It must be a slow news day to draw Washington, D.C.'s attention."

"I'll keep my fingers crossed for Daniel, Emma."

"Thanks, mine too, and thanks for the lift, Sam. I owe you one."

"And I'll collect." He winked.

Sam entered through the "Court Officials Only" entrance in the back. I walked around to the front. The courthouse was a massive brick structure rebuilt in the 1800s. The center section, though, was all rock and delineated the original building. Twenty steps ran the width of the building leading up to a pair of ten-foot-high carved oak doors. Those twenty steps were filled with people. Some news people chatted together as the cameraman set up his equipment. I recognized one, the newswoman from the nightly news, Catherine Somebody. She was sucking on a cigarette and blowing up clouds of smoke until a deputy pointed out the no-smoking sign. The townspeople turned out in droves, and I wondered how many were there hoping to see one of the Loves taken down a notch. As I stood waiting for the doors to open, I felt like I was being watched from every direction. Whenever I looked, heads quickly turned away. At least the news crew didn't know who I was yet.

The doors finally swung open, and we single-filed through the doors. We each had to pass through scanning checkpoints. First, there was a conveyor belt for any bags and anything we held in our pockets. This was followed by a personal scanner we walked through, like every airport in the country. It took forever. I feared the bail hearing would be over before I got there, but I was let in just as the judge entered the courtroom and the bailiff introduced him.

Bench seats, like church pews, lined the room. Most were full, but the two rows closest to the judge's bench held only one blue-haired lady. Just like in elementary school where none of the kids wanted to sit in front at the center of the teacher's attention. I sat down beside the older lady.

"The first matter on the court docket today is the bail hearing requested by the defense for Daniel Alvin Love. The charge is kidnapping. Counselors, I'll hear your thoughts," the judge said.

Henry Stone rose from his seat beside my brother.

"Your honor, we request a minimal bail to be set at ten thousand dollars. Mr. Love is a citizen of high standing in the community. He owns significant property in the county and his family has been here for generations. He is not a flight risk."

"Mr. Prosecutor?"

"Yes, your honor. I do not believe the citizens of our fine county would be best served by setting bail at all. This is a very serious and violent crime, and I'd like to remind the court that two women are still missing."

I noticed a flurry of activity in the far corner of the court and saw Sam rushing toward an exit door. He spoke to another deputy, and they left the courtroom together.

Henry Stone was back on his feet. "Your honor, I can only assume that my esteemed colleague has not acquainted himself with the facts, or lack thereof, in this case. I'm at a loss as to what grounds Mr. Love was even held on. A pittance of circumstantial coincidence is all the state has against my client."

The red-faced state attorney jumped up and his mouth flapped three times before any words came out.

"Your honor, the facts in this case, though circumstantial they may be, provide damning evidence of the crime and the perpetrator, Mr. Daniel Love. He is guilty, your honor."

The judge looked over to the court stenographer. "Strike the last part, Susan." Then he turned his attention back to the lawyers. "I'd like to remind council that this is not a trial. It is a bail hearing, and we are here to set bail. Do either of you have anything else to add? No? Then, please approach the bench."

The state's attorney's face was still red, and after

Henry Stone said something to the judge, it almost glowed. His remark, also unheard, did not sit well with Mr. Stone. He threw his arms in the air and stomped his foot, finally shaking a finger at his opponent. I had no idea the old man could be so animated.

The corner door opened again, and the sheriff strode through. He walked straight up to the judge, and whatever he said quieted both attorneys. The judge pointed them back to their seats.

"Bail is set at twenty-five thousand dollars." The judge pounded his gavel. "Bailiff, next case, please."

The sheriff escorted Daniel from the room to the oohs and ahhs of the crowd and a chorus of mumbled conversations. All eyes that weren't on Daniel seemed to be on me.

Everyone stood and moved toward the exit at the same time. That answered my question about what it was they were all here to see. I felt like I was swimming in a sea of humanity. Some huge man stepped on my foot, then I felt a hand at my elbow. I yanked my arm away before seeing it was Deputy Joyce. She nodded her head and pulled me back into the courtroom.

"Major Mattingley sent me back to get you out of here. The mob isn't dispersing as fast as we'd like, and the news crew is outside waiting…for you, I imagine. He said to take you out through the back entrance."

"Thank you, and thank Sam for me."

"You're welcome, but you can thank the major in person. He's waiting outside to take you to the hospital."

"The hospital? Seriously? It's only a tiny scratch on my hand, that's all."

Joyce looked at me as if I was speaking an alien tongue. "Ma'am?"

"It's Emma, but it's not about my hand, is it?"

"I don't know about your hand, but you might want to have that looked at too. They found Maria Clements, Emma. She's at the Newtowne Hospital Center."

Sam's cruiser was idling outside the back door. There was no crowd at all back there, but someone was standing in the alley videoing me as I climbed in the car.

"What's going on? They found Maria?"

"Yes, through pure luck. Your young friend Crab Grimes was wandering the woods behind his house looking for his dairy goat that scaled its fence. It's thick back there, but the kid said whenever the goat got out, the first place he looked for it was an abandoned homestead back there. He said some old apple and pear trees still bear tiny fruit on the years the opossums don't eat them all. There was still a decrepit barn standing there, and he heard a noise inside. The kid said he was scared, but thought somebody might be in trouble, so he peeked inside. That's when he found Maria. She was tied to a post, blindfolded, and gagged."

"How is she?"

"Not very good. The doctor said she was suffering from exposure, malnutrition, and dehydration. There was also concern about a nasty bump on her head."

"Hmm, I can relate to the last part."

Sam turned down the infamous Maple Street, also known as Louse Alley.

"Maria is under strong sedation and will sleep for hours, the doctor said. Thought you might want to visit the bail bondsman first. Deputy Douglas will call me if

129

Maria wakes up anytime soon."

"Thanks, Sam. That's a relief. I was torn between getting Daniel's bail money and hearing what Maria had to say. I wasn't sure which would help him more."

He parked in front of the old shop front. Yellow smoke-stained curtains were pulled closed over the windows, and layers of peeling paint adorned the door.

"Real fancy," I said.

"Yeah, let's go get it over with," Sam said and opened his driver's side door.

"No, I've got this. If you leave your cruiser unattended on this street, it probably won't be here when you come back."

"Emma, he's a creepy dude—"

"And you'll be one shout away if I need you. I wouldn't mind a bit if you were to wait for me, though. I don't savor the prospect of walking out of here alone."

Sam reached into his glove box and pulled out my gun. "Just in case then, and I'll be right here waiting."

The inside of the bailsman's office was even dingier than the outside. The walls and ceiling panels were coated with the same residual smoke stains that added a distinctive color to the curtains. The smell was an overripe combination of stale cigar smoke, whiskey, and body odor.

The proprietor of the place sat behind a metal flea-market-sale desk with his back to me while he chatted on the phone. On the desk was the phone, a soup can full of pens (I couldn't discern the brand) and a nude mermaid figurine curled up on a large shell. The shell held two crushed cigar butts. I sat at the chair in front of the desk and waited. He hung up and swiveled around on his office chair to face me.

He was a late middle-aged man. His hair was jet black, so black it could only come from a bottle in a man his age. He was balding in front but combed his hair from the side up and over to hide that fact. It wasn't working for him. His face was pallid and reminded me of the blind colorless fish I saw once while touring a cavern. He licked his lips.

"I'll bet you're Miss Emma Love. I can't say as we've ever met, not traveling in the same social circles, yet I did anticipate seeing you today."

"Good, then you know why I'm here."

He stood up and walked around his desk. He sat on the edge of it in front of my chair.

"I suspect I do, miss, but why don't you tell me about it…hmm? I'm known as a man who will help any damsel in distress."

"That's good to know, mister…"

"Call me Stanley. Please."

"Stanley then. I need to make bail for my brother, Daniel, for twenty-five thousand dollars. Can you help me with that?"

He leaned in closer to me. "That is exactly what I am here for, miss, to help people. May I call you Emma?"

"I'd prefer we stick to Miss Love."

"I see." Not giving up quite so easily, his hand reached out and landed on my knee. I brushed it off and stood.

"I don't have a lot of time, and I need this taken care of as soon as possible."

"Well, miss. There's paperwork involved. If you'll please sit back down."

"My boyfriend, Major Mattingley with the sheriff's

office is outside waiting patiently for me and I can't be much longer."

He stood up and walked over to the windows and pulled the nasty curtains to one side. I wouldn't have touched them with gloves on.

"Indeed, he is. I can't keep our fine police department from their appointed duties now, can I?"

I sat down. He scribbled on a piece of paper and punched numbers into his calculator.

"For a twenty-five thousand dollar surety bail, I'll require a non-refundable two thousand five hundred fee from you, Miss Love."

"I'll write you a check." I dug into my purse for my checkbook.

"On what bank, please?"

"It's the Newtowne Community Bank, right here in town," I answered.

The creepy dude picked up the landline from his desk and dialed a number. Stanley had it on speaker, and I heard a woman's voice answer.

"Newtowne Community Bank, Evelyn speaking. How can I help you?"

"Good morning, Evelyn. This is Stanley from Newtowne Bail."

"Oh. What do you need, Mr. Jones?" Evelyn asked, the cheeriness gone from her voice.

"I have a young lady here, Miss Emma Love. She needs my services and I'd like to ensure she has adequate funds in her account to cover a twenty-five hundred dollar check please."

"One moment."

I finished writing out the check and the phone came back to life.

"Miss Love's account is sufficient to cover the check, Mr. Jones."

"Thank you, Evelyn, and while I have you on the phone, I was wondering if we might…"

The phone went dead before he finished his thought.

"Everyone is rush-rush these days. No time to socialize," he explained.

I handed over the check. He stared at it as if it might disintegrate in his hands.

"I will provide the court with the surety bond, Miss Love. The court will issue a receipt for the bail bond that I will provide to our good sheriff. I suspect he'll be released in an hour or two."

"Thank you, Stanley. Have a nice day."

"Thank you, miss, and be sure to tell all of your friends about our service."

I left the bailsman with a sour taste in my mouth but with a sense of accomplishment also. Daniel would be released today.

I filled Sam in about my adventure with Stanley. He shook his head as he dropped the gear shift into Drive.

"He is a creep and bears keeping an eye on…and you told him I was your boyfriend?"

"That's all you took from my story? I said that so he'd get a move on and quit his aggressive flirting."

"Oh, I see…so you didn't mean it?"

"Well, I…maybe I…"

Sam's phone rang. "You're saved by the bell, Emma."

"Mattingley here," he said into the phone.

I didn't hear much of the conversation besides an

occasional grunt from Sam until he replied, "No, he needs to stay there. I'll get him relief before the end of his shift. Let me know when it's close on your end too."

"Everything okay?" I asked.

"Yeah. How about we catch up on that lunch we missed? In the mood for Mexican?"

"Sure, but don't leave me hanging. What's going on?"

"You're right, a guy should never hold out on his 'maybe' girlfriend." He smiled.

"Are you mocking me, Sam Mattingley?"

"Never. That was Deputy Douglas on the phone. He's at the office. He said Deputy Abell called in from the hospital. The doctor told him he might as well leave. Maria was dosed up pretty well due to her head injury. She might be out all night and incoherent for a while after that, but I felt we needed someone there. The perp is still on the loose, and the hospital doesn't maintain that level of security. Oh, and Douglas is going to call me as soon as Stanley gets to the jail so we can pick Daniel up."

"You have it all figured out, Major-Deputy-Assistant-Sheriff Mattingley. I'm thinking carnitas. I love what they do with roasted pork."

****

Lunch was grand. Sam ordered the seafood fajitas with shrimp and scallops. I stuck with my old stand-by carnitas.

While we waited for our food, Sam started the same game we enjoyed together years ago.

"What about the lady with the blue windbreaker, Emma?"

"Hmm, let's see. She's a practical woman judging

134

by the windbreaker over the dress clothes she has on under it. It is a brisk day today. I think she is having marital problems or thinks her husband is cheating. She keeps twisting her wedding band around her finger. She may be plotting an indiscretion of her own by the way she keeps looking nervously over her shoulder at the entrance. She's expecting someone she probably shouldn't be seen with. That's why she picked the shadowed booth in the corner."

"Not to mention the sunglasses worn inside?"

"Exactly. How about that guy across from us with the pin-striped suit?" I whispered.

"Despite the cheater's ring around his finger, I don't think he's cheating, but the lady with him isn't his wife. I'd say a first or second date after his divorce, perhaps. Wearing a suit, even a threadbare one, in a very casual restaurant, he's trying to impress her, and she's laughing too heartily at his jokes. She's nervous as well. I'd bet she's been on too many crappy dates since her divorce. They're both trying too hard."

We both laughed when a man entered with dark glasses, ducked his head, and made his way to the first lady's booth.

It was a good lunch. There's nothing quite as satisfying as sharing a meal with a good friend. It made everything taste extraordinary. The carnitas were always tasty; today they were sublime—tender, juicy, and spiced exactly the way I liked. Even the welcome basket of chips was the best—warm, crisp, and flavorful. Usually, I considered them only a means to shovel my favorite salsa from the bowl to my mouth.

"I'm glad we were able to do this, Emma. I think we needed a short break away from the madness. I know I did."

"I guess we better enjoy it while we can. Fried ice cream?"

Dessert was as fine as our meal, only sweeter. Midway through, Sam's phone rang, and the madness pulled us back in.

Chapter Twelve

We paid the check and rode through town after Deputy Douglas' call. Stanley Jones came through with the bail, and the sheriff's office was filling out the release paperwork. My brother was coming home.

The media circus grew outside of the jail entrance. Two news vans were now on site, and a young and eager Johnny Walker leaned against his dilapidated old Chevy, hoping for his big break. Once again, Sam saved us with a back-door entry.

Daniel was standing in front of the counter, and a deputy handed him a basket with his belongings inside.

"Here's your belt, wallet with $108 in bills, key ring with six keys, a cell phone, and seventy-eight cents in change. Please verify against the original list and sign for your belongings, Mr. Love. Then you're free to go," the deputy said.

"Good Lord, I have forty-three text messages on here. You might have let me keep my phone at least," Daniel said.

He turned around to head for the door and spotted me. "Emma, thank God." He then wrapped his arms around me. First time in a long time I thought he cared about me…or I was just a safe familiar someone.

One peek out of the back door and we knew it was no longer a safe exit. A cameraman stood in wait, his equipment at the ready with the Catherine "Somebody" perched at his side. Sam was right. They looked like vultures waiting for something to die…or waiting to give it a push in that direction.

"Okay, so we will lead you both out, run all the interference we can to my squad car. I'll drive you two hundred yards to the public parking lot where Simmons left your Bronco, Emma. Ready?" Sam looked at me and then to Daniel. Deputy Douglas gave the thumbs-up sign.

"All right, deep breaths and one, two, three," and he threw the door open. Before I cleared the doorway, we had microphones shoved in our faces.

"Mr. Love, do you have a comment for our viewers?"

"Emma, how do you feel about the charges against your brother?"

"Deputy, does the sheriff's office have a strong case?"

The deputies were pushing back against the throng, but it only served to energize them.

"Where is Gwen, Daniel?"

"Where did you hide her body?"

"Are there others?"

"Will Maria live? Why was she taken?"

There were probably twenty more in the fifteen seconds it took to cross the few feet to Sam's vehicle, but they became a blur of words, a cacophony of accusations. An over-enthusiastic audio girl got too close with her microphone as I leaned into the car, and it hit my lip, splitting it.

When we were safely inside with the doors shut, the sordid questions still echoed through. The reporters chased alongside the car as we pulled out on the street.

"Thanks, Sam. I appreciate that," Daniel said. "You too, Emma."

Daniel pulled his phone out of his pocket and started scrolling through his messages.

"I appreciate it as well, Sam, both you and the deputies. That could've been ugly…well, even uglier than it was," I said.

"Oh. Crap," Daniel said.

"What's wrong, Daniel?" Sam asked.

"I have a text message from the kidnapper."

Sam slammed the brakes and pulled over on the shoulder of the road.

"What does it say, Daniel?"

He handed the phone to Sam. "Oh, my God, my God," Daniel repeated.

Sam held out the phone so we could both see it. It read:

—$20,000 in blue Newtowne Pirates Jim bag on Monday at 9 am to Buddy's Burgers outdoor trash can. No tricks to. If so. She starves.—

"Same illiterate spelling, but a new delivery method. Let's hope the number is traceable," I said. "When was the text sent?"

"Thursday," Sam said.

"The evening after I was arrested," Daniel added.

"Besides the delivery, there's another difference between the two notes. The first message after they were both missing, the one through my window said 'their' fate, indicating Gwen and Maria. Naturally, we assumed Gwen and Maria were taken by the same person and held in the same place. The ransom text that Daniel finally received said 'she starves,' singular. I think the 'their fate' note, also known as the rock note, is a threat from someone other than the kidnapper. The writer of the text didn't know about Maria or knew she was safe well before she was discovered."

"Or he had nothing to do with the second kidnapping at all," Sam said.

"What are you both saying? You think there are two kidnappers loose in Newtowne?" Daniel asked.

"I think there's a pair of them working together, yes, but they aren't both on the same page," I said.

"What am I supposed to do, Sam? I can raise the money, no problem, but do you think this animal can be trusted? Will he release Gwen alive?"

"I don't know, Daniel. The official stance is to never pay a kidnapper, but most kidnap victims do get home again. On a personal level, as a friend, I can't say what I'd do. Sometimes you have to roll the dice, I guess. I don't think you should make any decision until Maria wakes up and we can question her. We have time. If you decide to pay him, we'll get the state police to provide a tracking device for the money. They've got all the good stuff." Sam eased his cruiser out into traffic.

"Nothing against your department or the state boys, but why hasn't the FBI been called in?" Daniel asked.

"To the best of our knowledge, the victims have not been transported across state lines. There are other provisions to necessitate their involvement, but so far none of them are applicable here."

"So, basically two women kidnapped in Newtowne aren't high profile enough for them?"

Sam shrugged his shoulders. "Despite the movies, the FBI seldom takes cases away from local law enforcement. I think this is your stop."

The parking lot was empty except for my Bronco and one all too familiar old Chevrolet. Sam parked next to the Bronco. Johnny Walker raced our way, pen and pad in hand.

"Mr. Love, Miss Love, can you give me a statement? I'll write it up just the way you say it."

I was already behind the driver's seat with the car started, but Daniel took the bait. He stood at my back bumper looking at the young man.

"I'll say this," he said. "I did not harm my wife. We had our problems like any married couple, but we've weathered them all. I love my wife, and I'm innocent. If anyone knows anything about Gwen's whereabouts, please come forward to the sheriff's office. You may save her life. Print that, young man." Daniel opened the passenger side door and climbed in.

"Have there been any ransom demands, Mr. Love?" Johnny yelled as I pulled away from the parking lot.

"Did I do all right?"

"I would have gone with no comment, but that's me. I would have left out the part about any marital problems too. He might twist that against you, but we'll see how honorable a young man he is. I haven't seen much lately that inspires any confidence in the Fourth Estate."

"Do they know all that's happened? Obviously, they don't know about the text I got, but you and Sam were talking about two notes. Was there another one?"

"I'll give the sheriff credit; he's playing his cards close to the vest. That's not easy with the pressure he's receiving from the press. He stated that two women were missing, and he identified them, but nothing else.

Sam says he's old school and thinks too much information might embolden the kidnapper, taint his case, or inspire copycats."

"What was it about a second note then?"

I explained about the rock through my window.

"It sounds like the glass company might be the only ones in town happy with us right now. We're good for business."

"I guess they might be eventually, but as you replaced your door glass and I have plastic taped over my window, it might be a while before they fully appreciate us."

We rode the last few miles to Love's Manor in silence.

****

Alicia was upstairs having her dinner with Nana when we arrived. Daniel paid her and though she insisted it was too much, her eyes lit up and she tucked it into her pocket. It was easy to see it meant a lot to her, although her help meant even more to us. I hugged her before she left and told her just that.

"It was no problem. You can call me anytime, Emma."

"You can count on me doing that."

Sam called to check in but had no new updates. Daniel came downstairs dressed in long pajamas and a robe.

"It's a little early for bed, isn't it, brother?"

"I am so beat, Emma. The past few days have been a strain in every imaginable way. I think I'll grab a sandwich and turn in unless you need me?"

"I'm good. Sam will be over later if you hear strange voices."

"The two of you have hit it off since you've been home, huh?"

"I guess we have. We've resolved a lot of old issues."

"That's great. Maybe it's a time for everyone to heal old wounds."

I looked at him, wondering where he was going with this.

"I know I haven't been much of an older brother to you, Emma, and I treated you wrong…so wrong. I guess pride and arrogance kept me from seeing myself for what I was. I've missed you, Emma…so much. I've kept tabs on your welfare for the past few years. I tried to make amends, even if pride only allowed it to be anonymously. Did you ever notice deposits made to your account that you didn't remember making? I knew when you came home months ago too. Gwen told me to reach out then, but I was afraid."

"Afraid? Of what?"

"That you'd reject me like I deserve."

"Daniel…"

"The past few days have hammered into my hard head everything that family means. Family is there through good times and bad…like you've been there for me through all of this, at my side despite everything. I don't know if you can ever forgive me, and I won't blame you if you don't. I doubt I would, but I promise I'll do everything I can do to make it right, to be your family again."

Daniel took a step toward me and wrapped me in his arms. After a moment, I slapped his back and held him at arm's length.

"We'll try to make it back," I said.

Daniel cleared his throat and wiped the back of his hand across his face. "Damn allergies," he said. "Are you going to be here in the morning for a while?"

"I think so. What's up?"

"I wanted to go to the bank tomorrow and withdraw the funds for the kidnappers."

"So, you've decided to pay the ransom?"

"No, not yet anyway, but I want to be ready, just in case."

****

Sam called me soon after Daniel turned in for the night.

"Hey, what's up?" I answered.

"Maria woke up, but she was in and out, so the doctor only gave me five minutes with her. She was so out of it that we didn't get much out of her, and that was mostly incoherent."

"What did she say?"

"When I asked her if she knew who kidnapped her, she said 'Who is she?' Then I asked her if she knew anything about Gwen and she kept saying 'Where's Gwen' whenever I asked her the same question. That was pretty much it before she started falling asleep again. Oh, there was one other odd thing before the nurse kicked me out. Maria said 'Loose lips sink ships.' What do you make of that?"

"No clue. I mean I'm familiar with the saying. I think the military used it as a warning for troops about what they let slip in their day-to-day conversations. It started during World War II if I remember correctly, but that's about it."

"That's about it for me too. She didn't give us much to go on. Hopefully, she'll be more lucid in the morning first thing. Anyway, I'm out of here and headed your way after a pit stop at home, if that's okay?"

"You can leave the sleeping bag at home."

"Oh, good to know…" I couldn't see the smile on his face any clearer if he was standing in front of me.

"Yes, we have plenty of thick blankets and the couch here is more comfortable than mine. Oh, I'm sorry. What were you thinking…?"

"I was thinking…maybe I can pick us up something for dinner on the way? Do you know what Daniel likes? He could use something different after jailhouse chow, I'm sure."

"Daniel is down for the count after a ham sandwich and a cold glass of milk. How does a frozen pizza sound? I saw one in the freezer."

"Pepperoni?"

"Oh, heck no, the works," I said.

"That'd be perfect."

"I'll see you soon then, Sam."

The pizza would only take minutes to cook, so I climbed the stairs to Nana's room while I waited on Sam. I'd neglected Nana for too long. At the light tap on her door, Nana beckoned me inside.

"There sure isn't anything wrong with your hearing, Nana."

She pointed at her ear. "It's good until my batteries die, Emma. You'd be surprised at what I hear. Some things I wish I didn't."

It warmed my heart to hear her say my name.

"Are we too loud and keeping you awake at night, Nana?"

"No, you children are as quiet as church mice…not

like when you were younger and full of vim and vigor. I miss the sound of all the tiny feet racing up and down the halls though. When are you and Daniel going to bring me great-grandchildren? I can't wait forever you know."

This wasn't safe conversational ground with Nana. Not for me, anyway.

"So, what do you hear that keeps you awake at night?"

"I told you about Daniel putting up the root crops, didn't I? Or was it Sarah I told? I get forgetful sometimes…"

"I think you told my mother. She mentioned it to me. I asked Daniel to tone it down or to do that during the day."

"There's a sweet child. He has been quieter these past few nights. The ghosts still wander around at night, but I didn't hear a word from Maya last night. Did you?"

"No. I didn't see her either, Nana."

"But you do still see her, don't you, Emma? Sarah says you have the sight, but you deny it. Poor Sarah. Sometimes it skips a generation."

"The sight?" I asked.

Nana looked at me or rather through me. "I had a lovely visitor today. She's going to be a nurse. I can't remember her name…"

"That was Alicia, Nana. She is so sweet. We like her a lot."

"Is she your babysitter, Emma?"

Okay, so I'm a child again in her eyes. "Yes, she is. She's my favorite one too."

"No, she's not. I don't believe you. Why are you

lying to me, Sarah?" Nana pursed her lips into a pout. It was rather dramatic with her false teeth removed. My mind was whirling with any answer that might ring true without upsetting her, caught as she was in a web of time from my youth.

"I'm sorry, Nana. Alicia is Daniel's little girlfriend from school. He didn't want anyone to know."

"His girlfriend? Does Gwen know about it? She doesn't need to stand for that. I didn't think Alicia was that kind of girl."

Oh, dear Lord, what have I done now? I thought.

"Oh no," I said, "She's not…not at all. Daniel talks about how sweet she is and how lucky we are to have her, so I tease him about her being his girlfriend. Not really his girlfriend. Nothing like that, Nana, heavens no."

"Emma, you shouldn't tease about something like that. People will hear it and that will ruin that poor girl's reputation. A woman, or a man for that matter, doesn't have anything harder to earn or easier to lose than a good reputation. You remember that."

"Yes, ma'am. You're right, Nana. I'm sorry."

"No more of that kind of talk then."

"No, ma'am."

"That's good, child. I'm going to close my eyes for a bit now. Give Nana a few minutes, and I'll be down to cook your dinner."

"Yes, ma'am."

How did a visit that started so well turn that bad so fast? It wasn't fair what she was going through. My heart wept for what she'd lost and for what we were losing as she faded away from us. Nobody promises us fair. Anyone who tells you differently wants something

147

from you or is a liar.

Sam pulled in as I walked down the hall. I hoped his mufflers didn't wake the whole house, but I heard Daniel stirring in his bathroom before I got to the stairs.

"Long day," I said and opened the door for him.

"Are you okay? You look like you saw a ghost or lost your best friend. I can't decide which it is."

"Both, I guess. I'm losing my Nana day by day and reliving haunted memories; it's like communing with ghosts."

"Are things worse?"

"It's a gradual thing. Face by face, memory by memory, her life is disappearing from her. She still remembers some of the crazy things she told me when I was a child though—even if she doesn't always remember who I am."

"I can't imagine what it's like for her or you. Maybe we can go talk with her after dinner? You can introduce me as your 'maybe' boyfriend." He smiled, but I didn't have any witty repartee to share. Not yet.

"Sorry, I didn't mean to be flippant," he said. "I was trying to cheer you up."

"I know—you and your humor in the face of stress, but just let me feel like crap for a while. I need that. It's like mourning a slow death, or the same death revisited over and over again."

"I've heard dementia is like dying a thousand deaths, for both the afflicted and their caregivers. I'm truly sorry, Emma."

"I'm being emotional and that's not me, but it's been an emotional day. The bondsman creep, Daniel's release, the hordes of reporters screaming at us, what seemed like a heartfelt apology from my brother, now

Nana…"

"Is there anything I can do?"

"Bake the pizza while I get a grip?"

Sam took me in his arms for a moment until I pushed back, and he let me go.

"I'll be back," I said. I ran into my bedroom and reached into my suitcase for the only thing I hadn't unpacked. It was a torn-eared pink teddy bear with a big red heart in the middle of its chest, a gift from Nana right after Maya died. I wrapped my arms around it and cried like I did years ago when I first left Love's Manor. Newtowne was good at bringing on the tears.

****

Sam was waiting on the couch when I came out of my room. The entire pizza sat on the kitchen counter, also waiting.

"Why didn't you eat? The pizza is cold, I'm sure."

"That's okay. I wanted to eat it with you."

"Silly boy." I laughed and the tension lines in Sam's face smoothed out.

"Yes, I'm all better now and ready to face another day," I said. "You don't have to worry."

He smiled a warm, caring, 'I'm here for you' smile. He didn't know, but it nearly set me to tears again. He was right; we had wasted so much time…

Chapter Thirteen

Rooster Rachel woke me early the next morning. I was in my bed but didn't remember how I got there. The last thing I remembered was eating cold pizza on the couch with Sam while he scrolled through the movie selections on Daniel's streaming service. He must have carried me to my room. I sat up in bed, but Sam wasn't there.

I heard male voices outside my door and slipped on my flannel robe. I cracked open the door and recognized Sam's and Daniel's voices.

"We don't know much else about what happened to Maria, as incoherent as she was, but the doctor assured us it would go better this morning," Sam said. "I'm hoping Emma will come along to listen in. The things she picks up on are scary. I know she's smart as a whip. But sometimes I think she has an invisible angel on her shoulder telling her things."

"If you asked Nana, she'd tell you it was something else, but I can see where that might be scary for a boyfriend."

"A maybe boyfriend," Sam replied.

Daniel's voice took on a sinister edge. "Now you just hold on there. If you're toying with my sister, I don't care if you are a cop…"

"Good morning, boys," I said and swept into the room. "Sorry, I slept in." Sam was at the stove cooking

150

pancakes while a red-faced Daniel cleaned up the ones on his plate.

"I'm sure you needed it," Daniel said, his eyes boring into the back of Sam's head. "Sam said he'd like you to sit in on his interview with Maria if you're up to it?"

"But you said you wanted…"

"I can go to the bank any time. There's no hurry there, and Maria's statement could be important."

"Well, if you don't mind, I would like to be there."

For the record, Sam makes a mean pancake. They tasted like they were made from scratch, but I could see the box mix on the counter.

"Okay, Sam, give it up. What's your secret pancake recipe?" I asked.

"Can you taste the actual pancake with it swimming in all that maple syrup?"

I lifted a forkful of the sweet goodness to my mouth while making rather sensual sounds. "Mmm, oh yes, I can."

"It's vanilla extract and cinnamon, and if it does all that, I'm buying cases of the stuff."

Daniel gave Sam another dirty look. What was up with him?

"Well, I need a shower. How about I meet you at the hospital? It's a new day, so many *maybes* and possibilities to think about," I said, staring at Sam.

He caught my meaning and frowned at me, so I let it go. He was a big boy. If he wanted Daniel annoyed at him, that was his choice…probably some male virility thing.

"Can you meet me at nine? The vital checks should be done by then, and that should stir her up."

151

"Perfect."

By the time I'd showered and dressed, Sam was off to do the same. I cleaned up the breakfast dishes and put them away. I didn't know where Daniel was, so I yelled at the house.

"I'm heading out, Daniel. I'll see you soon, and I'll fill you in."

"Emma, wait," he shouted back and came running down the stairs.

"Easy, brother. You'll fall and break your neck." He had such a serious look on his face that I thought he might tell me that Nana was kidnapped too.

"I know it's too late for me to start acting like a real big brother, and I don't want to be in your business, but please be careful. I like Sam…just don't fall too fast."

I assumed he was more concerned with his reputation than my welfare, and I'm sure he read that on my face.

"I don't mean to overstep, but I'm here if you need me, sis. That's it. Please tell Maria I'm praying for her swift recovery."

All the years of hurt landed on my shoulders at once, and my mouth engaged before my heart could hold it in check.

"There was a time I could've used that protection, Daniel, but I can take care of myself now." His eyes dropped to the floor, and my heart softened.

"I appreciate it though, Daniel. I do. It's nice having a big brother again. We'll get there." I hugged him and raced from the house.

I pulled into the hospital parking lot at 8:55 and Sam was beside his patrol car waiting.

"Ready to do this?" he asked.

"For sure. I'm hoping she's awake and chatty."

We signed into the visitors' log and made our way to the elevators. The smell of bleach and disinfectant permeated the building.

"What was up with you this morning, Sam?"

"How do you mean?"

"That look you gave me about the 'maybe' I threw out there."

"I think Daniel misunderstood a reference I made…"

"I know. I heard you, and I was trying to work around to diffuse the situation until you cut me off with that look. What was that all about?"

"Daniel was being protective of you as he should've been for years now. I wanted to let that feeling simmer with him for a while. Let him feel how good it is to protect his family. Not to be condescending or macho, but let him learn to be a man. He wasn't much more than a kid when your parents died too."

"Sam, I don't need—"

"Any protecting. Yes, I know, but everybody does sometime, Emma, and family is important."

The elevator doors opened on the second floor, and a beautiful young woman with amazing cornrows in her hair stepped inside. She was dressed in a set of baby blue scrubs with flowers and butterflies decorating the outfit.

"You guys going up to the third?" she asked.

"We are," Sam answered. "You wouldn't know if the young woman in number 312 is awake, would you?"

"That's my floor, honey, and I know everything

that's happening on my floor. Room 312 you said? That's Maria Clements' room I believe?"

"Yes, ma'am," I said. "Is she awake?"

"Awake? Girl, that woman is a regular chatterbox this morning. Acts like she's being paid by the word. The only time she's shut up is when I stuck a thermometer in her mouth, but don't tell her I said that. She's a sweetheart."

"Thank you, that's good news, Nurse…" Sam tried to read the name on her tag.

"I'm Jackie, Deputy…" She took her turn then staring at Sam's name tag.

"Sam Mattingley, ma'am. This is Emma." He nodded toward me, and I held out my hand. She shook it with a firm grip.

"Sorry, I don't have one." I pointed to where a name tag would be.

The elevator slowed in a jerky way. It gave me a queasy feeling in my gut, a step or two away from nausea, then stopped with a jolt.

"This is us," Nurse Jackie said. She led the way out and escorted us to Maria's room. Two hospital employees were there. One was doing a quick mopping of the floor. The other was holding out documents for Maria to sign. She had an IV installed in her arm and monitor lines leading under her hospital gown to her chest. Machines hovered behind her bed, beeping with regularity. She looked pale, as one might expect, and her hair…well, knowing Maria, she'd have a conniption if she could see it. She smiled when she saw us hovering in the doorway though.

"Hello. Get on in here, you two. The nurses here are the best in the whole of the USA, but I could use a visit with familiar faces."

"It's good to see you awake and in good spirits, Maria," I said. "If you're up to it, we'd like to ask you some questions about what happened to you."

"Where should I start?"

"I guess with why you left and checked into the hotel. That was you, wasn't it?" Sam asked.

"Yes, that was me. How did you know about that? Did someone see me? I thought I was incognito with my big old floppy hat. Who tipped you off? I guess I don't have much of a future career as a spy."

"Why did you, though?" I asked.

"Sorry, I think these meds have me a little strung out. Don't arrest me, Deputy Sam. It's all prescribed stuff." She giggled. "Oh yeah, well…why I went? I had to go. I got a note from Gwen."

"You did? What did it say?" I asked.

"Well, I'm not sure that I did, but I thought I did. There was an envelope on my bed that night. I don't know how it got there or anything. Does anyone else have a key to the manor? The note said 'I'm getting out of town. Come meet me at the hotel.' "

"Did you recognize Gwen's writing?"

"No, it was typed out and in a typed envelope, Sam."

"But you felt sure the note was from Gwen?" he asked.

"Of course, I did, or I wouldn't have gone there, would I? The note said not to tell anyone, especially Daniel, but not you either, Emma. 'Loose ships sink ships,' it said. Gwen told me one time that her father always said that when he wanted to keep a secret from her mom, like when he had a special birthday gift for her or something…"

"Do you still have the note, Maria?"

"I'm sorry. I threw it in the trash at the hotel as soon as I got there. Do you think that it could be an important clue?"

Sam and I exchanged glances.

"A lock of hair was inside…Gwen's hair. It had to be from Gwen. I was with her when she had the edge coloring done. We did the makeovers together. She looked so cute, but I don't think Daniel even noticed. You know how he is, Emma."

"What happened after you checked into the hotel? Did you see Gwen or the one who attacked you? Do you know who it was?"

"I didn't see anybody, Emma. I'm tired, guys. Can I take a nap now? We can talk later, I promise."

"Just a couple more questions, Maria?"

"Oh, Sam, please…?"

"Only a couple more. Promise. Can you tell us what happened in the hotel?"

"All right…I went out to get a bucket of ice from the machine down the hall. The next thing I remember was having a terrible headache. I couldn't even open my eyes, but when I did, I was tied up in that old barn."

"Did you see anyone after that…while you were in the barn?" I asked.

"I was tied up, blindfolded, and gagged. No, I didn't see anyone, Emma. Somebody came by to shove food in my mouth once a day. Can I take my nap now?"

"Almost there, Maria. This will help us find the kidnapper. Did they say anything to you? Could you tell if it was a man or a woman?"

"Sam, you promised…"

"I know, Maria. This is the last one, then you can rest."

Nurse Jackie stuck her head in then. "Everything okay in here? Doing all right, Maria?"

"Jackieeee, they won't let me sleeeep."

"Are you two about done in here? The patient needs her sleep. She's been through a lot."

"Yes ma'am. We only have one question left," Sam said.

Nurse Jackie nodded her head but remained in the doorway with her arms folded across her chest. She wore a look on her face like a momma bear defending her cubs.

"Could you tell if it was a man or a woman? Did they speak to you?"

"I don't knowww, Emma. Maybe a woman…maybe a boy. Whoever…disguised their voice, I think. They said they were protecting me from sin. Whether they meant from me doing a sin or having one committed against me, I don't know…"

Maria started crying.

"Time to go now, folks," Nurse Jackie said.

"Sorry, Maria. Get well soon. Daniel said the same." With that, we were ushered out the door.

****

We were already discussing Maria's responses before the elevator doors closed.

"What do you think, Emma?"

"There's a lot to take in, but not as much as I hoped there would be. The note referencing the loose lips thing doesn't mean much. Like I said yesterday, that is a saying that's been around since World War II. I wish she could've been able to identify the voice of the

157

kidnapper, and I'm not sure how accurate anything she said was. She was pretty doped up. Maybe more will come back to her as she recovers. I thought the most interesting part was what she said at the end. 'Protecting her from sin.' What is that?"

"A religious fanatic, I'd say," Sam answered.

"That and this person knows Maria well enough to think she needs saving, no matter how distorted their reasoning might be."

"And where was Gwen while this was going on?" Sam asked. "Why weren't they together? I think that strengthens your theory about it being two different people."

"It gives me more concern about Gwen, though. One of them has strayed from the plan, and the other one must have Gwen. What does that one have in store for her?"

"Yes, that worries me too. The amount of time the kidnapper gave us for the money drop-off is concerning as well. It's indeed given us more time to find out who he is, but is that a good thing? I am not a kidnapping expert, but if it were me, I would want to get the conditions and the demands out there as fast as possible. Then I'd give as short a delivery time as practical to leave the police reeling on their heels, less time to put a sting in place."

"Unless the money is secondary and the kidnapping was the point, to terrorize my family."

"I hate to even say this out loud, but what if something has already happened to Gwen? The kidnapper could delay the payout to heighten Daniel's stress, hoping he makes a foolish and impulsive decision."

"Do you think Maria was telling the truth about everything?" I asked.

"I think so, within the constraints of her shaky memory anyway, like you mentioned. Why wouldn't she?"

"I don't know. I had a feeling at one point that she wasn't being honest or omitting some salient facts. Did you notice how animated she was until the subject of identifying the kidnapper came up?"

"Not really, but with the meds she is on…"

"No, she was lying, Sam. She began pulling at her monitor wires and the IV. Both hands were fidgeting. Also, she was focused on the wall clock. She did not meet our eyes when that line of questioning began. I'd be willing to bet the way she drew out her words was more a pause to collect her thoughts than any mental or drug-induced exhaustion."

"Who would she be protecting? And why would she after what they'd done to her?"

"Maybe she wasn't sure but had suspicions and didn't want to tell us until she was sure? Maybe she thought this person was trying to protect her in their distorted reasoning. Maybe she is still scared of what that person might do to her or Gwen. I don't know, but it's another thing we need to figure out."

"That was a lot of maybes." Sam laughed. "You seem partial to that word."

"Yeah, maybe." I laughed.

"I don't know what Maria could be scared of, though," Sam said. "At least not as long as her bodyguard, Nurse Jackie is there with her."

"I know, right? If I was cornered by hoodlums in a back alley, I'd sure want Nurse Jackie at my side."

"What are your plans for the rest of the day?" Sam asked.

"I guess I should get back to Daniel's place, so he can head to the bank. He wants to be ready if he decides to go through with paying the kidnapper."

"Or kidnappers. Do you think he will…pay them, I mean?"

"I think he will, especially if we don't get any closer to the truth between now and the scheduled drop-off time."

"I guess we better come up with something before that then."

"Exactly. Where are you going from here, Sam?"

"I'm going back to the office and check the evidence bags from Maria's hotel room. I remember a bag of clothes, a phone, a purse, and the suitcase. I didn't see a note listed. Hopefully, the deputy bagged the trash too. I might get lucky."

Sam walked me through the parking lot to the Bronco. Both of our phones jingled at the same time.

"Oh no, they found us," Sam joked.

A glance at my phone showed Daniel's number.

"Is everything okay, Daniel?" I answered.

"Fine. I was hoping for an update on how it went with Maria. Did she give you anything helpful?"

I gave him the *Readers' Digest* condensed version of our conversation with her. While I described it, Sam was pacing back and forth in an agitated way. His voice went up and down in volume and his non-phone hand waved about, highlighting his points. Sam wasn't usually a "hand talker."

Daniel asked me something, but I was distracted and didn't catch it all.

"What did you say, Daniel?"

"Did I catch you at a bad time?"

"Not at all; just being nosy. What did you ask me?"

"About that Newtowne Raiders' gym bag. Would you mind stopping by the school to see if they have any for sale? I think they used to sell them in the library unless they expanded and added a gift store." He laughed.

"I wouldn't mind, but we have one already. I saw my old one in the basement from when I was on the cross-country team. I'll go down and get it when I get home. Then you can get to the bank too. I shouldn't be long."

"There's no rush. The bank is open until six o'clock today."

I disconnected the call and waited for Sam to end his conversation. As he finished, he held up his index finger. "One second," he said and dialed another number.

"Deputy, I need you to go to the evidence room and go through all the bags assembled from Maria Clement's hotel room. Fine tooth comb, Deputy, but be especially watchful for a typewritten note." He hung up and turned his attention back to me.

"I guess my afternoon plans have changed. There were only partial fingerprints on the paper attached to the rock from your place. The tech indicated a match based on twelve common points, which he explained was weak, but likely enough for a warrant if I'm nice to the judge. I submitted the prints as a priority, but some desk jockey admin guy decided it was only a vandalism case and put it on the back burner. Sometimes I wish I had the time to follow evidence all the way through the system."

"So, nothing then?"

"Oh no, sorry. We got a match all right. There's a ninety percent probability that the prints belong to…drum roll please…Robert Wathen. I'm on my way to see Judge Allen for an arrest warrant." Sam practically skipped toward his car.

"I'll see you back at the manor with good news."

Chapter Fourteen

On the ride back to Daniel's, I couldn't help wondering what possessed Robert to do something so childish and irrational. The childish part I understood, considering it was Robert, but he always considered consequences and options well in advance. It served him well over the years to get him out of his many jams when he was caught. Was I that big of a threat to him? I'd lived with his threat for years, so was he that vindictive? Did he hate the idea of losing so much that he went into a blind and thoughtless rage, a woman calling his bluff and fighting fire with fire?

The rock thrown through my window was one thing. He'd already made his thinly veiled threat to me in town, but could he be a kidnapper as well? That seemed too daring an escapade for someone like Robert. He was all bluster and brag, lacking both courage and creativity. It wasn't just financial gain. He had no worries about money, and he'd never worked that hard to make a penny. So, what would be the benefit of it for him?

I lifted my eyes toward the heavens.

"Please let this be over soon," I prayed.

I swore I heard Maya's voice then…a whisper in my imaginative mind, a recalled memory of something she said long ago.

"Believe in yourself, Emmy Girl. You'll find the

way."

I smiled at the trick my mind played, but if no divine power heeded my request, Sam might provide more answers this evening. I flipped on the Bronco's turn signal before Daniel's driveway and waved at our ever-vigilant reporter, Johnny Walker. He waved his arms and ran after me until I sped down the driveway.

Daniel was fixing Nana a sandwich when I went in. It was her favorite—thickly sliced tomatoes with mayo on white bread, heavily seasoned with black pepper and a sprinkling of salt. We always assured her the tomatoes were home-grown and not those "hothouse things," no matter what season of the year it was.

"Oh my. You'll be in Nana's good graces today, Daniel."

"Would you mind taking it up to her, Emma? She's in a chatty mood, and I'd like to get to the bank before half of the tellers break for lunch…lines get long about then. And you can take full credit with Nana." Daniel laughed and handed me the plate.

"No problem. Is she making sense today, or is she back in the land of far-away?"

"Both, off and on…you know how it goes with Nana, poor thing. Ask her about something from thirty years ago if you are after an accurate memory."

I heard Daniel drive off in his Mercedes as the garage door closed. I climbed the stairs to Nana's room and knocked gently.

"Come in, Daniel."

"Hi, Nana. It's me, Emma."

"Well, hello, child. Oh my, I see you brought my favorite lunch. Are those home-grown tomatoes from your father's garden, Emma?"

"Now, Nana, don't you think we know better than to bring you a sandwich with nasty old hothouse tomatoes? After all these years?"

"That's a good girl, Emma. You all take such good care of your Nana. I do not know what I'd do without you."

"Thank you. You are our favorite Nana, you know."

"Where is that sister of yours, Emma? I need to speak with that girl. I'm very worried about her."

"Is she in trouble, Nana? What did she do?"

"It's that boy she is seeing. What is his name, and who are his parents anyway?"

"I don't know…"

"He can't be from a good county family. He comes here too often and too late to visit with a young lady…sneaking around in the dead of the night. It isn't proper. You tell Maya to come see me when you see her."

"I sure will, Nana."

"Maybe I should tell Sarah what's going on, but I thought I'd give Maya a chance to straighten herself out first. I'm afraid my son would hit the roof if he knew about their shenanigans, so we'll keep him out of it for now. You tell her what I said, though, you hear me?"

"Yes, ma'am. I'll sure give her the message."

"That's fine then. I've told you before, a girl can't afford to tarnish her reputation. You remember that when you're grown up."

"Yes, ma'am. What are your plans for the afternoon, Nana?"

"I'm going to listen to the radio for a bit. My favorite show is on soon. Abbott and Costello. Those two foolish men make me laugh on the gloomiest of days. I think I'll make us a nice stew after. That would be good, don't you think? What does your mother have you doing today?"

"I think I'm done for today, Nana. I must go down to the basement. Daniel wants to borrow the gym bag I put down there."

"While you're down there, don't waste a trip. Bring your old Nana up two or three nice onions and a half-dozen carrots from the root cellar."

"In the basement?"

"Of course, child. Where else?"

Nana's eyes grew heavy then, and I stood up to leave.

"Would you turn the radio on to my show before you go, Emma?" she asked.

"Of course."

I inserted the Abbot and Costello tape into her radio's cassette player and hit the play button. A scratchy rendition of the "Who's on First" skit began. Nana smiled as she listened again for no less than the hundredth time. I suspect that each time it replayed, she heard it for the very first time.

****

I grabbed a flashlight from the hall closet and descended into the dank and dusty basement. I spotted the blue gym bag on top of the pile of boxes behind the old sea chest. I wanted to pull out some more of the papers from inside it as well. I was more interested in Maya's old drawings than I was in the ancient documentation about Love's Manor purchases. The artworks were cathartic memories of my big sister.

I reached over and pulled the gym bag from the top

of the pile, and the box beneath it fell to the hard-packed earthen floor, landing with a hollow sound. I placed the gym bag at the foot of the stairs and grabbed the fallen box to restack it…it was empty. I checked the two boxes that were stored beneath it, and they were also empty. Did my mother keep empty boxes here for a reason? Maybe to ship larger items? I couldn't imagine what those items could be, but maybe Daniel had some idea.

I held the tiny flashlight in my mouth to restack the boxes when I discovered an odd handle on the floor. I dropped the first box to investigate. A quick pull of the handle and a trap door opened revealing a narrow opening with a ladder descending into the depths of a hole. A musky smell floated up from the desiccated root crops I saw spread out on pallets at the bottom. At least the mystery of the unknown root cellar was solved, even if no other.

I crawled over the sea chest, put my foot on the first step of the ladder, and looked down again. It was twelve feet or more to the bottom. *What if I fall? No one will know I'm down there. Suck it up, buttercup; will you let a ladder beat you?*

I don't like ladders…The second step followed, and my knees started to knock. *Get a grip, Emma. You can do this. It's a stupid ladder.* The third one creaked in protest at my weight. Whether my imagination or reality, it seemed to wiggle beneath my feet.

"Whoa, girl," I said to no one. "This isn't about overcoming fear. Do you want to fall down this hole with nobody home and not a soul knowing where you are? Nobody needs another missing Love."

Yes, I hate ladders, and rickety ladders even more.

I retreated in shame, all the while cursing myself for my cowardice. I consoled myself with the knowledge I'd return as soon as another warm body, capable of dialing 911, returned home. I would beat the stupid thing. It would not beat me.

I dropped the trap door over the root cellar and grabbed a stack of our childish artwork from the sea chest to admire later. With the pictures under one arm and the gym bag in the other, I stomped up the stairs with my head hanging in temporary defeat.

****

My stomach growled as I made my way to the kitchen for a sandwich. When I'm involved with a project, forgetting to take meals is the norm rather than the exception. Daniel called as I was slathering bread with ketchup, mustard, and black pepper for my ham and cheese sandwich.

"Hi, Daniel. How did it go at the bank?"

"It was interesting. People there stared at me like I was an albino talking frog smoking a fifty-dollar cigar. I'm sure the tellers had to know what the money was for, but they had the good grace not to ask. Driving through town, the looks I got…I'm guilty as heck in the court of public opinion. I expected them to throw tomatoes at me or something."

"People are quick to judgment, Daniel. You'll get through this, and they'll soon forget all about it."

"I guess it's to be expected, but I wasn't ready for it. I called to see if you found the gym bag. If not, I thought I'd pick one up at the school while I was out and about."

"I did, and that's not all."

"What do you mean?"

"Remember the root cellar Nana is fond of talking about? I found it in the basement. There's a ladder going down to it and some long-forgotten root crops shriveled up down there."

"You didn't use that ladder, did you?"

"No. I thought I'd wait."

"Good. I remember the ladder incident all too well. What were you, maybe ten years old? You're kind of clumsy on ladders, Emma."

"I wasn't clumsy. I was eight and a nest of hornets was after me, and I…stepped off."

"And one broken arm later…"

"I know. I'm the one who got to wear a cast for the entire summer."

"Yes, but you fell off a ladder, and somehow it was my fault."

"I guess you should've been watching me instead of playing your dumb video games," I snapped, having enough of the conversation.

The phone went silent except for Daniel's sharp intake of air.

"I'm sorry, Daniel. That was uncalled for. Can we just forget about the damn ladder thing?"

"Yes, but you're right. I really should've been there. Is Sam coming over this evening?"

"I think so. He's getting a warrant for Robert Wathen's arrest, but I haven't heard back from him on that. I'm sure it will be an interesting story to hear. They were never the best of friends."

"What did Robert get himself into this time?"

"Ah, I forgot to tell you. You remember the note attached to the rock at my house, right? Well, the partial prints they got off it likely belong to Robert."

"It's good that Sam is following up then and not Robert's brother, the sheriff. Why would Robert do something like that? What did you ever do to stir him up? It's crazy."

"That's a story for another day, Daniel. Suffice it to say, my issues go way back with Robert. Have you forgotten?"

"No, not that I haven't…of course not…but it was so long ago, and you were the aggrieved party, not the other way around."

"Well, I switched it up a bit since I've been back."

"I see…Enough to make him come after you like that?"

"That's the question I've been asking myself all morning."

"Well then, Robert Wathen is one less thing to worry about now. Okay, I'll be home in five minutes. Stay off the ladder, please."

I finished fixing my sandwich and sat at the kitchen table to eat. I heard Daniel pull in as I washed my plate. Going to the door to greet him, I saw a second vehicle following close behind him. It was the beat-up old Chevrolet mini-hearse. Johnny Walker had come a-calling.

"I know what you're going to say, Emma," Daniel said as I threw open the door.

"What are you doing, Daniel?"

"He seems like an honest kid, and he has a few questions for me…for us. If we don't give the vultures something, they'll just make up something worse to say about us. From what I saw in town, they can't think much worse of me than they do already. Will you sit in with me?"

I nodded in the hope I could keep Daniel from saying too much as the reporter approached the door.

"Miss Love, it's great to see you again," Johnny "Scotch" Walker said in greeting.

"Mister Walker," I replied. "Please come in and have a seat." I led the way into the great room.

"The wainscoting is beautiful," Johnny said. "Cedar?"

"Cherry," Daniel answered. "One of our ancestors cut and milled the planks from off the farm."

"I'm sure you aren't here to discuss lumber or interior design. Mr. Walker," I replied.

"No, ma'am, and please, just call me Johnny."

We took our seats. Daniel and I sat together on the overstuffed couch, and Johnny plopped down in the armchair nearest the door. He looked rather nervous, as you'd expect from the interviewee, not the interviewer in this situation. I reminded myself he was a very young reporter.

Johnny fumbled through his notebook, and several pages fell to the floor. One drifted our way. It was marked "Love's Interview Questions." I picked it up and handed it to him.

"You might need these."

"Yes, well…" he stammered, his face flushed. "Is it all right if I record this?"

Daniel and I nodded.

"Let's begin, then." He pulled a mini-recorder from his pocket and pressed record. "Mr. Love, do you have any idea where your wife is?"

"I think we've covered this, but no, I do not."

"Are there any developments in the case that haven't yet been released?"

"I'm not aware of any…"

"Would you say so if there were? Recent ransom demands, for instance?"

"I'd have to depend on advice from the police before any comments along those lines."

"So, there have been no demands to date?"

"I didn't say that."

"I see…Do you know of anyone who would wish your wife harm?"

"No, Gwen was well thought of in the community. She led several charities involving support for children and was active in the Christmas in April events."

"And you, Mr. Love? What kind of relationship did you have with your wife? Had you argued?"

"I don't think that's your business or your readers' business, but we got along fine."

"I see…So, there's no truth in the rumor that Mrs. Love was having an illicit affair?"

"No."

"Is there anyone who might wish harm to you personally or to the rest of your family, Mr. Love?"

"You must understand, Johnny. We were blessed with this beautiful home and farm, but we didn't build it. Our ancestors worked hard to do so, and we are the beneficiaries of their labors, vision, and largess. Our family has been here a long time and weathered many storms, economically and physically. Many farms folded during the depression…ours endured. We purchased, what was at the time, valueless land to keep other less fortunate families from bankruptcy.

"We have endeavored to improve our holdings for the benefit of our future progeny, just as those before us did. Despite being good neighbors and advocates for the less fortunate, I'm sure some resent our good fortune without weighing the cost to our ancestors."

"May I quote you on that, Mr. Love?"

Daniel looked at me. I thought about what he'd said and nodded.

"Of course."

"From what you've told me, you're not aware of any recent threats or a particular individual who's made threats against your family?" Johnny looked at me.

"No."

"What is your relationship with Robert Wathen, Miss Love?"

"Robert Wathen? There's a name from the past. I knew him in my school years, but we didn't hang out. Why? What does he have to do with any of this?"

"When the state police dragged Robert Wathen to jail a few hours ago, he was agitated and screaming obscenities. It was your name he was cursing, Miss Love."

"I have no idea…"

"I hoped you could shed some light on that, Miss Love. Most of the media were there and they all had questions too."

"I'm sorry, but I cannot imagine the cause for his animosity. Are you sure it was my name he yelled?"

"Yes, ma'am. Anyone there would tell you the same."

"What did Robert do?" Daniel asked.

"The state police were very closed-mouthed about the charges, but it will come out." Johnny looked at me.

"Are you sure there is nothing you would like to say, Miss Love? Maybe get ahead of this thing before it blows up?"

"Mr. Walker, we invited you in as a courtesy for an interview, but you've turned it into an interrogation. I think we are done here."

"You're right of course…my apologies. I'm new to this and didn't mean to offend. Before I go, did you care to make a statement, Mr. Love? An appeal for your wife perhaps or…"

"I'll say again, I would never and have never hurt my wife. If anyone knows anything that might lead to Gwen's safe return, please notify the sheriff's department. You will be rewarded for your good citizenship."

Johnny Walker flipped off his recorder and stuck it back in his pocket. Smiling ear to ear and thanking us for the interview, he made his way to the door. We waited until his rust bucket started down the driveway before we spoke.

"Wow…just wow," Daniel said.

"Where did all that come from and what's the deal with Robert? I haven't done anything to him, though I could have if I'd wanted."

" 'I'm new to this, and didn't mean to offend.' Is that what he said, Emma? Must have one heck of a mentor or teacher then. That kid is going places."

"Yes, but at our expense, I'm afraid."

Chapter Fifteen

My phone was lit up with voicemails and text messages from Sam. I clicked on the last voicemail that asked me to call him back when his number popped up as an incoming call.

"Are you okay?" he asked before I answered.

"Yes, why? And what is going on with Robert Wathen? Who knows about what I had on him besides the two of us? Why is he cursing me out?"

"Whoa. One question at a time. I was worried because I've been trying to reach you. First, nothing went through at all, not even my text messages, and after that everything went to voicemail. I don't know who, if anyone, knows about what you had on Robert. Maybe one of your sources when you were investigating him? Why?"

"I don't think that's it. Must be someone else. Sorry, I've been incommunicado. I was in the basement, and there's no reception there, and then we did this interview with the Walker kid—"

"Please tell me you're kidding? I know you didn't tell him any information we haven't released, but what about Daniel?"

"No, it went okay, except he already knew things he shouldn't…like asking about my so-called relationship with Robert Wathen, Gwen's possible extra-marital fling, and a fight between her and my

175

brother."

"Maria…I'll bet she's given the press more than she did us."

"Maybe, but she didn't know anything about the Robert part…and what's up with him?"

"I don't have any real news on that front. I'm sitting on my heels waiting on Judge Allen. He should be in chambers any time now though."

"I think it's a bit late for that, Sam. The state police arrested Robert already."

"The state boys? What was the charge?"

"Our young journalist didn't know that yet but assured us that he would soon."

"I'll call you right back."

Sam disconnected.

"Okay, bye. Nice talking to you, Sam," I said into the dead phone.

I walked upstairs and peeked in on Nana. She was asleep in her chair. I pulled her blanket up over her, and as I turned to leave, my phone vibrated in my pocket. I hurried out of the door and closed it without a sound before answering.

"What did you find out, Sam?"

"He was arrested all right. I asked about interviewing him for our case, but he is being grilled in the interrogation room. I'll have to wait my turn at him. They got him on misappropriation of funds from his non-profit. I guess he didn't cover his tracks or get out from under it soon enough. From what my source over there says, he's all but spitting blood and repeatedly cursing your name."

"I didn't say anything, Sam. I swear it. Did you…by chance, I mean, mention it to anyone?"

"Of course not. You told me about that in confidence and though it would cost me my job, I'd not break my word to you. I'll admit I did begin investigating him for other concerns."

"Don't tell me. I don't even want to know."

"Probably for the best."

"We should talk to Maria again too, Sam. I'm not sure what her plans are once she's released from the hospital."

"I think I'd wipe the dust of Newtowne from my sandals and head out if I was her."

"I agree, but I'd like to see if she has any better recall of what happened."

"And what she's said to the press."

"Exactly. Are we going to see you tonight, Sam?"

"We? Are you asking for Daniel or yourself?"

"Hmm, I don't know. Do you have something going on with my brother too? Should I be jealous?"

****

Downstairs, Daniel was stuffing the Newtowne Pirates gym bag with bundles of cash.

"That's a lot of money, Daniel. Let's hope you don't have to use it."

"I know, but Gwen is worth it. I haven't been the best husband to her. Not as attentive as I should've been. She deserved better, but maybe I can at least do this right. I just hope she is okay."

"We all do, Daniel. Sam is coming over later, but he wants a crack at questioning Robert as soon as the state cops give him a chance. Robert is blaming his situation on me from what Walker and Sam said, but I didn't do anything to the creep."

"Was he arrested for what you had on him? Is that

what you meant when you said you'd turned it around on him?"

"That's one of the things. Robert Wathen is just an all-around bad unit."

"You need to be careful, sis. That family has a lot of friends and supporters in the county. Some of them are violent thugs. The sheriff isn't a bad guy, not like Robert anyway, but he turns a blind eye toward his friends and family."

"Thanks, Daniel. I can take care of myself if need be. I was the top marksman in the concealed-carry permit class. I've been beaten up in a few mixed martial arts classes as well, and I picked up a few pointers there at the expense of a sore body and a lot of bruises. Plus, Sam has my back. There's no need for you to worry."

Daniel gave me a pouty heavy-lidded look. Was it concern I saw on his face, or fear that I'd sully the family name…again?

"I can't lose you again, Emma. Sam isn't the only one who has your back. If you need me…for anything, I'm there."

I wasn't sure how to respond to that. I nibbled at my lip and nodded.

"Oh, Emma, I took out those old drawings you had in the gym bag and put them on the kitchen table. I saw Maya's and Jessie's efforts at the top of the pile. I always wondered about those two."

My phone buzzed and I clicked on the text message from Sam. It read:

—Robert's refusing to answer any questions without his lawyer there. The lawyer is out of town until tomorrow. Be there soon. Bringing Mexican for dinner. What does Daniel like?—

I texted back.

—Same as you, the seafood fajitas. See you then.—

I retrieved the artwork from the table and went to my room. Stretching out on my bed, I looked the pictures over while I waited for Sam's arrival. The latest crop of drawings was from Maya along with a few done by her friend Jessie Dawson. Seeing those, I determined to visit Abby Dawson soon to share my findings. I knew it would bring back memories, both happy and sad. The pictures were the usual family and home depictions and several of the two girls (I assume) together. They were holding hands and skipping along…Red hearts were drawn all over the pages. It was easy to see that they were best friends back then. I don't recall ever having a girlfriend like that growing up. From the bright red crayon smiles drawn on their faces, I felt like I'd missed out.

I looked at my watch, impatient to share my basement discovery with Sam and explore it further. Daniel offered to help me investigate, but I saw his apprehension and knew of his basement phobia. I wasn't old enough to recall the incident, but my mother told me what happened years later after I teased him about being a chicken. Daniel was about six years old, and my parents were outside weeding the flower beds. Nana was there too, but she fell asleep in her rocking chair while reading a book. Daniel saw this as his opportunity to explore the basement—the forbidden zone. He closed the door behind him, so he'd not wake Nana, and it locked behind him. He wasn't tall enough to reach the string-pull light cord and spent over an hour crying in the dark…all alone. I guess some events will stick with you forever…

The Mustang's throaty growl echoed outside and disturbed my reverie. I went to meet Sam at the door, but Daniel was already there welcoming him inside.

"Hi, Emma." Sam leaned over and gave me a head and shoulder half hug, both hands full of food bags. "The food is hot, and I had to smell it all the way here. Can we dig in before my stomach digests itself?"

"We can't have that, can we, Emma?" Daniel asked.

"I'll set out the plates."

I didn't contribute much to the dinner conversation. My mind was already exploring the dark recesses of the newly discovered root cellar. I don't know what I expected to find there, if anything, but it was a mystery to solve and like Robert Wathen, it was also calling my name. Sam and Daniel didn't seem to notice my inattentiveness, caught up as they were in a discussion about muscle cars and the Super Bowl prospects of various football teams. I could almost smell the testosterone levels rising.

I finished my carnitas, or all I could eat of it, before the men did and washed my plate at the sink.

"Did you choke that down?" Sam asked.

"She's in a hurry to explore, Sam. Emma is an inquisitive soul and always has been. I can tell you that waiting for you, her fellow explorer, was a real challenge for her. I did offer to go to the basement with her, so she didn't break her neck down there, but she had mercy on me and waited."

"What's going on in the basement?"

"After all these years, I've located the mysterious root cellar down there. I went to check it out, but the ladder was kind of shaky, so I decided to wait for a spotter while I climbed down."

"I'm your man," Sam assured me. "Are you hoping to save a few carrots and potatoes after all these years? Maybe a bottle of vintage wine worth a couple of million bucks?"

"I not worried about anything as mundane as desiccated root crops or as dramatic as your unknown liquid treasure, Sam. I just want to satisfy my curiosity."

"Who knows. Maybe there's some deep dark family secret down there," Daniel added.

"If you two ever finish your meal, I can go find out."

"You heard the lady," Sam said and wolfed down a huge mouthful of fajitas.

"Whoa there, Deputy. I need a spotter who can pull me out if the ladder breaks, not one of the county's finest choking to death on Daniel's kitchen floor."

"I can't help it. My mother told me years ago I should never keep a lady waiting."

****

Flashlights in hand, Sam and I went into the basement together. Daniel waited at the top of the stairs directing us to yell if anything went amiss. At the top of the root cellar entry, we flicked on our lights.

"Wow, a lot of work went into that cellar," Sam said. "It just has a hard-packed dirt floor, but the walls are floor-to-ceiling mortared river rock. Looks like the same mason who built it did your fireplace in the great room."

"Okay, I'm going down, Sam."

"How about I go first? If it holds me, it will for sure hold you."

"No, this is my quest. I'll yell up if I find anything interesting."

"I really don't mind, if you—"

"Sam!" I said louder than intended.

"Everything okay?" Daniel asked.

"All is good," Sam replied, then to me, "Okay, Emma. Yell if you need me."

I guess we all have our ingrained fears. I wasn't ashamed of that fact, but I wouldn't let fear conquer me, or cage me. I might've chewed my lip, still sore from the microphone slap, when my foot eased into the third rung of the ladder. It twisted under my weight, but the remainder of my descent was without issue. The root cellar was much larger than it appeared from above. Along with the pallets of produce on the floor, the walls were covered with deep shelves holding baskets full of foodstuffs. There were boxes of home-canned jars of corn, tomatoes, pickled beets, and green beans.

"What's down there, Emma?"

"About what we thought—a bunch of root crops that have seen better days and dozens of mason jars full of veggies. I don't think we'll be fixing any of it for dinner anytime soon. Wait a minute. What's that?"

At the far end of the room, my light flickered across a wooden structure. It looked to be a round door about five feet in diameter. I giggled out loud. "It's a hobbit hole." I walked over to investigate. The shelves on the walls closest to the door stored more boxes of mason jars, all filled with water. I opened one and took a sniff and my eyes watered. I heard something moving behind me and I whirled around, my flashlight's beam catching Sam between the eyes. He held up his hand to ward off the light.

"Emma, I was yelling for you, but you didn't answer. Are you all right?"

"Check this out, Sam." I shined my light at the door and handed him the mason jar. "Take a whiff and tell me what you think."

Sam stuck his nose in the jar, drew in a deep breath, and crinkled up his nose. "It's moonshine. Does your family tree include a bunch of moonshiners from prohibition days?"

"If not, they sure kept a large supply on hand."

"What's behind door number two?" Sam asked.

"Let's go find out."

The oak wood door grated against the stone around it and the hinges made a familiar horror movie 'S-C-R-E-E-C-H' before yielding. Behind the door was another room, not as large as the cellar, but it had its own fireplace. A huge rusted pot with coils of tubing sprouting from its funnel-shaped lid sat inside. Wooden barrels were stacked to the side.

"Is that what I think it is?" I asked.

"I think we've answered the question of whether your ancestors were distillers or just imbibers." Sam laughed. "Running moonshine is how a lot of folks kept their financial heads above water in those days. Maybe we've discovered the secret of the Loves' family fortune."

"Not that funny," I said, pressing my lips together to stop my smile from forming. "I think I remember where this chimney comes out past our yard at the edge of the tree line. Mama told me she thought it was a vent for the septic system when they couldn't get piping back in the day."

Sam was waving his light around the four walls. "How far back does this go? There's a hallway or a tunnel off that side. See it?"

"Let's go find out."

The hall went about ten feet before it began to shrink. By the time we reached the end, it was no more than three feet wide and five feet high. We were both hunched over when we spotted a ladder leading up. Sam didn't wait for me to protest and scurried up the ladder.

"There's another trap door up here," he said.

I heard a thumping as he pressed against it.

"It's stuck…locked from the outside I'd bet. They wanted to keep little people from falling in."

"Or keep revenuers out," I said.

"Where do you think it comes out?" Sam asked.

"It must be back in the woods twenty yards or so? We'll step off the distance back to the still. I remember where that old chimney comes out, and we can step off the distance in the morning. I'd never find it in the dark."

We climbed out without incident. The ladder rungs held, and we found Daniel waiting at the top of the basement stairs.

"I was beginning to wonder about you two. Did you find that priceless bottle of wine down there among the old vegetables?"

"I had no idea it was such a large cellar, but no wine…plenty of moonshine though," I said.

"Moonshine? Really."

"Yes, we uncovered the secret of the Love family fortune," Sam joked again. "Did you know your ancestors distilled corn mash, Daniel?"

"That is a family tale that I don't remember being recounted at any Sunday dinners. Is there a statute of limitation on illicit whiskey production, Sam?"

"I think you're safe, Daniel. There was even a moonshiner's tunnel leading outside somewhere too. We couldn't get out that way though; the trap door was locked. As for the booze, I guess we should dump the stuff sooner or later. It's well-aged, that's for sure."

"Congratulations then. The two of you have solved both the secret of the family fortune and of the mysterious root cellar. Well done."

"That's not the only mystery solved," I said.

"What do you mean, Emma?"

"Nana speaking of ghosts whispering to her at night and the root cellar being restocked; the sound of rats in the basement and movement on the stairs. They weren't all the sounds of an old house settling."

Both men looked at me as if I was speaking in a south county dialect.

"How about a glass door broken out from the inside?" I saw the light of understanding flicker in their eyes.

Chapter Sixteen

I woke from the recurring "Maya at the pond" dream curled up in Sam's arms. He was beginning to be a fixture in my life, and I wasn't sure how I felt about that. I had no intention of using him, but I confess to postponing any further thought on long-term relationship status until our case was solved. Sam stretched out beside me and opened his eyes.

"What are you staring at, my lovely lady?"

"Hmm, 'my lovely lady'?"

"Would you prefer my 'maybe lovely lady' better?"

"Just 'lovely lady' works fine." I smiled.

"What are your plans for the day? No lone spelunking, I hope?"

"No. I thought I might talk with Maria again this morning at the hospital while you're questioning Robert. Then I want to find the tunnel exit, and if there's time, I want to visit Abby Dawson. I found some drawings that her daughter Jessie made. She drowned with Maya, if you remember. Best friends until the end. How about you?"

"As you said, I hope to get in a chat with Robert. I'm not sure how long that will take, and I have a ton or two of paperwork to catch up on after that. If there is time, I wouldn't mind having a chat with Robert's wife, Amanda. You remember her? She was a year behind you. Amanda Young was her maiden name."

"I remember Mandy, although we didn't hang out together. From what I did know of her back then, she deserved better than Robert Wathen. What makes you think she'd talk to you about Robert, though?"

"What do you tell me all the time? I have a gut feeling about her…we'll see if it pans out."

Sam was in a hurry to get to the sheriff's office. He even skipped his morning coffee, planning to grab a cup en route. I had plans for a busy day as well, but coffee came first. I made enough for several cups. Daniel slept in, but I knew he'd want a cup when he did rise. I'd tasted Daniel's coffee before. I wouldn't serve it to my worst enemy.

I poured myself a cup and sat at the table while I skimmed yesterday's paper. There was little about Gwen's case. Johnny Walker's byline included a picture of Daniel leaving the courthouse and accurately related his statement about Gwen. There was another picture of Robert being dragged into custody. The cameraman caught him with his mouth wide open, likely with my name on his foul lips. Walker's interview piece with us would likely be in the next edition.

I folded the paper and took a long sip of coffee. I had time. A woman must set priorities while recognizing her limitations. Needing a strong jolt of Colombian roast before facing the day was one of my many shortcomings. The world and our problems could wait that long.

My first order of business was to locate the outside entrance to our root cellar. I dressed in a heavy blue blouse with sweatpants, then slipped on a gray hoodie. I was a regular fashion plate, and I didn't care. The cold snap was waning but there was still a bite to the air in the early mornings.

I found the chimney opening where I remembered it to be, then paced off the distance we'd measured in the tunnel the night before. A thick carpet of oak leaves covered everything and made the search difficult. I scraped away leaves with my boots until they hit something solid. The first time, it was a heavy maple root jutting out of the ground, then a half-buried coke bottle caught the toe of my boot. The third time was the charm. I brushed away freshly fallen leaves and found my second hobbit-hole door. It had hinges on one side and a hasp screwed into the other side, but no lock. A large carabiner is all that held it secure. There was no rust on it. Slipping it off, I pulled the door open and looked inside. The ladder stood ready…for anyone's entry.

I returned to the house to change clothes before going to chat with Maria again. Daniel was sitting at the table sipping his coffee.

"Slow down, Emma. Are you in a rush? Did you see my picture in the paper? Guess I'm famous."

"I think the word you are looking for is infamous," I said, "not a good thing."

"Oh, I got that, believe me. I didn't realize how fast friends and neighbors could turn on someone, not until my visit to town yesterday."

"I know, Daniel. It will blow over when we get Gwen back home."

"If we do, you mean?"

"No, not if…when. As soon as I change clothes, I'm heading to town to talk to Maria again. Sam is hoping to question Robert. Hopefully, we'll get some answers."

"Would you mind if I went with you? I have a couple of questions for Maria also."

"I don't mind, but your reception in town will be just as negative as before. Are you up for that?"

"I love this old house, Emma, but if I'm held hostage in it, it's no longer a place of refuge—it's a fancy prison cell."

"Give me fifteen minutes to shower and change, and we'll head out…in my Bronco. Your Mercedes draws too much attention."

"Take your time. I already called Alicia to see if she'd cover for a couple of hours. Nana loves it when she comes for a visit anyway."

After a hasty shower and wardrobe change, black yoga pants with a blue knit blouse, I was ready to go in time to answer the knock at the front door. Alicia was all smiles, as was normal for her. After greeting her and voicing our appreciation to her yet again, Daniel and I headed for the hospital.

We signed in at the reception desk and headed to the elevators and room 312. Not surprisingly, Nurse Jackie was in attendance. She gave me an evil-eyed look.

"I won't have you upsetting my patient again today, Miss Love. We hope to have her released today. Isn't that right, Miss Clements?"

Maria nodded. "Hello, Emma, Daniel. How are the Loves this morning? Is there anything new on Gwen?"

"Nothing to speak of," I answered. "We were hoping you might have a better recollection of what happened to you though?"

"I think I told you everything already. I just don't recall much. I was blindfolded."

"Did you recognize the man's voice who took you?"

"No, I'm not sure who he was."

"So, it was a man's voice? You said before you couldn't tell if it was a man or a woman because they disguised their voice. That's some progress."

"Umm, I guess…"

"Could you tell how old the man was?"

"A younger man, I think, but I didn't recognize his voice. It could have been anyone."

"Are you protecting someone, Maria?" I asked.

"No, I wouldn't…but maybe he was protecting me."

"From what?"

"He said people were after me because of my sins."

"What sins?" I asked.

"I don't know…" Maria began to fidget under her covers.

"Has the press been here to see you, Maria?" Daniel asked.

"Yes, I'm very popular now, you know. Why do you ask?"

"What did you tell them?"

"About you and Gwen, you mean, Daniel? I told them the truth. You don't have anything to hide, do you?"

Daniel shook his head and his face flushed red. Maria had turned the conversation away from herself to put us on the defensive. I couldn't have that.

"What do you know about Robert Wathen?"

"Who…?"

"Were you having an affair with him also?"

"No, I…"

"Did you intentionally lead my family and the police to think you were kidnapped before the actual event occurred?"

"No."

"Why did you leave without a word or a note then? Were you in on it from the beginning?"

"Of course not. There was Gwen's note…"

"Did you conspire with Robert Wathen to provide a note to misdirect the police investigation?"

"No, I did not. I hardly know him."

"What are your plans when you're released, Maria?" I asked. She looked stunned at the changed direction of the question.

"I…I am not sure. I'd like, if Daniel lets me back into the house, to pack my clothes and head to Annapolis. I have a friend there, and I need a fresh start. Would that be okay, Daniel? Sometime later today?"

"You aren't waiting for us to get Gwen back home safe and sound? Aren't you two an item?" Daniel asked.

Maria looked around the room to avoid our eyes or in search of a sympathetic ear. Her face assumed a stoic appearance, and she stared straight into Daniel's eyes.

"I'm sorry, Daniel. It wasn't meant to go this far." She rubbed her eyes. "You just paid no attention to her. What did you expect? It was Gwen's idea."

"What was her idea? The kidnappings?"

"No, our so-called love affair, the affair that never was. Gwen wanted to make you jealous, Daniel. I guess that part worked out as planned. I was supposed to meet her at the hotel. We already had the note typed up. She said, 'It's only for a little while, but I'm not sure he'll even notice that I'm gone.' But breaking out the door glass…that wasn't part of the plan, and I was worried. Then they found the necklace with the blood…Gwen told me she was going to sneak out that night. She said, 'Daniel will think we ran off together when you join me.' We were going to hide out in town for a couple of days, then she was going to come back to you, Daniel. Don't you know? How stupid are you? Gwen loves you, but only the good Lord knows why." Tears rolled down her face.

"Why didn't you just leave together then?" I asked.

"Gwen wanted me to wait a day to gauge Daniel's reaction…to see if they still had a marriage worth saving."

"Where is Gwen now?" I asked.

"I wish I knew." She shrugged her shoulders. "My kidnapping and hers though…despite Gwen's plan, they became real. I swear it."

Nurse Jackie appeared at the door. "I'm hearing loud voices in this room. I'm sorry, Miss Clements, we had two new patients to get settled in. Is everything copacetic in here?"

"I think we're done, Jackie. I'd like for them to leave now," Maria answered.

"Y'all heard my patient. Let's move out."

I nodded at Nurse Jackie and turned back to her patient. "Thank you, Maria. You've been a great help. We'll talk soon."

Daniel didn't have much to say as we left, lost in his thoughts. On the elevator ride down, I had no reception on my phone, but texted Sam when we were back in the parking lot.

—New development from Maria. Says her affair with Gwen was a hoax to inspire Daniel's jealousy. Being released today. Leaving for Annapolis. Will flesh it out when we speak. Any Robert news?—

The phone buzzed with an incoming message before I had it back in my pocket.

—Interesting but complicates things. Daniel's ransom text was from a burner phone. Can't trace. Going in to see Robert now. No news there yet. I think we can work on a surprise for Maria. Need her here.—

Once safely ensconced in the Bronco, Daniel became chatty.

"What did Sam have to say? Did he have anything new to report?"

"Not a lot yet," I said and handed him the text messages to read.

"What did you think?" Daniel asked.

"Stinks that it was a burner phone, so that lead is a dead end."

"Yeah, it is…but I meant what do you make of what Maria said."

"I don't know. I think most of what she said was true. She must know that what she and Gwen did can lead to repercussions for her. I can't imagine she lied about that part, but I can't help thinking she's hiding something…or someone."

Daniel sat in the passenger's seat staring out of the window. I fastened my seatbelt and with a twist of the key, the Bronco came to life.

"Are you all right, Daniel? Is there something else on your mind?"

"I don't know, Emma. I hope what she said is true. I've been praying for it to be true." He turned away from the window, and I saw wet streaks on his cheek before he wiped them away with his shirt sleeve.

"Daniel…?"

"Do you think Maria was lying…about Gwen still loving me?"

He looked at me as if I held some secret…a magical incantation that could save him before all that he held most dear was ripped away.

"I don't know, Daniel…Mom used to say everything works out for the best in the long run. If it's meant to be…you know, all that? Most times I think that's true though. If I had to bet? I'd say everything she said after mentioning wanting to leave town was honest. It didn't feel like a lie, and Maria has many tells, as the poker players say, when she's making up a story. I didn't see or hear any of those after that point. What I did hear was Maria quoting Gwen and giving a more detailed account than she did earlier. Her posture was more open, and even though she didn't want to tell the truth, I think she was honest through all of that."

Daniel smiled and gazed back out of the window.

"I've been such a fool," he said. "What have I done?" I didn't answer, leaving him alone with his thoughts. I slipped the gearshift into reverse and backed out of the parking spot.

"There's a new seafood place in town. Joyful Seafood I think it's called. How about we stop in for lunch? It might cheer you up a bit, brother," I suggested.

"I don't know. We should get back. Nana is—"

"In good hands with Alicia Wood. You said so yourself, that Nana looks forward to her visits."

"I could maybe eat something light. I guess."

"Joy of Seafood it is then."

I turned into their parking lot and circled around until I found a space. I backed up enough to wiggle in closer to the center of the parking spot, and a horn blared behind me. I gritted my teeth and swung around in my seat…and there sat Sam's cruiser. I rolled down my window.

"I thought you were busy interrogating?"

"It didn't take very long, I'm sorry to say. Are we having lunch? Daniel's treat?"

Daniel gave a thumbs-up sign, and we went in together. The restaurant had a homey comfortable atmosphere. Pictures and carvings of various sea-dwelling creatures lined the walls. Ornamental fish nets were draped in the corners holding captive decorative shellfish. The hostess met us at the door.

"Hello, Deputy Sam. We haven't seen you for a few days. Are there just three in your party?"

"Yes, we're it. Thanks, Monica." She led us to a corner table.

"Is this a regular stop for you, Sam? Is the food good?"

"Well, it is seafood." He laughed. "Seriously though, it is very good, and the waitresses are sweet and attentive. I think it will catch on in Newtowne. The special today is steamed shrimp, by the way."

He pointed to a chalkboard behind me. Steamed shrimp, scallops, and crab legs were listed as the day's specials.

A young woman with long brown hair arrived to take our drink orders. She wore an apron with a crab embroidered across the front and couldn't leave before telling Sam how good it was to see him again.

"How often did you say you come here, Sam?" I asked. "Everyone seems to know you."

"I'm afraid it's the price of bachelorhood. People tell me I'm a fair cook, but I can't tolerate my own cooking. Makes me nauseous. Except for cooking on the grill, of course."

"Of course. While we're waiting, fill us in on your chat with Robert."

"Like I said, there isn't a lot. They let me in to see him and right off, he was belligerent. He only wanted to talk about his case with the state police and what you told them. I told him that I knew for a fact you had nothing to do with it, but he didn't believe me. I asked him about the note he left at your house, and he seemed genuinely surprised. Then I asked about the property damage at your place.

" 'Ah, so that's why she turned me in,' he said. I didn't mention the content of the note either. I did inform him about a fingerprint on the note matching his and asked how he could explain that.

" 'Print match?' he said. 'Kids are always rooting through my trash at the curb on collection day. Anyone could have grabbed some paper out of the cans. Some kid found a nudie magazine I threw away a month back, and I've had to chase him off every trash day since. I started shredding my bills and identifying paperwork. You can't be too cautious these days.' "

The young server came back with our drinks and took our food order.

"Thank you, Alice," Sam said.

I smiled.

"Did he have much else to say?" I asked when Alice was out of earshot.

"Robert said he'd give us a sample of his handwriting if we had an expert on tap to do a comparative analysis. Of course, the note wasn't handwritten, so that might've been a ploy on his part. He asked if I knew a good lawyer. He didn't seem in the least concerned about your note if indeed he did know about it. It's circumstantial evidence at best. With the low degree of certainty of a match and how easily he explained it away…I'm just glad the state has him on the other charges."

Our meal arrived, and we ate in companionable silence, each of us lost in thought. The men opted for the shrimp special, and I couldn't resist the crab legs…messy but so good.

We were clearing our plates of the last vestiges of our meal when Alice was back at our tables telling us about their dessert options. We all declined.

"Sam, before we leave, what did you mean in your text? You said Maria's confession about making Daniel jealous complicated things? What things?"

Sam looked at me with one raised eyebrow and a barely perceptible head shake.

"Oh, nothing…just another trail to follow," he answered. "That was a great meal, wasn't it?"

"I never thought I'd get ahead of you on one, Emma," Daniel said. "You're quick, even getting the punchlines of jokes before I do. What Sam meant but is too professional or considerate to say in front of me, is the suspect list has grown by two. My alibi was that Maria knew I was away from the house during Gwen's disappearance. Now Maria's previous testimony and her honesty are in question, as well as where she was at the time. It wasn't a bulletproof alibi, but it did cast serious doubts. Maria's alibi was that she was also kidnapped, but if she kidnapped herself, that puts us both back in the prime suspect seat."

Chapter Seventeen

We all left with another preferred restaurant…well, Daniel and I did. Sam already had it on his favorite's list. We said our goodbyes in the parking lot.

I looked forward to a chat with our old family friend, Abigail Dawson, and sharing the treasured memories I'd found. Sam had a date with Robert's better half (although I didn't understand his reasoning about questioning the wife). Daniel planned to stay home in case there were any further communications from the kidnapper and to relieve Alicia.

When I turned into our driveway, the omnipresent mini-hearse was waiting for us. Johnnie Walker waved us down with the latest edition of the *County Examiner* paper in hand. I wound down the window to grab it.

"I don't know if you're subscribers or not, but thought you deserved a free copy after allowing me to interview you," he said. "But I want you to know that I—"

"Thank you, Johnny," I said and drove around him toward home, wishing later that I'd run over his foot.

Alicia said she ate her lunch with Nana. They had a good chat, and Nana fell asleep after. Daniel paid her with much thanks. I gathered Maya's and Jessie's drawings and headed for the door.

"I'll see you later, Daniel. I'm walking over to Abby's. It's a good day for a stroll."

The sky was a clear blue, and the earlier threat of rain vanished with the clouds. I edged around the tree line to ensure I had my bearings on the new hobbit hole entrance and walked right to it. I thought I'd reattached the carabiner, but it was sitting in the dirt beside the door. I needed to pick up a stout lock to replace it with. We didn't need any children falling in, or animals…or any uninvited guests either. I hooked the carabiner back on and continued my journey. The soil was firmer than the last time we'd plodded across looking for signs of Gwen, making the short journey much easier (and my boots cleaner).

The chimney had curling tendrils of smoke rising from it, just like in the girls' drawings. I tucked them tighter under my arm and went up the front steps.

The fenced backyard was missing the many ornamentals in bloom, but I did see a huge tarp covering something. That was new. I walked around to the front of the house. Before I could knock on the door, Abby was across the threshold pulling me into a bear hug.

"What brings you out on such a lovely day, my girl? It's the Lord's Day too, and where is that handsome deputy you were with during your last visit? I hope you didn't run him off. I think he's a keeper."

"Sam is still working on Gwen's case, Abby."

"Oh, dear Lord. I thought for sure they'd found that girl by now. I meant to stop by and ask about her, but I don't get around like I used to. You know we don't get the latest news out here."

"No, she's still missing. Progress on her case has been slow, Abby."

"That poor girl. Well, you come on in here, and let

me see if I have something sweet for you." She wiped her hands on her apron and ushered me inside.

"I love the apron," I commented. "No flower dress today, but you're keeping up the tradition with the apron. Are those poppies?"

"No, they're miniature climbing roses just like I have in the backyard. I only have the apron today, but I do love my flowers. It's nice having them around, especially this time of year when even the mums are giving up the ghost. Don't you agree?"

"Maybe you'll show me your roses before I leave?"

"Nothing to see back there but thorns this time of year, Emma." Abby frowned.

"Well, it is a beautiful apron."

Abby retrieved a platter of peanut-butter cookies from the counter and placed them on the table between us. A thick hard-backed book was on the table near her seat with the back cover showing.

"I'm sorry they're not chocolate chips, but you dig right in, Emma. We don't stand on ceremony around here."

"Is Mister Dawson back home from his fishing trip yet?"

She swung around in her chair, reaching under her seat and coming up with a flyswatter. Sitting back up, her elbow brushed against the book, and it fell to the floor between us, I bent over to retrieve it, but she snatched it up.

"Thank you, Emma. That's some of Michael's Bible reading; thought I'd have a look at it. I don't read much, you know…no time."

She swung the fly swatter at the far end of the

table.

"Got him. The flies have been terrible here this year," she said. "But you asked about Michael. I don't know what to tell you about that man. He calls me every other night telling me one fish story after another. I'd be worried to tell you the truth, but he's up there in the mountains with some good God-fearing men. I don't believe they'll lead him astray."

"I guess Jack is off doing teenage boy things?"

"No, my Jack is a good boy. He listens to his Momma most of the time. He bought himself an old clunker car that he's working on out back. I don't know if he'll ever get it on the road or not."

"I'm sure Mister Dawson will help him when he comes home."

"Of course he will. I had Jack run errands in town for me, but he will be back in a bit. That's enough about us, though. How are you and Daniel doing with everything?"

"Daniel is holding up well. Very concerned of course, but he hasn't given up hope."

"And how about you?" she asked. "I heard some young hoodlums vandalized your little house and with you hardly moved in. Makes no sense. Kids will do anything these days. I guess I've been blessed, but a parent must teach children right from wrong."

"It sure isn't like it was when I was a child, and that is one of the reasons I came for a visit today. I have some old drawings done by Maya and Jessie. My parents saved them all these years, and I wanted to share them with you."

"Aren't you the sweetest thing to think of me? Can I see them?"

"Of course," I said and passed them over to her.

Abby smiled at the first several pictures from the girls' earliest efforts, then frowned when the more recent ones appeared.

"They were the best of friends, weren't they, Abby?" I asked.

"It certainly seems so." She handed one to me. It had lip prints in the shape of kisses on the edge of a drawing of the two girls in a field of flowers. "Maya must've given her lipstick. We didn't allow it for Jessie. She was too young," she said.

"I imagine they got into Mom's makeup drawer when my parents weren't home. She never managed to get it all off, and she'd get in trouble. She tried putting it on me too, but that was during my tomboy stage."

"Michael thought she was like that…pulling others into her mischief."

"I didn't mean—"

"Of course, dear. I understand. Maya was such a sweet child…they both were. But Michael thought Jessie was growing up too fast because of Maya; she was so mature for her age. I think Michael would have kept Jessie six years old for the rest of her life, poor man. I don't think he approved of their friendship, truth be told."

"I see. Well, I guess I better get on home, Abby. Would you like to keep the pictures? I have more back at the house."

"I better not," she said. "I think the memories would upset Michael. You know how fathers are with their daughters."

"Yes, ma'am, I do."

Abby gave me a zip-lock bag full of cookies to

share with Daniel at home.

"Please tell your brother we are all praying for him and for Gwen's safe return. Michael asked me to pass along the same thing."

"Thank you, Abby, and for the cookies too. You've always been the best baker in the county." She gave me another bear hug at the door, and I walked home with a lot to think about.

****

I found Daniel sitting in the great room with the *County Examiner* crumpled up in a pile at his feet.

"What's going on, Daniel? Are you starting a fire with the old paper?"

"Oh no—this is this week's edition. You'll want to throw it in the fireplace too when you read it." He reached down, pulled one sheet of the paper away from the rest, and handed it to me.

"Read this garbage," he said.

I saw the headline he pointed out. It read "Love Lost, the Thief of Love" under Johnny Walker's byline. His leading paragraph gave the facts of Gwen's disappearance and Daniel's release from custody. Everything after that was a hatchet job. He claimed to have interviewed resentful neighbors about us. He intimated that their grievance with us was the Loves' fortune being made during the Great Depression. His version was that our ancestors bought up failing properties from desperate people for pennies on the dollar. He described our family as an elitist old county family. He mentioned our "intense interest" in the Robert Wathen case, theorizing that our curiosity was due to "old family rivalries against one of the most respected families in the county." He wrote of our pride in our heritage and charitable giving, then stated "for the record" that he found no evidence of it other than the volunteer hours and charitable contributions by the missing Gwen Love. He concluded with the question "Was Gwen Love's selflessness and charity the source of the Love couple's estrangement? Where is Gwen Love?"

"Nice," I said. "Obviously, Johnny Walker is not our friend. Let Sam read it before you let the fire eat this trash."

"You won't have to wait long then. It sounds like that noisy Mustang of his pulling in now."

I met Sam at the door with a question.

"What did you find out from Amanda Wathen…anything?"

"Well hello, Emma…Daniel. Yes, we had an interesting discussion."

"Come sit in the great room. It's more comfortable, and we have something to show you too," Daniel suggested.

"So, what did Amanda have to say?" I asked as we sat down.

"I was surprised at how forthcoming she was. Guess who the mysterious tipster was for Robert's misappropriation case? If you guessed Amanda, you'd be right. She copied documentation and sent it along to the state police in a plain brown envelope…no return address of course."

"Why would she do that?"

"It seems Amanda suspected Robert of cheating on her. On one of many evenings that Robert told her he'd be working late, she figured out his email password. Guess what she found there?"

"The pictures I sent him and the warning about his accounts?"

"Bingo. She said she filed for divorce this morning. I'm not sure why she decided to entrust me with that information when she'd gone to so much trouble to hide the source in the first place. Maybe I have a trustworthy face."

"Or maybe she knew you and Robert weren't the best of friends since way back," I said.

"That too. She has a hot poker up her backside about Gwen too, Daniel. She said Gwen stole her boyfriend in high school, and it seems she still holds a grudge about it. Can you imagine? From high school! When I was leaving, she said she was 'almost sorry' about what was happening with Gwen. I think despite her current ill feeling, she and Robert are peas in a pod and meant for each other."

"You don't think she would've done Gwen harm, do you?" Daniel asked.

"She did mention she thought Gwen was the one Robert was having an affair with until she saw your pictures, Emma. She said Robert flirted with her whenever he saw her. I don't know, Daniel…betrayal stirs intense emotions and often ends in violence. I see it too often."

"You're saying we have another possible suspect, if I'm hearing you right?"

"Assuming there's more than one kidnapper involved. Amanda Wathen is a hard and angry woman, but I don't think she could subdue Gwen on her own."

"One sharp hit on the head is all it takes, as I found out," I said.

"Could she then drag Gwen out of the house,

across your yard, and load her in a car by herself? No, if Amanda did it, she had help."

"Remember, it was what the cops call an inside job. The outside doors were all locked. How did she or anyone else get in the house unless they knew about the bootleggers' tunnel that you found?" Daniel asked.

"Maybe she did," Sam said.

"How?"

"I wasn't aware that your grandparents ran moonshine, Emma, but I know for a fact that Robert and John's grandfather did. They seem proud of that fact…even brag about it. Maybe your grandfathers worked as partners? That might be the beginning of your families' falling out if they disagreed back then."

"I hoped we'd be eliminating suspects by now, not adding more," I said.

"Or reviving old ones," Daniel added.

"Tomorrow is the kidnappers' ransom day, Daniel," Sam said. "What are you planning to do? We'll want to put some things in place if you intend to do the drop-off, but no pressure either way."

"I think I have to, Sam. Gwen is more important than the money. I think it's the fastest and safest avenue. Do you disagree?"

"I'm good with whatever you decide." Sam reached into his jacket pocket and pulled out what looked like a computer chip. It was square, black, and no bigger than a dime. He handed it to Daniel.

"What is this?"

"That is to put in the gym bag. The tech guys tell me it's a mini-GPS module. The battery life and range are both excellent. Slip it in the bag, and we'll be able to follow it wherever it goes."

"Great. I'm glad you're on the case, Sam. You too, Emma. I don't know how I would've gotten through to this point without the two of you. I owe you both…big time."

"You're welcome, Daniel," Sam said, "and you don't owe me anything. Just doing my job. I sure would like a sandwich though. Lunch seems like a long time ago."

"We have the fixings for sandwiches, or we can do leftovers night. We have a couple of slices of pizza, four crab legs, and half of my carnitas. There's some soup left that Alicia made for her and Nana too. Pick your poison."

"You guys enjoy," Daniel said. "I had a sandwich a while ago, and I'm going to hit the sack. I have a long day tomorrow."

****

We must've been hungry, as barely a word was spoken while we tore into our rewarmed repast. Afterward, we settled down in the living room and switched on the boob tube for background noise more than anything. There was still a lot to discuss. I showed Sam the newspaper article with the infamous Love interview.

"What do you think we should do about this?" I asked when he raised his head from reading.

"It isn't very complimentary, is it? I'm not a lawyer. I don't know what's required to bring a civil suit for defamation. From my viewpoint both as a cop and a friend, though, I'd let it go for now. At least until we get closure on this case and get Gwen home. No reason to stir the hornet's nest. If it was me, I'd hold my head high but keep a low profile."

I nodded my head. "Do you know if Maria was released from the hospital?"

Sam smiled. "She sure was, but her freedom didn't last long."

"C'mon, Major Mattingley. Don't leave a girl hanging."

"We wanted her to stay in town and I agree with you that she still knows something that she's not telling us, so I had her arrested."

"For what?"

"Even though she's on our suspect list again, we didn't have enough there to hold her, but we did have a decent case of wasteful employment of the police."

"That's a thing?"

"Yeah, it's been a criminal offense since the 1960s. It's meant to prevent knowingly making false reports to the police, but she did cause a wanton waste of time by going along with the kidnap scheme…through her admission."

"Do you think she's involved with Gwen's disappearance?"

"No, but I'm not ready to dismiss her as a suspect either. Most of all, I want to know what she knows…what she's kept from us. The threat of six months incarceration and a fine might help persuade her to give it up." Sam said. "Same question to you now, Emma, but about Daniel."

"I hate to say it as his sister, but speaking just as an observer of the facts, I can't dismiss him either. I don't see him as someone capable of this."

"I'm curious. What did he say after Maria made her confession today? Did it perturb him?"

"That is one of my concerns. He said that he'd

'been a fool' and 'what have I done.' I assumed it was the whole bit about neglecting his wife. But I can't be sure.

"I heard today that the gossip was going around about the vandalism at my place. Do you know if that was let slip by anyone?"

"I'm confident it wasn't released by any of the deputies. Did the gossiper know what the vandalism consisted of or about the note?"

"Not that I'm aware of."

"I'd say idle gossip by someone with too much time on their hands. They saw the damage as they walked by your place and couldn't wait to tell someone. Do you have nosy neighbors?"

"Everyone has nosy neighbors." I laughed. "Another reason I love the country. The ratio of snoops is just as high, but there aren't as many of them."

"Here I thought you came back because you missed me."

"You wish. Do you remember Michael Dawson? Wasn't he one of the Boy Scout leaders back in the day?"

"He was a troop leader for a couple of years. Why?"

"I'm a little concerned is all. He's been up in the mountains fishing. Abby doesn't seem worried though. She said he calls her every other night, but he was supposed to be back days ago. Do you know where his fishing camp is?"

"I do, or I know where he took all of us on a scout trip years ago. It was up near Flintstone, Maryland. I don't know if he still goes to the same place or not. I haven't crossed paths with Mr. Dawson in a while now."

"Do you know any of the nosy neighbors up in those parts who might be able to check on him?"

"Emma, you don't have enough on your plate that you want to get in the middle of what's probably a domestic dispute?"

"It would mean a lot to me." I hated myself for the extreme pouty face I made at that moment.

"Would my involvement elevate me to the next level beyond 'maybe boyfriend?' "

"Oh yeah, at least 'potential boyfriend' if not 'probable boyfriend,' but I'll have to check with the judges."

"I'll see what I can do."

Chapter Eighteen

I was awake more often than asleep that night. I woke from one dream covered in sweat but could recall nothing of it, except it involved my parents' accident. Later I woke with the touch of a cool hand on my face. I lay there with my eyes closed, enjoying Sam's touch. When I heard the faucet running in the bathroom, my eyes flew open. For a brief moment in time, I stared into Maya's soulful eyes. *Remember!* I blinked and she was gone. The mind enjoys its tricks.

Daniel was up and roaming the halls above us for a good part of the night. I didn't much blame him. The money exchange could be the pivotal point in getting Gwen home safely. If all went smoothly and the kidnappers acted in good faith, Gwen might be home tonight. If not…well, I didn't want to think about that.

Daniel met Sam and me for coffee in the living room that morning. Daniel seemed in good spirits for a man with a dark cloud following him and a life-or-death sort of day ahead. My brother was always an expert at hiding his emotions. Only the bags under his hollowed eyes betrayed the lie of his smile. Daniel sipped his coffee slowly as if he had all the time in the world and a day of luxurious indolence ahead of him. But he checked his wristwatch for the tenth time in the five minutes since he'd joined us.

"It's almost eight o'clock," he said. "Should I go

now and get this over with or wait until nine to deliver the bag?"

"Let's wait a bit," Sam said. "I want to rehash a few things with you first."

Daniel nodded.

"Did you put the GPS transmitter in the bag?"

"Of course, I did. It's ready to go."

"Good. A trooper will be stationed in an unmarked vehicle parked at The Dollar Shop two hundred yards away. The trooper is trained to monitor the GPS signal, but the sheriff's department is overseeing the operation. There will be no marked cruisers within the town limits this morning. To avoid arousing suspicion, there will be no police presence at the drop-off point either. I'll be in place on the county road across from Buddy's Burgers changing a tire on the shoulder of the road. Don't put the phone to your ear. Just leave the connection open so I can hear you in case there's any issue."

"What do you think could go wrong?" Daniel asked.

"I don't anticipate any problems, but we want all our bases covered. We aren't taking any chances. There's a small microphone attached to the outside of the trash can as well as a small camera hidden on the wall. Deputy Douglas will be monitoring them. If anything doesn't feel right, just get back in your car and drive away."

"None of it feels right, Sam."

"The threat to you is minimal. The kidnapper will know he's being watched, despite our subterfuge. I expect it will be a long day for all of us while we wait for him to make his move."

"He said Gwen would starve if he was caught. Do

you think he would let that happen?"

"I can't say one hundred percent, Daniel, but the chance of recovering Gwen safely is reduced every day she's missing. Once we know who the perpetrator is, we can narrow our search to find her. Kidnapping is a low-life crime, but murder is worse and draws a much longer sentence. I'd talk if it was me."

"Can we go over everything one more time? I'm not sure I remember where everyone will be."

"I don't want you to worry about all of that, Daniel. I just wanted you to be aware of what we have in place. You only need to concentrate on three things." Sam clicked each item off on his fingers:

"Accept the call from me when you pass the stoplight, but don't put the phone to your ear in case he's watching. Leave the connection open.

"Pull up beside the trash can, but don't park. Drop the bag in the trash and leave. Don't dawdle or look around acting suspicious. Just get in your car and leave.

"Drive straight home. We'll keep you and Emma up to date on what's happening throughout the day."

Daniel nodded his head. "Okay. My part seems simple enough. Can Emma ride along with me?"

"It would be better if it was just you, Daniel, but if you don't feel comfortable with any of this, we can have a plain clothes deputy make the drop-off. If it's you though, the kidnapper might be less suspicious and cautious."

"Well, Lord knows we can't make the kidnapper uncomfortable." Daniel offered a weak chuckle. "No, I've got this, Sam."

"I'm heading to my lookout point on McIlhenny Road. Give me twenty minutes before you leave,

Daniel. If you have a change of heart for any reason, you have my number."

"I'll be there," Daniel said.

I followed Sam to the door, smiling at his wardrobe selection. He had on ripped-up jeans like the kids wear, an old sweatshirt, and work boots. The ensemble was topped off with a grease-stained gray jacket and an equally greasy Pittsburgh Steelers ball cap, a team he hated.

"That's as good a disguise as I could've dreamed up for you, Deputy."

"What do you mean? This is my Sunday-go-to-meeting outfit."

"You're going to need a long shower tonight after wearing those clothes. Where did you get the Steelers cap? I'm pretty sure you didn't find it hanging in the closet with your Ravens paraphernalia."

Sam laughed. "I borrowed it from Deputy Joyce, if you can believe that. I have a hard time visualizing it on her head. She claims it's a good luck charm, and she never washes it, or the magic might wash off."

"I can tell." I caught myself chewing my sore bottom lip and moistened it with my tongue.

"It's going to be fine, Emma. I'll make sure Daniel gets home safe."

"Make sure you do too. We can't be sure what this person is capable of…I'd really like to be there, Sam."

"We talked about this, Emma…"

"I know and I get it, but I'll be on pins and needles all day."

"As soon as Daniel makes the drop, I'll call you. It will be all right. Quit worrying."

"Hmm, don't say that, Sam. That sounds like

famous last words if I ever heard any."

I kissed him goodbye and then checked the time. If I had to be out of the loop, at least I could ensure we kept a tight timeline. Twenty minutes he said. Sam waved before climbing into his Mustang. It started with a roar. As he slipped the gearshift into reverse, both the car and Sam's well-laid plan were put into motion.

Twenty minutes later, I escorted Daniel to the door. It was easy to read his nervousness. Several bathroom visits and his short fast intakes of breath told the tale.

"You are going to get through this, Daniel. I'm here for you. Sam is too. We're both a phone call away. If you get too stressed, turn around and come home. No one will blame you or think poorly of you."

"I wish you could be there, Emma. God, I'm a wimp."

I hugged him and he held me for a long while, trembling as he released me.

"I know it's a lot, Daniel, but I'll be eight minutes away. Sam will be even closer. I'm dressed. I have the Bronco's keys in my pocket. Nana is sleeping, so if you need me…"

"I know. Thanks. I'll see you soon, sis." Daniel turned and walked to his Mercedes, gym bag in hand.

****

It was a good day for a third cup of coffee, but what was left in the pot was old and cold. I opted for the instant decaffeinated that had resided in the cabinet for way too long. It was crusty on top, and I broke off chunks of the stuff to add to a cup of water I'd zapped in the microwave. It tasted awful…

Coffee done, I paced back and forth between the kitchen and the living room, pausing to look out of every window and checking the time with each repetitive circuit.

My phone rang as I checked my watch for the last time. A twenty-minute wait that took five hours.

"Sam, what's happening?"

"So far, so good, Emma. Daniel made the drop. The GPS signal is working. He went out the back way past the dumpsters for some reason, but he looked as cool as a cucumber. Ask him if he saw anything weird back there. It's in a blind spot, and I'll ask a plainclothes deputy to have a look if he did."

"He's on his way home then?"

"He is en route to you, Emma. He should be there in under ten minutes. Call or text me when he's home safe," Sam said.

"Will do. Keep us posted."

"Talk to you then," he said, and the line went dead.

I went back to pacing until I heard tires on gravel and went outside to meet Daniel.

"Sam said it all went according to plan. Any problems from your end? Did you see anyone or anything that seemed suspicious?"

"No, I think everything went off without a hitch. I'm just glad my part is over. How long do you think it will be before Gwen gets home?"

"Fingers crossed for soon, Daniel. Sam said you didn't drive straight out but circled around past the dumpsters."

"Yes. I'm glad he was keeping a close eye out for me. Sam's good people, Emma." Daniel kicked a stone in the driveway. "I guess I was nervous and couldn't wait to get away from there. I didn't take the time to turn around to leave by way of Main Street. I went straight out taking the back streets away from town."

"Good. Nothing fishy going on in the back? Sam says it's a blind spot. Did you see anyone?"

"Nothing and nobody." Daniel turned, nodded at the house, and stepped in that direction. "Is there any coffee left? I could use something stronger, but I'll settle for that."

I sent Sam a text —*The eagle has landed*— on the way inside.

—*Thanks. No movement here yet*— he texted back.

I had a glass of grape juice and sat with Daniel as he slurped at the dregs of coffee from the bottom of the pot.

"I have a feeling it's going to be a long day as Sam said."

"Probably," I said, "and I'm praying it all ends well."

"I know it is Sam's job and all, but I couldn't care less if they catch this guy. He can take the money and skip town or whatever…as long as Gwen comes home safe."

"Gwen is Sam's priority also, Daniel. He knows what he's doing."

Minute-long seconds turned into hour-long minutes. The three hours until Daniel and I sat down to lunch were days long, but at the first bite from my sandwich, the phone jingled.

"Is it from Sam? What does the text say?" Daniel asked, and I held it out so we could both read.

—*Money is on the move. A kid picked it up. He looks like your young friend Crab!*—

—*He must be retrieving it for someone, Sam*— I responded.

—*We know. Keeping a discreet distance while following whoever he passes it off to. Not pushing him. No hurry. The tracker pinpoints the bag's location to within ten feet. All is working to plan.*—

—*Thank you, Sam. Hungry for all updates. Sitting on my hands—waiting is hard.*—

—*Will do. Talk soon.*— he answered.

"The money bag is moving? Do the cops have eyes on it?

"They're following it through the GPS tracker. You read the text, didn't you? They want Crab, or whoever the kid is, to take it to the person who enlisted him to retrieve it."

"Who is Crab again?" Daniel asked.

"He's a young lad I met in town. Josh Grimes is his real name. He and two of his friends, the infamous Eric the Red and Pete the Sneak, helped me put up the missing posters for Gwen and Maria. I don't know Eric's and Pete's last names, but I could tell all three of them were good kids, raised right, you know? If Crab is mixed up in this in any way, then he doesn't know what's happening. Somebody tricked the poor boy."

"That 'poor boy' is on the loose with twenty grand of my money. It's one thing if it funds Gwen's safe return; it's another thing altogether if it becomes some adolescent's toy, comics, and video game fund. Call Sam and ask him to grab that kid before he gets away. I don't have much trust in that GPS thing either. It's too tiny to do much. The battery will die any second."

"Easy, Daniel. You're letting it all get to you, and I won't ask Sam any such thing. He knows what he's doing. The state boys have used those tracking devices before. If there was a longevity issue with them, they'd know. We've come too far to screw it all up now."

"It's already screwed up."

"What do you think the kidnapper would do if he found out his money mule was caught? I hope they are also considering what might happen to Crab after the delivery is made."

Daniel shook his head and gathered the lunch dishes to wash.

By now, I was so attuned to the passage of time that I heard every second ticking off on the grandfather clock down the hall in the great room. I followed the sound there and pulled out my laptop. Maybe there might be a funny video to take my mind off today's events and speed the passage of time. I clicked on one, watched it for a minute, and clicked on the next. None were able to distract my thoughts and concerns. They all seemed silly on a day like today, with so much at stake.

I heard Daniel walking toward me and looked up.

"I guess you're right…about everything," Daniel said. "I think I'm going upstairs to check on Nana and try to take a cat nap. It's been a long day already. Thanks, Emma. But come tell me if there's any news."

"No problem, Daniel. Get some rest; you've earned it."

With the silly videos doing nothing for me, I went to my bedroom for my spiral notebook and curled up on the living room couch with the laptop. I clicked on my favorites and selected NeighborsSnoop.com. I didn't think there was too much more dirt I could find there, so I reverified what I'd already noted. I needed to talk to Sam about the Michael Dawson record. Something didn't add up there. He'd been a teacher and a Boy

Scout leader, and all charges were dismissed, still…Everything else checked out as my notes indicated.

I thought I'd try my luck with a few other recent and questionable actors. I tried Amanda Wathen and came up empty. Remembering her maiden name, I tried again under Amanda Young, and the search bore fruit. There was one charge of aggravated assault from five years ago and a second one the year following. Mrs. Wathen once had an anger management problem…did she still?

I remembered the comment the sheriff made about Maria and pulled up her old record for solicitation. It appeared to be her first and only arrest. I guessed her to be about sixteen in the mugshot. She looked like a frightened teary-eyed little girl, not a hardened criminal.

My next search was for rental cabins and fishing camps near Flintstone, Maryland. I remember Sam saying it was the area where Michael Dawson took them as Boy Scouts. I racked my brain to remember the name of one of his old fishing partners. I remembered one; he was another teacher from our school…then it popped into my head as fresh as the day I met him in biology class, freshman year…Raymond Stewart. I wondered if NeighborsSnoop.com had anything on him…

I don't remember feeling drowsy, but sensed the passage of time when I heard footsteps descending the stairs. I checked my phone and saw that I'd lost over two hours. My text messages were empty, and there were no missed calls. Why hadn't Sam called?

Daniel stuck his head in the door. He looked

miserable. I was afraid he might pass out or, at the least, toss his lunch up on the carpet.

"Emma, we need to talk," he said.

"What's wrong, Daniel? You look like hell."

"I feel like it too."

"So let's talk," I said.

"Remember what you said? That I would screw everything up if I asked them to stop the kid?"

"You agreed with me after you thought about it though, right?"

"Yeah, but I screwed up, Emma. I screwed up."

My phone rang and I saw that it was Sam calling, and I showed Daniel.

"Answer it."

"What's going on, Sam? I have you on speaker with Daniel."

"It's all gone wrong, Emma. Everything has gone to hell."

Chapter Nineteen

I looked at Daniel, expecting an "I told you so" look. Instead, his face turned ashen. He choked back a sob and took a deep breath. It didn't stop his hand from trembling.

"I messed up, Sam. I didn't put that tracker in the money bag. I put it in a separate gym bag that was just like it and threw it behind the dumpsters."

"What…why would you do that, Daniel? You know that was the bag we were tracking? Don't you get that?"

"I wasn't worried about the money, Sam, only getting Gwen home safe."

"What do you think we're all trying to do, Daniel? What could have gone through your head to think that would help?"

"The kidnapper sent me another text late last night, Sam. He knew or guessed that we were putting a tracker in the bag. His text said to put the GPS chip inside a duplicate bag. He said to toss it out of sight on the back side of Buddy's Burgers behind their dumpster cage, and if I didn't, he'd kill Gwen. He promised to release her as soon as he has the money in hand."

"I don't even know what to say to that, Daniel. When the GPS stopped moving for an hour, we moved in. What do you think we found when we got there? I'll tell you. The signal led us to an elderly couple's home.

The tracker was taped to a box that a delivery driver left outside of their front door. They hadn't even brought it inside yet. No money, no bag…nothing. We spent all day following a box of extra-large adult diapers. That's what you got for your twenty-grand investment. We have a cruiser headed out now to pick up the Grimes kid. I hope he can tell us something.

"I'll get back to you as soon as I can, Emma. We have one unholy mess to try and unravel. Can you take me off speaker, please?"

Daniel's eyes watched his fingers pulling at a loose thread on his shirt sleeve. I hit the speaker button.

"Okay, Sam. It's just me. What's your next move?"

"I don't know, Em. This hurt us badly. I hope Gwen doesn't pay for Daniel's duplicity, and I pray your buddy, Crab, is safe and sound at home. This hurt a lot."

****

Now it was Daniel's turn to pace the floor while I sipped a cup of decaf and tried to make sense of it all. I was so angry at Daniel, the anger only slackened by the knowledge of what he had been through…and was still going through. Like Sam, I hoped young Crab was safe and that he could shed light on the events he was involved in.

I heated us each a can of soup. Daniel only liked soup when it was as thick as mud, so I put a roll of crackers by his bowl.

"Sit down and eat before you wear a path through the carpet, Daniel."

"I've screwed up, Emma."

"You mentioned that, and yes, you did. We all do, then we try to make it right. It's Adulting 101, isn't it?"

"How am I supposed to make this right?"

"I don't know yet, brother, but the Big Guy or the Universe or whatever you believe in always gives us a shot at redemption. Yours will come too."

"But will it come in time to save Gwen…?"

I didn't know how to respond and said nothing. When our humble repast was done, I returned to the living room and my laptop. I checked my phone and saw there were no new calls or text messages, but the battery symbol was in red…18% charge. My charger was plugged into the wall by my nightstand, so down the hall my electronics and I went.

Daniel's footsteps resumed the pacing from one end of the hall and back. I hoped he'd find his way down to the game room or his office, but back and forth just outside my door. I didn't think I had anything else to offer him as consolation and prayed for good news soon.

A sharp rap on my door. "Emma, can I come in?" Daniel asked.

"Yes, what is it, Daniel."

"I have something to show you. The kidnapper sent me another text."

He held out his phone to me and I read, —*Thank you, Daniel, but it's not about the money. It never was*—

"What do you think it means?" he asked.

"Maybe it means he's satisfied and will release her now."

"Do you think so?"

"Yes, I think that's it," I said, but I couldn't look him in the eyes.

"Thank you, Emma."

I nodded, and he left the room. Before I could text Sam with the new revelation, my phone sprang to life. I didn't recognize the number but couldn't risk ignoring it.

"Hello?"

"Emma, this is Sam. I have you on speakerphone at the sheriff's office. I'm with Mrs. Grimes and her son, Josh. We were hoping you could come down here as soon as possible. Josh says he won't speak to anyone unless you're there too."

"I'm leaving as soon as I get my shoes on."

"Thank you, Miss Love," I heard a scared little voice say.

I slipped on a pair of clogs and made one phone call before heading to town.

****

I pulled into the small parking lot at the sheriff's office. Sam met me at the reception desk as I entered the building. He looked tired. He held one hand over his stomach…the weight of disappointment. He squeezed his eyelids shut for a moment when he greeted me.

"I appreciate you coming, Emma. Today was an epic screw-up, the worst of my career. I should have put the GPS in the bag myself."

"Daniel would have just taken it out again, Sam. He was convinced it was the best route to ensure Gwen's safe return. He wasn't thinking with his head, only his emotions."

"But if I'd kept the bag in sight…"

"If you'd followed the bag or Crab that closely, it would've tipped off the kidnapper. You know he or she was sure to be watching. Don't put this on your shoulders."

"Feels like my fault, Emma."

"Daniel knows it's on him, and he's beating himself up over it. You don't have that luxury, Sam. We have my sister-in-law to find. We're down, not out."

Sam nodded. "You're right, Coach. I appreciate the pep talk. There's a young man in the interview room who really wants to see you."

Sam led me down the hallway to a door marked "Interview Room" in bold letters. I glanced through the door's window and saw Crab seated by a young flaxen-haired woman with her back to the door.

"Are you ready?"

"Let's do it, Sam."

"Mrs. Grimes, this is Emma Love, a close friend of the sheriff's department. Emma, this is Josh's mother, Cathy Grimes. Josh, I believe you and Miss Love already know one another?"

"Yes, sir." Crab stood up, held out his hand, and shook mine.

"I sure do appreciate you coming, Miss Love," Crab said.

His mother stood then as well. She was what they call a natural beauty, her face unretouched by make-up, yet it was her eyes that set her apart. It was easy to see where Crab inherited his from. She had the same hauntingly hypnotic blue eyes.

"I'm not sure what's going on here or whether my son is under arrest, but he seems convinced that you can help. You've made quite an impression on him."

"Sam? Have the deputies explained to Mrs. Grimes?"

"I'm sorry, Mrs. Grimes. Josh is here to answer

some questions we have and is not under arrest. I'm sorry if that wasn't explained to both of you. It's been one of those days, and I hope you'll accept the department's apology."

Cathy nodded and looked back at me. I was dialing my phone, and when Henry Stone picked it up, I put it on speaker.

"Mr. Stone, this is Emma Love. You asked that I call when I arrived because you couldn't be present for the conversation with my young friend, Josh Grimes?"

"Yes, Miss Love. Everyone, please be aware that I am recording this conversation. Can you tell me who is present?"

"There's Josh Grimes, his mother Cathy, Major Sam Mattingley, and myself. Thank you for listening in, Mr. Stone."

"No problem. Just tell Daniel I'll bill him." He laughed, but I knew he meant it.

"To start then, Josh, could you tell us what's happened today?"

"You can call me Crab, Miss Love, but I didn't steal nothing. I just stuck the thing that was in the bag to a box like the deputy told me to do. I asked them to let me talk to Deputy Fife because he can explain everything, but the cops just laughed at me."

I forced back a smile also. "What does Deputy Fife look like, Crab?"

"I don't know what he looks like, ma'am. Deputy Fife left me, Eric, and Pete a note in our mailboxes."

Sam stood up and stepped out of the room.

"What did the note say, Crab?"

He reached into his pants pocket and handed me a crumpled-up piece of notepaper. I read the typewritten note out loud.

"Josh, I'm told that you are a smart young man. Would you like to help the sheriff's department and make some money too? You can help us to catch a bad guy and be a hero. Your friends Eric and Pete are helping us too, and I'm trusting you all to keep this a secret from everyone, even Mom and Dad. They will be so proud of you.

"There will be a blue bag in the trash can outside of Buddy's Burgers. Grab it Monday morning and take it back behind the dumpsters. Eric and Pete will be waiting for you. There will be a lot of money in the bag. Take it out, and put it in Eric's bag but look for anything else that might be in there. Sometimes the bad guys do that to confuse us. It could be a small plastic thing about the size of a stamp. Leave that in your bag. I know you're honest, but make sure you don't lose any of the money. The deputies will count it after we catch the bad guys, and I don't want you to get in any trouble. Take the bag across the woods to that store where the delivery vans park. If you find something in your bag that isn't money, tape it to one of the boxes inside the vans. If you don't find anything, throw the whole bag in the van. I know this is a lot to remember, so keep this note to remind yourself of the instructions. Remember, this is a top-secret operation, and we trust you not to tell. If you do tell, or if you can't complete the mission, good people will get hurt. The twenty-five dollars in here is for you to keep for helping us out. Thank you, Josh, you're a hero. Your friend, Deputy Fife."

Sam stepped back into the room. I handed him Crab's note to catch up on things.

"Is everything that's written here what you did,

Crab?"

Henry Stone interrupted for the first time. "Your son doesn't have to answer that question, Mrs. Grimes."

Cathy Grimes leaned over and whispered in her son's ear.

"What do you advise, Mr. Stone?" I asked.

"Deputy Mattingley, what is your department's intention with this witness?"

Sam held up one finger as a sign to wait while he finished reading.

"Deputy Mattingley, did you hear my question?" Stone asked.

Sam placed the note on the table. "The sheriff's department has no intention of prosecuting, and I'm sure the District Attorney will agree, assuming Josh tells us the truth. Give me a moment."

Sam stood up and walked to the corner of the room and dialed a number on his phone. We heard him describe what had transpired so far in the interview room. He then nodded several times, thanked the person on the other end, and hung up.

"The District Attorney has no interest in prosecuting, as the young man acted in good faith. Again, that's assuming he tells us the truth. She did ask for Honorary Deputy Josh to advise the department about future requests for top-secret missions."

"You can answer the question, young man," Henry Stone said.

Crab gave me a questioning look. I knew with all the back and forth, he'd forgotten what I asked. I picked the note up from the table and held it up.

"Did you do everything that's written on here, Crab?"

He looked at his mother, and she nodded her head. "Yes, ma'am."

"What were the other two boys supposed to do?"

"I don't know, Miss Love. They got their own letters, and we were afraid to ask each other. It was top-secret and all, so it was need to know only."

"Do you know where they went with the money bag after you left Buddy's Burgers?"

"All that money was in Eric's bag. It was more money than I ever saw in my life, over a hundred dollars, I bet. Pete had a bag too, but I think it was empty. It was blue too, but it wasn't exactly like ours. It didn't say nothing on it about the Pirates."

"Did you all three leave Buddy's Burgers together?"

"We crossed the road and went through the woods together. I stopped and did what I was supposed to do at that delivery place. There was a little black plastic thing like Deputy Fife said and I taped it to a box. I used some freezer tape that Mom keeps in a kitchen drawer at home. I don't know what Eric and Pete had to do. Then I went home."

I looked at Sam.

"Deputy Joyce is almost here with the other two boys."

****

Crab and his mother were thanked for their cooperation, and Joyce arrived soon after. She escorted everyone inside, Eric with his dad and the mother accompanying Pete.

"They wanted to come in together, Major Mattingley. Is that okay?"

Sam nodded. "I don't have any issue if Mr. Stone

231

doesn't?"

"I'm good. It's all on Daniel Love's dime."

Sam gestured to the four new arrivals toward seats around the table. We were one chair short, and he left, returning with a rolling office chair for himself.

"I'm sure you're wondering what's going on, dragging you from your homes at this time of night. The answer is that your two boys, along with Josh Grimes, were involved with and witnesses to an important case we're working on. The District Attorney has stated on the record that no charges will be brought against your boys if they tell us the truth. We have the lawyer, Mr. Henry Stone, on the speaker phone and if you have any questions or concerns, feel free to address them with him at any time. Miss Love is here as a friend of our department and as a character witness for all three boys. Are there any objections to her sitting in?"

Both parents shook their heads.

"We didn't do anything wrong," Eric said. "We did exactly what the deputy said. Nobody will be hurt now because of us."

"Was that Deputy Fife?" I asked.

"Yes, Miss Love. Do you know him? Did he send you a note too?"

"No, but Josh showed us his. Do you still have the note, Eric?"

Eric pulled his out of his shirt pocket. It was just as crumpled up as Crab's, with the addition of ink-smeared type.

"Sorry, it's all buggered up. I slipped in the stream where I left my bag. I was looking for tadpoles."

"Where did you leave the bag, Eric?" Sam asked.

I read from the note, "Eric, you are to leave your bag in the yellow trash can at the wine-making place by McIlhenny Run across the woods from the burger joint. I know you like catching frogs there."

Sam stood and went to the door. He waved Deputy Joyce over and whispered something in her ear. She grabbed a second deputy and ran out of the office.

"Did you put the bag with the money in the can like the note says, Eric?" Sam asked, but the boy just looked at me.

"It's okay, Eric. Deputy Mattingley is on our side," I said.

"I put it in the trash can there like Deputy Fife said. I thought it was kinda funny to leave all that money there like that, but I didn't want to ask anyone. It was top-secret."

"Pete, do you have your note too?" I asked.

Pete looked as if he might burst into tears.

"No, ma'am. I threw it away in our trash can at home."

"That's fine, Pete. There's nothing to worry about."

"Would you mind checking when you get home and calling the station?" Sam asked Pete's mother. She nodded.

"Do you remember what Deputy Fife asked you to do, Pete?"

"Oh yes, ma'am, but mine was top-secret too, like Eric's, so I threw it away."

"I know, but we all have top-secret clearances, so you can tell us."

"The note told me there were two bags by the dumpsters behind the fast food place. One had a picture of a pirate on it for Eric, and the other one was just a plain ol' blue bag. That one was mine."

"What were you supposed to do with your bag?" Sam asked.

"The deputy said to walk around the town square with it for two hours, but I was so tired of walking after about an hour and a half I went home." Pete pulled two bills from his pocket, twenty-five dollars. "So, I didn't earn this fair and square. You can take it back. I'm sorry I messed up everything…did I make anybody get hurt?"

"No, everyone is fine, Pete, and you did just great. I'd like to trade you my twenty-five dollars for yours though. The deputies need to practice checking for fingerprints…you know, secret agent training. Is that all right? I want you to keep the money too. You deserve it for helping us," I said.

"Pete, where is the bag now?" Sam asked.

"It's at our house," the mother answered. "I'll give it to your deputy when he takes us home."

Chapter Twenty

I stretched out on the couch pondering the day and wondering what we could've done differently. Over and over, I recounted our colossal failure. Robert Burns said "the best-laid plans of mice and men often go awry" and Steinbeck revitalized the thought. Awry didn't begin to describe the day's fiasco. The hope that Sam would bring news to salvage a vestige of investigative progress is all that kept my eyes open. It was a long day.

My head jerked up and down on a neck turned to rubber in my effort to remain conscious. The yo-yo bouncing only stopped with the sound of Sam's Mustang rumbling down the driveway.

From the look on his face, I knew his day hadn't improved since we'd parted company after interviewing the three boys.

"Nothing, I'm guessing," I said.

"No prints on the money, or the notes. Crab's bag had Daniel's prints, but that's it…not at all helpful. The kidnapper must've scrubbed everything and then used gloves. The money was gone, of course."

"A total bust in other words."

"Total. I'm going to hit up Maria in the morning. Maybe a night in jail will loosen her tongue."

"I'd like to show you something I've been working on, Sam." I pulled out my notebook and showed him some of my research.

He scanned the first page and turned to me. "Where did you get this, Emma?"

Flipping open my laptop, I pulled up NeighborsSnoop.com and passed the computer to him.

He looked through it, inputted a few names, and smiled. "There's almost as much information as we have with the NCIC database. Are you sure that this site is legal, Emma?"

"To the best of my knowledge, it's legal; it's creepy and invasive, but legal. I really wouldn't care at this point. The drawback is that it's not always one hundred percent accurate, and I want you to verify a couple for me. Would you do that?"

"I'll bet what you have noted for Michael Dawson is one of them you want me to investigate. CIMT, it says, or moral turpitude. That was a long time ago and covers any number of things, Emma. It's not a very specific charge."

"That's what I'd like you to find out…if it's *our* Michael Dawson and what the actual crime was. If it was pleaded out or if the charges were dropped, would your system tell us that?"

"Most likely. Who is Raymond Stewart? That name sounds familiar."

"It should, he was my freshman-year biology teacher. Didn't you have him too?" I asked. "And yes, he's the other one I'd like you to follow up on."

"Yeah, that's where I know his name from. You're dredging up a lot of dirt from the past."

"I just have a gut feeling that Gwen's kidnapping is somehow tied to the past, Sam. Maybe there's an old case or some injustice that was done and it planted the seed for this crime…"

"I'm all about leaving no stone unturned, especially at this point. I wouldn't want to be a criminal with you after me."

"Thanks. So you'll do it?"

"I'll see what I can find out in the morning, Emma. After a huge mug of coffee that is. I think I'm going to need it."

****

I opened my eyes the next morning when Rachel the rooster decided the best place to greet the new day was inches away from my bedroom window. I opened my eyes to see Sam staring at me.

"Good morning, Emma," he said.

"Back at ya, Deputy. I predict today will go a lot better than yesterday. What do you think?"

"I think it wouldn't take much to meet that criterion. Did you want to sit in when I talk to Maria this morning?"

"I'm going to sit that one out, if that's okay, Sam. I have a few phone calls to make. Despite yesterday, I think we are close to solving this. We may even crack the case today."

"That would be great, as is seeing your confidence. You've been a major asset in this from the beginning, even if you won't admit it. You see a lot that everyone else misses, including this bumbling deputy."

"You're anything but, Sam. Unless you're fishing for compliments? But I think the puzzle pieces are starting to fall into place."

"Do tell?"

"I'm not ready to share just yet…but soon."

"Just don't do anything impulsive, Emma, please.

Call me if you happen to flip over the right rock and the cockroaches scurry out."

"I promise, Sam. What are you smiling about?"

"I'm thinking of that time we were hiking back to Mr. Hill's pond to go fishing. Remember that big sow with piglets that broke out of the fence?"

"I certainly do."

"She was blocking our path and charged us. I guess she thought we wanted to barbecue one of her piggies. Scared me to death. I lost two years' growth that day, but you just stood your ground, head held high. That old momma sow didn't know what to make of you. She sniffed your feet and walked away, her piggies in line behind her."

"Believe me, I was scared too. Probably too scared to move."

"Not that I could tell. I don't recall your ever being afraid of anything, Emma. From surprise algebra tests to charging porcine monstrosities, you were always up for the challenge."

"I've been scared, Sam, and I've been hurt," I said. My mind flooded with the memories of Maya falling in our pond, the policeman telling Nana our parents were dead, the night at Sam's party, and having to strike out on my own when I wasn't much more than a child…

"I'm sorry, Emma," he said. "Not intending to pull up bad memories, but to remind you that people are crueler than any hog ever was."

I nodded. "I'll call if I need you, Sam. Scout's honor."

"Now how about I get a couple of mugs of coffee brewing?"

"Is your coffee making better than your cooking?"

****

Sam left, and I sat down in the living room for a second cup of coffee. The door to Daniel's office opened and closed. He was up early. He walked past the living room and backtracked when he noticed me out of the corner of his eye.

"I'm surprised you're up after the day and night we had yesterday…thanks to me," he said.

"Shake it off, Daniel. I have a gut feeling it's all going to break today."

"Miss Confidence, are you?" he said. "Glad to hear it."

"Hmm, that's the second time I've heard that today already. Do you and Sam think I'm some insecure and timid little wallflower or something?"

Daniel smiled. "Wallflower? No, not at all, but answer me this. If you could go back in time to when I threw you out of our house, with you the injured and innocent party, what would today's Emma do?"

"Honestly? I still would have left. I think I'd break your jaw first though."

"Exactly. That's the Emma sitting in front of me today…I'd bet you could've too. You were first in your self-defense class back then, just like everything else you tried."

"Everyone changes, Daniel."

"I know. I remember when I first got my driver's license. The first thing I wanted to learn to do was squealing tires and burning rubber…like all the cool guys did, until I had to buy my first set of new tires. I lost the desire then. My life did the same turnaround when Mom and Dad died. I stopped squealing the tires of life…stopped letting go. I needed control. So, I've always worked at maintaining traction, not losing it. I'm losing traction now, Emma. I'm not sure how long it will be before I spin out of control and flip the car."

"You're looking at it the wrong way, brother. We only had a setback. Borrowing your metaphor, we stopped for gas. Now we have a full tank and an open road for the next fifty miles."

"I hope you're right…and, Emma?"

"Yeah?"

"All those years ago? I wish you'd delivered that punch."

****

When Daniel went to the kitchen to pour his coffee, I pulled up the NeighborsSnoop.com site and looked up the phone number for Raymond Stewart in Flintstone, Maryland.

A woman answered the phone on the second ring.

"Hello, Stewart's residence."

"Mrs. Stewart? I'm trying to reach Raymond Stewart. Is he available?"

"I'm his daughter, Gloria. Can I tell him who is calling and what it's about?"

"My name is Emma Love and I'm working as a consultant for the St. Merriam's County Sheriff's Office. We're hoping Mr. Stewart can help us with a case we're working on."

"Dad hasn't lived in St. Merriam's for over ten years. I'm not sure if he can help you, Miss Love."

"I understand, but my questions are pertinent to the time that he did."

"Hold on, and I'll find out if he wants to speak with you."

"That would be appreciated."

I heard mumbled voices and an old-time country music ballad in the background, and then the coarse raspy voice of a long-time smoker picked up the phone.

"Hello? Miss Love, did you say? I don't believe we've met?"

"We have, but it was a long time ago, Mr. Stewart. I wouldn't expect you to remember me. I was one of the many Newtowne High students blessed to have you for Freshman Biology."

"If I gave you a bad grade, and you need it boosted up for college, I can't help you. If you've called for my opinion on gender reassignment, like our county paper did last week, I have no comment on the subject. I was a biology teacher, not a doctor. If that doesn't cover your question, then what can I do for you, Miss Love?"

"I called to ask about Michael Dawson. I know the two of you were very close back in those days. Mrs. Dawson says he still goes to a fishing camp with you and some other friends?"

"I don't know anything about that, Miss Love."

"What is it you don't know, Mr. Stewart? About the fishing camp on Flintstone Creek, or who goes there now? Are you saying you don't go anymore?"

"I don't remember anything about any of it. What are you asking me for anyway?"

"I'm sorry to hear that, Mr. Stewart. Wasn't that your daughter Gloria on the phone? She sounds sweet. I bet it's great to have her there and following in your footsteps teaching too. I'm glad to know the Allegany school board gave her a chance after that nasty drug conviction in Colorado. It was a blessing when Colorado dropped the charges after her community service, first-time offense, and all. Shame the school out there let her go though."

"She's a good girl and a great teacher, Miss Love. She made one mistake."

"Oh, I do understand, Mr. Stewart. We all make mistakes. Did you think…oh my, you have the wrong impression. I'd never breathe a word to a soul." I meant it too, but he couldn't know that.

"I remember you, Miss Love, and I remember your family too. As I recall, your family was well thought of around Newtowne. I imagine there was a reason for that. You were a straight-A student and lived in that big mansion on the hill, but you weren't stuck up like the other wealthy kids. That's why I remember you. I respected you for it, but I'm not so sure that respect was well founded at the moment. I want nothing to do with Michael Dawson, miss. We had a falling out years ago."

"Why, Mr. Stewart? What happened?"

"I'd rather not say as there's nothing I can prove. What exactly is it that you need from me, Miss Love?"

"Thank you, Mr. Stewart. I want to know if Michael Dawson still uses the old cabin on Flintstone Creek. I'd like to find out if he is there now or if he has been there in the last week."

"I haven't seen Michael Dawson in several years, ma'am, but I do know he still comes up from time to time. I don't go to camp when he's there, but I'll find out the information you want and call you back. Do me one favor in return, Miss Love. When we're done here, lose my number."

I felt dirty after this exchange…literally. I beat myself up for being an empathetic fool, but I still took a shower to wash off the spiritual grime. If my bluff of a veiled threat frightened Raymond Stewart and helped get Gwen back home safe, I'd take as many soul-scrubbing showers as necessary.

****

A side benefit to a shower is I do my best thinking there. It's a break that gives me time to collect my thoughts and to assemble the puzzle pieces. I remembered Michael Dawson's Bible study book that Abby yanked out of my hands. It felt as if she was hiding something…Michael's secret interests? Did she suspect her husband of another case of moral turpitude? I tried to recall the book's title, and as I washed the shampoo out of my hair, it came to me.

In my robe with dripping hair, my laptop search engine gave me a summary review.

"*The Return of Sodom and Gomorrah* is touted as a fast-paced exposé of Western culture and its inevitable end if we do not return to God's righteous path. The author asks, 'What does the Lord in his holy word say about prostitution, homosexuality, and adultery?' We soon learn the author's take on that question. Thieves, conmen, fornicators, and sinners of all stripes populate every page of what the publisher calls a religious thriller.

"Author Pittman Baker takes the reader on a ride through a doomed future that he says waits for us all in the not-so-distant future. *New Christian Variety* says, 'Not since Dante's *Divine Comedy* has an author so eloquently described the wages of sin as is seen in modern-day America.' This reader suspects they only read the book blurb or the author purchased a lifetime subscription from them.

"Despite the interest from a handful of divisive

outlier churches, all major Christian religions have denounced Pittman's work, condemning it for its repetitive and controversial plea to readers that ends each chapter. 'Destroy the wicked now or be cast down with them.'

"Follow the author's advice—cast this book down; or better yet, don't bother picking it up at all. One star for the cool 3D hellfire graphics on the cover and because I'm feeling charitable."

Michael Dawson had odd taste in literature. Abby must be wringing her hands just reading that stuff. It did make me wonder how much influence the father had on the son. Jack was still a person of interest in my mind. He fit the profile of a subordinate kidnapper…or killer.

Engrossed in my research, I glanced at my phone and saw I had one missed call and received a text from Sam that read:

—*Maria is about ready to break. All jittery. Still says she can't identify the kidnapper, but he wore a hoodie with it pulled down over his face. Getting closer. Call me when U R able.—*

I tried to do just that, but the call went straight through to voicemail.

I sent a text instead. —*Ask what color hoodie*—

Daniel brought me a sandwich for lunch on his way up to do the same for Nana.

"Find out anything new I should know about? Never mind; don't tell me. I can't be trusted with it anyway."

"Look, Daniel, I love you, and I don't mean to be harsh, but this feeling sorry for yourself needs to stop now. I may need your help soon, or Sam might. Most of the time your instincts are spot on. This time they weren't. Emotions clouded your judgment. So, get over yourself. You'll get a chance to make it right, but not in that frame of mind. Can you do that?"

"I promised you, Emma, if you need me, I'll be there. I meant it."

"Good man." I gave him a thumbs-up sign, and he smiled.

Chapter Twenty-One

After Daniel left, I tried Sam's number again.

"Hey, Emma. Did you get my text?"

"Yes, did you get mine? Did you ask Maria about the hoodie's color?"

"Yes, to the text, but I haven't gone back in with Maria yet. I thought I'd let her stew in her own juices for a while."

"I have another thought for when you do, Sam. No matter what color she says it was, tell her we know it was Jack Dawson and would she care to comment on that or face obstruction of justice charges. They had some kind of weird relationship, or Jack thought they did anyway. I know she feels sorry for him, so worst case scenario, it might get her to give up the responsible party to protect Jack."

"It might work. I'll give it a go with her and see if anything shakes out. Something you might find interesting. Michael Dawson was arrested for moral turpitude, but the records don't specify for what offense. The case was dismissed and no reason was given for why. He was discharged from a middle school across the river in Chapman County shortly afterward. It was the school year before he started here at Newtowne Elementary. I called Chapman County, but the school administrator there won't release any information without a warrant."

"Privacy laws are important. They protect the innocent but sadly, they shield criminals too."

"A necessary evil, Emma. You'll get used to it after a while."

I told Sam about Michael's choice of reading material.

"If his life is in step with his reading, he's a whack job. No law against that though. I better sign off. I'll check into your biology teacher, and I'll let you know what I find out."

"No need to, Sam. He was very cooperative, as it turns out. He is going to call me back. Let me know how it goes down with Maria, and I'll do the same with anything Raymond Stewart tells me."

"Okay. I'll call when I have anything. Be safe," Sam said, and the line went dead.

The phone rang immediately, and I answered without looking, thinking Sam had forgotten something…

****

"Miss Love? It's Raymond Stewart."

"Good afternoon, Mr. Stewart. I wasn't expecting your call this soon. What did you find out?"

"I tried all the guys we share the fishing camp with, but I only got through to Bobby Wallace. He's the only one at camp now anyway. I'm surprised I got through because the reception there is terrible. Most of the time, that's a good thing. But Bobby said he's been there for two weeks. I guess he and his old lady had a big fight, and he's hoping she'll cool down. The fight was about him fishing too much, so I'm doubting his wisdom on that. He isn't too smart, you see, but Bobby never lies. He said Michael called him the first of the month to say he'd meet him at the cabin, but he hasn't shown. He claims the trout are darn near fighting to jump on his hook, and Michael didn't know what he was missing. I don't get around so good anymore, Miss Love, but if you need me to, I'll go up there and have a look. It's just that last half-mile you gotta hike in…"

"That won't be necessary at all, Mr. Stewart. I can't tell you how much this means to our case. You may have helped save a life."

"I'm glad then. Does this make us all squared up, Miss Love?"

"It does. and thank you, Mr. Stewart. I've already lost your number."

We hung up, and I tried Sam's number again, but no answer.

"Raymond Stewart called me. Michael Dawson is *not* at his fishing camp. Hasn't been all week…so where is he? In hiding? Call me as soon as you can."

After the call, I curled my feet under me on the couch to wait for Sam's return call. In minutes, I slipped away…

****

I was at the pond at the bottom of our hill snooping on Maya. She didn't want to play games today, or not with me at least. She had things to do. I didn't know anything more important than playing, and I wanted to find out. She sat alone at the pond's edge tossing tiny pebbles in the water and watching the ripples.

Maya spread a blanket out on the grass and wildflowers. She was wearing her yellow bathing suit with bumblebees stitched across its top. I thought Maya was going to swim in the pond. I started to get up to ask if I could swim too, but I was afraid of snapping turtles.

Maya didn't swim though. She stretched out on the blanket like she was taking a nap. Napping certainly wasn't more fun than playing. Twice while I watched, she sat up and looked around like she was looking for someone. I hoped she didn't know I'd snuck up on her. She'd tell Mom, and I'd be in trouble for spying.

The third time Maya sat up, I saw a figure walking toward her from the shallow end of the pond. It was a girl I recognized, Jessie Dawson, our nearest neighbor. Maya stood up and waved, and Jessie ran toward her. Maya hugged her. Jessie's bathing suit was white and decorated with bumblebees also. They stretched out on Maya's blanket and stared at the sky. They were talking about something, but I couldn't make out the words. They sounded excited. I thought it must be about a boy at school or a movie star.

They were like that for a long time, lazy and doing nothing.

'Let's go play Space Invaders, *Emma,' I thought.*

I watched for a while longer, but it was dull. My head was nodding, and I slipped forward into some thorns. One scratched my cheek. I made a noise, then remembered where I was and looked toward the pond. Both girls sat up. Had they heard me?

Maya whispered something in Jessie's ear. I don't know why; nobody was there to hear her. Jessie put her hand behind Maya's head and pulled their faces together…their lips touched. They were kissing like in the movies, the kind of movies we stole peeks at from behind the doorway when our parents thought we were asleep.

I stood up with a big grin, planning to tease Maya about having a girlfriend, but my vision was fuzzy. A

249

man was hiding in the thick brambles and spying just like me. He stood up…who was he? The man ran at Maya and Jessie, but the flowers swelled up and swarmed around the three of them in a protective embrace.

The man punched into the ball of flowers, and…they became a dress billowing in the breeze. That didn't make sense. The flowers fought back and drove the man to his knees.

Maya and Jessie screamed. The man broke free and the girls fell back. They rolled into the pond with a splash, flapped their arms, and screamed again. Maya grasped at the weeds on the pond's edge…and sank into its depths. Maya!

Then she was there, touching my arm. This couldn't be real. *Wake up, Emma*! I shook my head, but she held on tight to my arm.

"What did you see, Emma? Remember!"

The mist that was Maya lifted above my bed and drifted away as if in a breeze. She was gone.

I sat at the edge of my bed trying to make sense of the apparition or the hallucination. In either case, something I could not ignore. What was it trying to tell me? Remember what?

I'd missed a call from Sam again, and a text message was lit up as well. I pulled it up.

—Looking into Michael Dawson's arrest record again, and the date rang a bell. Dawson was arrested the same night and on the same street corner as Maria Clements was. Going to question her now. Call me back.—

His phone rang four times and went to voicemail.

"Where is Michael Dawson? I'm calling Abby.

Call me back. Tag, you're it," I said.

I remembered the look on Maya's face in my semi-dream state and it all clicked!

I dialed Abby then, but she didn't answer. It was Tuesday, the day the grocery store began its sales ad. The day Abby did all her grocery shopping.

I went upstairs to talk with Daniel. He wasn't in his room, so I peeked in at Nana. My brother was sitting in the chair beside her, his head resting on his chest and fast asleep.

I went back downstairs and left a note on the kitchen table, then tried Sam again. When he didn't answer, I assumed he was still in with Maria and texted him. My phone's battery was in the red with twenty-one percent left. That should be enough. I went into 'Settings' and switched to low power mode.

—Leaving the house for a while. Call me when you finish with Maria.—

With Abby shopping in town, it was my perfect opportunity to check out what was under the tarp in her backyard.

Chapter Twenty-Two

I started across the field, then changed direction to follow the stream at the back of the property. I didn't want to be seen approaching if anyone happened to be home or if a vehicle drove by on the county road.

I considered that Michael might be at the house, but I had to take the chance. It didn't look like he'd ever left Newtowne. What was he up to that he needed to keep his presence a secret?

My phone rang…Sam. I pressed the green button to accept the call, but the reception was terrible in the stream bottom. His voice sounded excited, but his words were blurred and full of static.

"I'm not sure if you can hear me, but I can't hear you. It's a bad connection. Can you text me?" I glanced at my phone's charge, eighteen percent. The message alert jingled, and I opened Sam's text.

—*Just finished questioning Maria. She didn't take the bait on Jack and the hoodie, but boy what she did tell me! Call me ASAP. Just don't text and drive. Where are you?*—

I tried his number again, and again it wouldn't connect.

—*Sorry, Sam, I can't call, still won't go through. What's up?*—

I couldn't tell Sam what I was up to. Sirens and flashing lights would descend on the Dawsons' house, and all hope of slipping in quietly would be gone. We'd be stuck sitting on our hands waiting for who knows how long for Judge Allen to issue a search warrant…and then anything could happen.

Another text from Sam.

—Scoop of the day: Maria is Michael Dawson's illegitimate daughter! That's why Dawson's case was dismissed. Maria was arrested when she met up with someone else fifteen minutes later. I guess he was willing to take his lumps at his school rather than admit the truth about Maria. Jack is her half-brother. Remember she said she told Jack he was like a brother to her the first morning Gwen was missing? Guess that one flew over our heads. Gwen knew about Maria's parentage also. Maria says she didn't think that was pertinent to the case. Believe that? This changes everything. Sets us back to the beginning. Call me as soon as you have bars.—

The phone registered a fifteen percent charge.

****

I reread the message twice and thought about it. Rather than setting us back or putting us in search of new perpetrators, I thought Maria's clue might've just solved our case. Michael's God was an Old Testament, burn-in-hell, vengeful God. As an adulterer with a severe guilt complex, where would he stop to right his wrongs? Poor Abby. Was she trying to protect his reputation?

No smoke rose from the Dawsons' chimney, and Abby's car was nowhere to be seen. I stood at the backyard fence and listened. Hearing no stirring inside the house, I walked around to the front door and knocked. When there was no answer, I twisted the knob and the door swung open. I stuck my head in.

"Is anyone home? Abby? Are you here?"

No response. The humming of the refrigerator's motor was the only sound.

Back around to the fenced-in yard, I climbed the fence and went straight to the tarped vehicle. I yanked off the covering and my suspicion was confirmed. It was Michael's old Ford F150 pick-up.

I peeked inside, not knowing what I might find, and expecting nothing. If Gwen's other shoe had fallen inside, it was gone now. If Michael had gone fishing, no relevant signs jumped out at me. No blood or tiny fragments of glass were in evidence.

A Bible passage was attached to the dash. It read, " 'Vengeance is mine…for the day of their calamity is at hand, and their doom comes swiftly. Deuteronomy 32:35.' " Two round stickers proclaiming "I voted" were used to tape it on.

I needed to have a look around inside of the house, but what if Michael or Abby came home?

I looked at my phone and saw a twelve percent charge remaining, but it indicated two bars of reception there. I dialed Abby's cell phone number.

"Hello? Is this Emma? What are you up to, sweetheart? There's nothing wrong, I hope?"

"Everything is fine, Abby. I was wondering if you would be home later this afternoon or early evening?"

"I sure will. If not, I'd make sure I would be for a visit from my favorite neighbor. I just started my grocery shopping though. I need to stock my pantry before my man comes home. You know Michael; that man has an appetite. I should be done in say an hour and a half. Jack is with me, and it will take me a bit longer. He wants to drop a couple of job applications for weekend work and the evenings after school. Then it's straight home for us. That boy has fallen behind with his schoolwork."

"Take your time, Abby. I wanted to talk with you about Mr. Dawson too. I'm worried about him."

"Oh? Why is that, sweetheart?"

"He's been gone so long. I don't think he's…I know it must be hard on you with him being gone all week."

"Don't you worry your head over us, Emma. I'm used to these trips, and Michael is always in such a good mood when he does come home. I'll see you say around four thirty or five?"

"That would be perfect."

"I'll have cookies," she assured me, and we said our goodbyes. Ten percent remained on my phone.

I was in the clear with Abby for at least an hour, but Michael? He might be hiding out somewhere. In a small town like ours, it would be hard to remain unnoticed for so long when so many knew you by sight. If he was at the house, he had to be hiding in the basement, and if so, he already knew I was here. I reached down to my hip and felt the comfort of my 9mm, then walked back to the front door.

****

I didn't take any chances when I entered the house. The door slid open without a sound. I stepped over the threshold, placing each foot with care. It was the silent predatory stalk my father taught us…but I wasn't hunting squirrels or rabbits today.

I swept each room, one by one. The kitchen and living room were empty. I walked down the hall and stopped to look in the bathroom. Pulling aside the shower curtain, I anticipated a jump scare, but there was nothing. I guess Hitchcock's *Psycho* movie affected us all. The bedrooms were next. The first one on the right had to be Jack's. Rock-and-roll posters covered the walls. Some high school "required reading" novels in pristine condition were stacked on a shelf beside a selection of CliffsNotes and several dusty and long-forgotten miniature cars. A dozen dog-eared superhero comics covered the homemade nightstand.

There was only one other bedroom to search. Abby's bedroom was at the end of the hall. As I would've guessed, the room was filled with flowery decor. The window curtains were covered with bursts of daisies. The bedspread featured sunflowers, and a bouquet of silk roses bloomed forever beside her bed.

A plaque hung on her wall. It read, "The man that committeth adultery…the adulterer and the adulteress shall surely be put to death. Leviticus 20:10."

One side of her bed was tousled, but the other hadn't been slept on—Michael's side, I guessed. His book, *The Return of Sodom and Gomorrah*, sat on his nightstand along with a huge copy of the Bible. On his wall hung a framed picture of the temptation of Christ in the Judean desert. "Lead us not into temptation" was written across the bottom.

The master bedroom had its own attached bath, and I stepped forward with care. It was the last hiding place on the main floor. I looked left and right, the barrel of my pistol following my eyes, then moved toward the shower curtain. As I pulled it back…*Thump*!

I jumped back several feet and bumped into the sink. It wasn't a loud sound, but it stood out in the silent house. I caught my breath and stepped forward again, pistol outstretched. There was nothing inside the shower.

Thump!

This time I recognized the direction of the sound. It was coming from under my feet…in the basement.

At the top of the stairs, I considered flipping on the lights but thought better of it. I closed my eyes to give them time to acclimate to the darkness and took the first step down, the second, and then the third. The fourth step squealed when I put my weight on it.

Thump!

I sat down to present a smaller target while hoping to quiet my descent. I slid down two more steps, then three more. I could see the entire room now, but not the source of the sound.

Thump!

I saw it now, a dark shape huddled around a metal support beam in the center of the open room.

"Michael? I'm armed, but I don't want to shoot you. Stand up slowly and put your hands behind your head." The huddled figure didn't move, then…

Thump!

My finger tightened on the trigger. I reached into my inside jacket pocket and pulled out a small pocket flashlight. I held it tight against my 9mm Ruger.

"I'll ask you again. Stand up, and put your hands behind your head." I flicked the light on prepared to shoot.

It was Gwen.

Chapter Twenty-Three

I spotted another light switch on my way to her side. Gwen was gagged, and her hands were fastened together in front of her with a thick cable tie. A rope ran between her arms and was tied in a loop to a metal support beam. She was dirty, and her cheeks and eyes had a hollowed-out look.

I pulled the gag down first.

"So…happy to…see you," she said.

"Same here, Gwen, but I need to get you out of this place."

I tried to untie the rope from behind her, but the knots were too tight. After several tries and two broken fingernails, I knew it was futile.

"I'm going upstairs to get a knife out of the kitchen to cut you free, Gwen." I saw the fear in her eyes. "Don't worry. Michael isn't here. He may be out of the picture, and Abby won't be home for a while. Don't worry. I'll be right back."

"Michael." She pointed toward the far wall of the basement and wiggled her jaw. "My jaw is…so stiff."

"I'll bet it is, and you're right. Michael is elsewhere. If he does show up, I'll be ready." I showed her the pistol, then ran up the stairs to the kitchen.

It was time to call in the cavalry. I opened my phone, went to text messages, and selected Sam's number.

—I'm at Abby Dawson's. Gwen is in the basement. Dehydrated and confused. Come quick and bring EMTs.—

I hit send, then opened several cabinet drawers until I located the knives. I felt the edge of a couple until confident I had one sharp enough. It was a small paring knife, but it would do the job. The rope was thick, and cable ties are tough. I slipped the knife through my belt and under my shirt to keep my hands free.

My phone buzzed. I looked, and a red note beside the text to Sam read, "Not Delivered." I hit the *Try Again* option and swung around at the sound of the opening door.

Abby stood there with a double-barreled shotgun pointed at my chest.

"Well, isn't this the sweetest surprise, Emma? I didn't expect you this early."

"Same here," I said.

"I guess you came to see my husband, didn't you? You know I can't let you do that. I've always looked out for him."

"It's over, Abby. You don't have to protect him anymore. We know what he did to Gwen and Maria. Did he do something to Maya and Jessie too?"

"Sweetie, that was a tragedy for both of our families."

"It's in my dreams, Abby. It haunts them still."

"I'm sorry, Emma, but you need to hand me that gun of yours now, and your phone too."

"Abby, I…"

"Now, Emma!"

I handed her the gun, holding it out by the barrel.

She grabbed it, and my protection was gone.

"Phone too," she said. I gave it to her, and she searched through it. My connection to the world and its comforting illusion of sanity vanished. I was no hero…best private investigator in the state, huh? Yeah, right.

"Turn around and put your hands behind you."

I did as I was told, arching my back so the knife wouldn't stand out…praying she wouldn't notice it. The tip of the blade dug into my butt on the left side. I bit my lip to hide the pain and felt the cable tie pull tight around my wrists.

My eyes scanned the room, searching for any avenue of escape.

"Stand up," Abby said, then waved her gun directing me to the basement door.

"People will be looking for me, Abby. Don't do this."

"I have your phone, sweetie. It doesn't look like that deputy friend of yours knows where you are. You were always such a smart girl, Emma. What were you thinking? Then you left the tarp off Michael's truck. I knew someone was in here snooping, but I thought better of you, Emma. It would be a real shame to shoot you as a home invader."

"Daniel knows. He'll call the cops."

"And I'll send them packing until they return with a search warrant, child. I happen to know that Judge Allen chartered an all-day cruise with friends; he's trolling in the Chesapeake for striped bass. I heard they're really biting this week. It will be late before his honor gets home…if hc doesn't have a few beers with his friends afterward, that is. The Allen family always had a weakness for alcohol, you know. Do you think you or Gwen will be here for them to find after all of that happens?"

"Please just tell me this first, Abby. I know you're a God-fearing woman, not a killer. Why did Michael push Maya and Jessie into our pond to drown? You tried to save them."

"What are you talking about, child? Michael made mistakes, but he was a good man. All I've ever done is try to protect my family, Emma. You can understand that, can't you?"

"Where is your family, Abby? Where are Jack and Michael?"

"My men are fine, Emma, but you should worry about yourself now. I'm sorry. I truly am. I must pray over what to do with you."

She pointed her shotgun at the basement door again.

We walked down the stairs to where Gwen waited for her rescuer…for me.

****

Abby threaded a rope between my arms and tied it to the same post as Gwen. She turned her back on me and walked over to the washer and dryer set. Gwen was holding her chin against her chest so Abby wouldn't notice her gag was pulled loose.

"Let us go, Abby. We know you're innocent. Don't get caught up in Michael's crimes any deeper than you already are."

Gwen tapped the toe of her boot against my ankle and shook her head.

I looked at Abby. She was bent over reaching into the dryer.

"Stop. I know, Gwen," I said, low enough that Abby couldn't hear.

Abby pulled a dish towel out of the dryer and carried it back to me. She shoved the middle of it into my mouth and tied it behind my head.

"I've always loved talking with you, Emma, but you'll have to stay quiet for a while now. This will all be over soon."

As soon as the basement door closed behind Abby, I was contorting to pull the knife out of my belt. I put my face up to Gwen's and thrust out my gag. The dehydration took a toll on her senses, and she didn't catch on to what I wanted her to do. I shook my head and thrust out the gag to her again. The light of understanding flickered in her hollowed eyes. She opened her mouth and bit a mouthful of dish towel. She tried a few times without success. Abby had it tied tight. I turned my head for her to have a go at the knot. Again, she bit into the towel, and my head bounced back and forth like a chicken plucking corn, but finally, I felt the knot break free, and I spit out the towel.

"It's Abby…the one. I…think she…"

"Don't talk, Gwen. You need water. I know it was Abby. I don't want her to know I know just yet though. It had to be one of the two of them. At first, I thought it was Michael. He was the one with the arrest record…I believed he forced Abby to help him or that maybe she didn't even know. The real reason his case was dropped canceled out that train of thought. When I found out Maria was Michael's daughter, there was little doubt. I knew Abby was the brains behind it and Michael was being dragged along. I think she killed Michael. He might have tried to stop her…like he did at the pond with my sister. Abby slipped and spoke of Michael in the past tense. He was a deeply religious man of the fire and brimstone persuasion, and he committed adultery. That's what Abby has held over him. I suspect that Jack is the one who kidnapped Maria though. In his distorted reasoning, he was trying to protect his sister. I think Jack is in trouble somewhere too."

Gwen was nodding her head and pointing at the wall. "Michael," she repeated.

****

No matter how hard I tried, I couldn't get my knife positioned in a way where I could saw at the rope, not to mention the cable ties. My eyes were adjusting to the single dim fluorescent light that Abby left burning. I looked over to a workbench I hadn't paid attention to before along with the large utility room-style sink beside it. Beyond the bench on the earthen floor was a pile of dead flowers. Abby's floral obsession knew no bounds. The top of the bench held several larger tools: an electric drill, sander, and a circular saw were all I could identify from that distance. There was a pegboard panel behind the bench with a hammer, screwdrivers, and assorted pliers hanging from it.

"Would've been nice if I'd seen that the first trip down here," I said and shook my head.

"Hmm?" Gwen replied.

"You'll have to do this, Gwen. Work on the cable tie." I turned my back to her and dropped the knife in her lap, then got on my knees in front of her. She caught on right away this time, and I felt her cutting and prying against the cable tie. I felt the edge of the knife bite into my palm and the warm sticky flow of blood.

"You're bleeding," Gwen said and paused.

"No, Gwen, don't stop. It's just a scratch."

She began again but sawing at the tie rather than prying. Would it ever cut through at this rate?

"Pry at it, Gwen. Sawing isn't working." I listened for any movement upstairs but heard nothing. I said a silent prayer that Abby went out to pull the tarp back over the truck…and carried my cell phone with her. I felt sure Sam's technical guys would be searching for my phone's GPS signal by now…if Daniel hadn't yet read my note.

The cable tie around my wrists broke loose with a popping sound. I was free. I ran over to the bench and spied a pair of snips and cut Gwen loose. Deep red lines were carved into her wrists from her bondage, and her hand and fingers were swollen. She stood on shaky legs. I helped her stumble toward the sink. She cut on the faucet and sucked at the water greedily.

"Not too much at once, Gwen," I said.

I'd noticed the basement doorknob was a simple bedroom-style lock that could be easily picked with a thin flat-head screwdriver, but I'd also seen the deadbolt on the other side. I'd have to use the crowbar for that…a noisy proposition, but one hung from the wall behind the workbench…waiting. A small enough screwdriver was harder to find, but a search through the drawers below the bench bore fruit.

I looked down at the odd array of flowers on the floor. At the end of the pile was a simple wooden cross. We'd buried our childhood dog with one just like it, but this one didn't have "Ranger" scratched across it. It said, "Michael P. Dawson." There was a single date listed, but no year, "October 16th," one week ago today.

I listened again at the base of the stairs and heard nothing, so I started up them…step by silent step. Halfway up, Gwen started hurling all the water she drank. The sound was as loud and raucous as a primordial beast in its death throes. I knew it would draw Abby's attention, and I hurried back down the steps.

"Abby had to hear that," I whispered as Gwen's heaving subsided. "Are you all right?"

"Better. Wet my whistle."

"Sit down where you were, in case she comes down here."

"Where are you going?"

"I'm going to listen at the foot of the stairs for a minute. I'll be able to hear her if she throws back the lock."

I waited until I felt sure Abby was sleeping, praying, or outside the house. There wasn't a sound from above. I waved to Gwen to get her attention and pointed to the sink. I mouthed the word "Easy," and she nodded.

The screwdriver was in my pocket and the crowbar clenched in my right hand. It might have to serve double duty as a weapon. Up the stairs, I climbed again. I stepped over the creaky fourth step down and up to the third. Pausing there to listen again, I slipped the screwdriver into the lock and turned it. Now for the scary part.

I glanced down at Gwen. She was at the sink with the water dribbling out. She splashed it on her face and sipped a few handfuls. Still no sound from our captor. It was now or never.

Popping a deadbolt lock from the opposite side of

the door isn't a quiet operation, and I knew of no way to make it so. I slid the hooked point into the crack of the door and yanked the crowbar with everything I had. The door flew open with a bang.

Chapter Twenty-Four

I fell back from the released force, catching myself on the handrail before I fell down the stairs. Gwen hurried up the stairs behind me. We both stood there, stock still, waiting for Abby's fury to be unleashed upon us.

Nothing…

We stepped cautiously onto the landing. I held the crowbar up in a death grip in the position that a baseball player holds a bat. The inside of the house was close quarters. Gwen stood a chance of getting away if I could get the jump on Abby. Her shotgun was a short-range weapon.

"Are you able to run if you have to?" I asked.

"I'll run…Emma. Like the hounds…of hell are after me."

"Daniel's missed you, Gwen. He sure loves you." I wasn't sure if we'd get out of Abby's alive or not. I wanted to leave her with a good thought in case…well, just in case.

I led Gwen to the front door. Abby's shotgun and my pistol were on the kitchen table along with a bag of cookies with my name on it. I grabbed the pistol.

"I don't think Abby is a threat to anyone anymore, Gwen."

I led her to the steps and motioned for her to go first. As she stepped down off the last one, we could hear approaching sirens. She turned around and smiled.

"Thank you, Emma." Her eyes ran with tears.

"Straight down the driveway to the EMTs, Gwen."

"Where are you going?"

"I'll meet you there."

****

I needed to find out where Abby was, and I didn't have a good feeling about it. I checked the bathroom and Jack's room, then progressed to Abby's bedroom with my pistol at the ready.

Abby was on her back in the bed. Her hands were folded across her chest and resting over Michael's thick Bible. She was pale, and I couldn't detect her breathing. An open pill bottle was on the bed beside her.

"Abby?" I was at her side without realizing I'd taken a step. I felt her wrist for a pulse but felt nothing. I tried again at the carotid artery in the neck…still nothing. I started chest compressions. After fifteen, I heard Sam's voice at the door.

"Emma, where are you?"

"In the back. Where are the EMTs?" Then like magic, two of them were there. I stepped to the side. "That makes thirty chest compressions," I said.

"Thank you, ma'am. Checking the airway, Tom," the young woman said.

"Pulse is faint," Tom said. "We need the folding stretcher, Louise. We won't get the wheeled gurney around the turn and down that hallway." He looked over his shoulder at Sam. "Could use a couple of extra bodies, Deputy."

Sam scurried out as the EMTs worked their magic, returning with the stretcher and two deputies I didn't know. Tom and Louise turned Abby on her side, slipped the stretcher under her, and rolled her back over. They strapped her in and asked us if we were ready. Louise and the two deputies grabbed the handles on Abby's right side and Sam, Tom, and I took the left.

"Grab the empty bottle from the sleeping pills, Tom," Louise said.

"Grab that too," I said to Sam and pointed at the slip of paper sticking out of the Bible.

****

When we had Abby loaded into the ambulance, the siren screamed, and it roared down the driveway. I turned to Sam.

"Is Gwen all right?"

"She is. Are you okay? What did you do to your hand?"

I held it up to look at it. Dried blood was caked on it and stretched down to my elbow.

"It was just a scratch. Hard getting out of those cable ties."

"And the blood on your backside?"

I turned my head to see a patch of blood on the butt of my jeans the size of a softball. "A tiny knife wound."

"What were you thinking, Emma? You could've been killed."

"I wasn't though, and I'm fine. Besides, I knew you'd come charging in like some medieval knight in armor. You didn't disappoint."

Sam shook his head. "Emma, please don't do anything like this again. I don't know what I'd…"

"How did you find us, Sam? Did you track my phone, or did you get a call from Daniel first?"

"We did track your phone to here, but Daniel also called while I was on the way. He arrived just as I pulled in. He was running across the field in his house slippers with a rusty old single-shot shotgun in his arms. He looked like that proverbial medieval knight of yours, or more like Don Quixote, ready to storm the castle or beat down windmills. He left on the first ambulance with Gwen. He was torn up about it until Gwen assured him you were safe."

"Dad taught us to shoot with that old shotgun. Daniel never did quite get the hang of it though."

****

Sam offered me a ride home, but I didn't think we were done here.

"Do you think we could sweep the place one more time, Sam?"

"What are you expecting to find?"

"Not what, but who. It looks like Michael was buried in the basement, and I'm worried about Jack. We haven't seen him, but Abby told me he was with her in town earlier. So, where is he?"

"Maybe she dropped him in town somewhere?"

"No, she said she would be later getting home because of running him around dropping off job applications, but because he had schoolwork to catch up on, it was 'straight home for us' after that."

"If he was with her, but never went inside, he's either outside or still in the car."

We turned at the same moment and stared at Abby's old car, then trotted over to it. I looked inside and saw the keys still in the ignition and bags of groceries on the floor, but nothing else. Sam went to the back and pounded on the trunk.

Someone pounded back.

I grabbed the keys and tossed them to Sam. The

trunk lid popped open, and Jack stared back at us with a drugged-out, uncomprehending stare.

"Momma?" he said.

Sam ran to his cruiser to call another ambulance to our location.

****

After the ambulance left with Jack, Sam repeated his offer to drop me off at home. "If you think you've got everything covered here now, of course."

"That would be great, but I'm curious what was on that slip of paper you pulled out of Abby's Bible?"

"Too much going on, Emma. It slipped my mind." He pulled it from his jacket pocket, unfolded it, and held it out so we both could read.

Dear Heavenly Father,

You told us if we didn't have a sword, to sell our cloak and buy one to protect ourselves and our families. I have tried to protect my family from the Dark One, but I failed and punished the innocent. Thank you for listening to my prayers. I have sinned and fallen short of your glory, but I know what must be done.

You blessed me with a wonderful husband and two innocent children. I failed our first-born, Jessie, and she fell into sinfulness because of it. You warned us that bad company corrupts good character, but my eyes were blinded. My only choice was to return her to innocence and her soul to you. Your righteous punishment was to keep another child from us for so many years.

I tried to bring Michael back to your light, but the temptations of the flesh from the Serpent of Old weighed heavily on him. When he fornicated with another, I read your words, "Do not condemn, and you

271

will not be condemned. Forgive, and you will be forgiven." I prayed Michael would come to see the errors of his ways while I heeded my heart and helped him to hide his sin.

When his lustful eyes gazed upon Gwen, I could see he was smitten, and I couldn't hide from the truth any longer, but still, my heart was twisted. With clearer eyes, I would have sent Michael to his glory then…before he destroyed his immortal soul. Maria told Gwen about Michael's wickedness, and I had to protect him. Then you opened my eyes, dear Lord. You showed me the errors of my ways. I'd punished the innocent for the acts of the sinner. With your guidance, I sent Michael home to you. Please have mercy on his soul.

Now I must make amends for my sins and for turning my face from you. I'll not further stain my eternal soul with the deaths of two blameless women. I throw myself at your mercy and beg for your forgiveness. John passed along your words that no man has greater love than to lay down his life for another. I lay mine down so that they might live. Forgive me.

Your faithful servant, Abby

Sam looked at me and shook his head. "That's quite a suicide note."

"It's quite a confession as well. Do you think they'll all be okay? Gwen, Abby, and Jack?"

"Gwen was dehydrated, but she's young and will bounce back quickly. Abby's already had her stomach pumped out unless I miss my guess. From the timeline you gave us and the time it took for her to write her note to God, I can't imagine she'd digested much of the pills."

"And Jack?"

"I've seen opioid overdoses go both ways. He's young too, so he has that going for him."

"Where are you going from here?" I asked.

"To the hospital to check on Gwen and see if she's up to giving me her statement. I doubt there's an update for anyone else yet. You?"

"I'll take that ride to the house now. I want to get the Bronco, and I'll meet you there. Do you know if anyone is there with Nana?"

Chapter Twenty-Five

Alicia showed up in record time. She'd heard the ambulances from her house and thought Nana might be involved. She waited by the phone for our call. She was fast becoming one of my favorite people.

When I found Gwen's hospital room, Daniel and Sam were sitting at her side. She was cleaned up, and an IV needle was sticking in her arm. The bag hanging by her bed was almost empty. Her color was already improving, but her eyes couldn't hide the terror she'd lived through.

"Feeling better, Gwen?"

"So much better than a few hours ago." She laughed. "You're my hero, Emma."

"Mine too," Daniel said.

"She was mine already," Sam echoed.

"All righty then. I love you all too." Sam raised his eyebrows, and I smiled back at him.

"How long are they saying you'll be held captive here, Gwen?"

"Not as long as the last incarceration, I hope, and the conditions are a lot better here."

"The nurse said she thought she'd be released tomorrow," Daniel said.

"We asked about Abby and Jack, but they wouldn't tell us much. They aren't listed as critical now though. The nurses are waiting for a regular room to be available for them," Sam said.

"No police guard at their door, Sam?"

"I don't think either of them is in any danger of leaving, but I will have a deputy in the hall to watch their doors tonight. They might be here for a few days."

****

I didn't see Sam that night, but I knew he was busy with all that had transpired that day. I wondered if he made it to his bed or if he fell asleep sitting at his desk. I slept the sleep of the dead, and it was well past ten in the morning before I opened my eyes. I had a sweet, peaceful dream—Maya and I playing *Space Invaders*, and as usual she let me win.

I couldn't imagine Rachel the rooster respecting my need for sleep. I sat up, for a moment confused by where I was, then remembered I spent the night in my bed for a change.

I checked my phone for messages, but there were none, and coffee was waiting to be made in the kitchen. While it was brewing, I sent Daniel and Sam a text.

—Any updates from the patients?—

Daniel answered immediately.

—At the hospital now. Hoping they release her soon. Alicia's still with Nana—

I replied, *—Keep me posted.—*

The coffee was still percolating, and I realized I'd made too much for just me. Old habits might die hard, but new habits form fast. I opened the bag of English muffins, but as I slipped one into the toaster, I noticed the green furry mold.

"No breakfast for Emma this morning," I said to no one.

I sipped my coffee, not chugging it down in huge

gulps as was the norm lately. A leisurely cup was what I needed, and I was grateful for it. I thought about Abby and felt nothing but sorrow. She was guilty of a list of crimes, and too many had suffered and died at her hands. How did everything get so twisted up in her head? How did anyone, especially in the name of God, commit such atrocities while considering themselves righteous? Abby was the poster child for an insanity defense.

Sam's response came through as I washed the percolator and my coffee cup.

— *Good morning. Do you think you could meet me at the hospital?*—

—*Sure, what's up?*—

I waited for his response, and the phone buzzed in my hand.

"Hey, Sam."

"Hi. How did you sleep?"

"I slept too well if anything, thanks. What's going on at the hospital?"

"Abby was awake and alert when I got here this morning. She said she'd answer any questions we had and sign any confession on two conditions."

"Excellent. How can I help?"

"One condition was we give her son immunity for anything she tells us, and the other is that you are there for it. The D.A. already signed off on not prosecuting Jack with conditions. The boy has suffered enough. I imagine years of therapy will be in order though. Can you meet me there in an hour?"

"I'll be there."

****

I made it in well under the hour and used the extra

276

time to visit with Gwen and Daniel. Gwen was perky and animated. Daniel was all smiles but held on to her hand as if she might float away and eyed everyone who passed in the halls as if they'd abduct her.

"Has the doctor been in yet? Are you still getting out today?" I asked.

"He said they were doing the release paperwork an hour ago, but here we still sit."

Our old friend Nurse Jackie stuck her head in on us.

"Well, if it isn't Miss Love," she said. "Gwen here has been telling me you're a hero, and I thought you just enjoyed harassing my patients. Is she harassing you, Gwen?"

Gwen smiled and shook her head.

"My sister is a walking, talking contradiction in many ways, Nurse," Daniel said, "but she's one hundred percent hero."

I reached across the bed and hugged Gwen. "See you later at your house?"

"You better, Emma. Daniel said he'll pick us up a bottle of that good wine they got in at Newtowne Liquors to celebrate. Bring Sam." She winked.

I stepped out into the hall and saw Sam approaching. He waved as he walked past Gwen's room.

"See you guys in a few minutes," he said, and we continued to Abby's room. "Ready?"

"No idea what she wants me there for, but I do have a few questions for her," I said.

Abby was sitting up when I tapped at the door frame. She noisily slurped at what appeared to be chicken noodle soup from the lunch tray in front of her.

"Can we come in?" I asked.

She looked up from the soup. "I guess I should thank you, Emma. I hope you'll forgive me if I don't. I know your heart was in the right place, but I expected to wake up in glory with the Lord, not in this sterile and soulless place."

Sam turned on a recorder and set it on her nightstand. "Abby, I need to record our conversation. Do I have your permission?"

Abby nodded.

"I need you to answer out loud, please."

"That's fine."

"The District Attorney has indicated that Jack will not be prosecuted for anything you tell us, short of a violent felony. Kidnapping is in that category, but she's agreed that's off the table due to his youth, his having no prior record, and the fact that Maria Clements is now claiming it never happened. That's assuming Jack was involved in Maria Clements' disappearance. Do you understand?"

"I do. In a way, I'm glad it's over. I did think you'd catch on sooner with all the slip-ups I made, Emma."

"We did our best, Abby."

"Lordy, you were slow, sweetie. I unconsciously gave you the clues, but I'm afraid my Jack might've hit you on the head a bit too hard."

"Abby…" Sam started.

"It's okay, Sam. The D.A. isn't likely to prosecute with an uncooperative victim."

"I'm sorry about that part too, Emma. I meant it when I said you were my favorite neighbor."

"What clues do you mean?" I asked.

"I gave you Gwen's shoe that very first day. I

mentioned that I'd warned your brother about the shenanigans going on, and I know you saw Michael's truck out in the backyard the day you came by for a visit. I could've said he was back home working on it, and he was out for a walk, couldn't I? That Maria had it coming to her, but not Gwen Love. I was waiting, giving her time to see the perils of her sin. I knew she would eventually; she was a good woman. When Maria told Gwen her tale though, it left me no choice. I had to protect my family and it was my undoing. I'd never hurt an innocent."

"Maya and Jessie were no more than children. You killed them too, didn't you, Abby? Jessie was your daughter and Maya was so full of life. She never hurt anyone. Aren't you forgetting about them?"

"You think your Maya was so innocent? She pushed her perversions on my sweet little Jessie. Michael tried to stop me, but he was a weak man. It was left to me to protect my baby girl's soul."

My eyes filled with tears at the memory of their sweet smiling faces, their drawings filled with love, and their two precious lives ended when they'd barely started. It was too horrible to consider. I excused myself and rushed to the adjoining restroom. I threw water on my face and washed away my tears, then went back into the room. It was quiet except for the beep and hum of the machines.

"She wanted to wait for you," Sam said.

"We can begin again now if you like," Abby said.

"Did you give Jack an overdose of opioids, Abby?" Sam asked.

"He threatened to turn me in…his mother. I'd forgotten to give him his medication. You'd be

279

surprised how easy it is to get, even in Newtowne. He thought he could go against me, but he had his father's weakness. He hid that perverted woman from me and God's righteousness. She bewitched him and he protected her from me. I gave Jack a double dose that day. I hoped to help him see the path to righteousness again."

Chapter Twenty-Six

The interview ended after that. I told Sam I'd meet him in Gwen's room. I barely made it there in time before I hurled the coffee I'd had for breakfast. I wish it would end there, but the contractions in my gut would no sooner stop than the wrenching waves of uncontrolled weeping. Daniel looked in on me twice before I could beat down the horrors.

My head ached, and there were no tears left to flow when I stepped back into the room. Sam was there now, but no one said a word to me, their souls as tormented as mine. I sat alone in the corner chair and stared out of the window. Sam walked over and sat at my feet. He rested his arm against my leg and gently rubbed my knee.

Nurse Jackie stepped in then. Arms folded across her chest, she stared at each of us in turn.

"My oh my, did I just break up the party? Miss Love, look at you. You're supposed to be the harasser, not the one getting hassled. Do I need to run Gwen and these fellows out of this room? I'll do it, you know."

I laughed. A loud obnoxious, out-of-control donkey braying laugh. It wasn't that her joke was that funny, but my emotional storage area was well past peak capacity. It overflowed as laughter. With my tears spent, release came in any form.

Poor Nurse Jackie looked at me like she was doing

a visual fitting for a straitjacket, and that made me laugh even more.

"I'll be back in a minute," she said and whirled around.

"You don't think she's going up to the psychiatric ward, do you?" I asked.

"Oh no, she better not try before we have that bottle of wine tonight," Gwen said.

The mood in the room had changed, and what we hadn't let go of, we would smash down and try not to remember. *Suck it up, buttercup.* That's what Daddy said when I skinned my knees or stubbed my toes. Suck it up, Emma. Tomorrow is another day.

****

Nurse Jackie returned with the discharge papers in hand. She pointed out the spots where Gwen needed to sign and wished us all a "blessed day" when it was done. She turned toward the door and nodded to me.

"Miss Love? Do you have a minute?"

I stepped over beside her, and she leaned over to whisper in my ear, "I know what you did, Miss Love. I know what was done to you. You are either the strongest woman I know, or you do one helluva job impersonating her. If you ever want to talk or just need a friend, you call me. Okay, sugar?" She handed me her business card and if I had any tears left, they would've started again. Instead, I hugged her.

"Please call me Emma."

"Only if you remember I'm Jackie." I nodded again.

The flowers, cards, and Gwen's personal belongings were gathered, and we headed down every hallway with a bright red "Exit" light at the end of it. A nurse who was poorly trained in the finer points of wheelchair locomotion pushed Gwen ahead of us.

"Look who we have over by the nurses' station, Sam," I said, pointing.

"Isn't that your reporter buddy?"

"None other than Johnny Walker in the flesh."

As we passed by, he lifted his head from the conversation he was having with the duty nurse and spotted us.

"Miss Love, Deputy Mattingley. Great to see you. I'd like to apologize—"

"Are you wearing your competitor's apparel, Johnny? Isn't that a *Chapman County Herald*'s cap on your head?"

"Yes, ma'am. I wanted to tell you—"

"That you got a big promotion after the slam piece you did on our family?"

"No, ma'am. I'm not with the *County Examiner* anymore. My editor…he didn't like how I portrayed your family. He said it wasn't newsworthy. He changed everything, made it ugly, and I quit. I tried to tell you that day, Miss Love—"

"I'm pleased to hear there's still honor among journalists, Johnny." I held out my hand and he shook it with a smile. Sam and I turned to leave…

"Miss Love? I don't suppose you or Deputy Mattingley would have a quote for my readers?"

Sam shook his head.

"Wait, Sam," I said. "Johnny deserves a quote for being so honorable."

"Thank you, ma'am."

"Tell them that the kidnapper was caught because of the inspiring detective work by the deputies of the St.

Merriam's County Sheriff's Department, also known as the First Sheriff because it's the longest continuously running sheriff's department in the good old USA. Tell them everyone is recovering nicely. You can even tell them that Emma Love is back, has a boyfriend, and thinks she may be in love." I pulled Sam to me and kissed him.

Johnny tried unsuccessfully to switch his phone from recording to camera mode.

"Did you hear about the killing at River's End, Miss Love? Will you be involved with that case?"

"Maybe, but that will be a story for another day…"

A word about the author…

David W. Thompson is a multiple award-winning author, an Army veteran, and a graduate of UMUC (now UMGC). He claims his first writing efforts were "Dick and Jane" fan fiction when he was a child- no doubt with a unique twist. As a multi-genre writer, he's been awarded membership in the HWA--Horror Writers' Association, the MWA--Mystery Writers of America, and the SFWA -- Science Fiction & Fantasy Writers Association. He lives in picturesque southern Maryland, blessed with nearby family and dear old friends. When he isn't writing, Dave enjoys time with his family, kayaking (flat water, please), fishing, hiking, archery, gardening, winemaking, and pursuing his other "creative passion"- woodcarving.

NOVELS:

Legends of the Family Dyer Trilogy:

I) *Sister Witch: The Life of Moll Dyer*- 1st place Magical Realism Critters Readers Poll 2017, Golden Quill Award Best Book of 2018, Readers' Favorite Finalist Historical Person Category 2018, eBook Selection New Apple Awards 2018

II) *His Father's Blood*- Readers' Favorite Silver Medal Urban Fantasy 2019, Literary Titan Award (2018), Readers' Favorite Silver Medal Paranormal Fantasy 2021, International Book Awards Finalist Horror 2021

III) *Sons and Brothers*- 1st Place Magical Realism Critters Readers' Poll

Julianna's Choice (as Davina Guy (Paranormal Romance))

NOVELLAS

Call of the Falconer (Dystopian Novella)

Haunted Southern Maryland (Paranormal History)

Haunted Potomac River Valley (Paranormal History)

SHORT STORIES

'Possum Stew (Short Story Collection)- American Writing Awards 1st Place Anthologies, Finalist Chanticleer Awards Paranormal Fiction, Firebird Book Award for Best Anthology

What If #2 (Anthology GBB Authors)

www.david-w-thompson.com

Thank you for purchasing
this publication of The Wild Rose Press, Inc.

For questions or more information
contact us at
info@thewildrosepress.com.

The Wild Rose Press, Inc.
www.thewildrosepress.com